Satan's Lullaby

Books by Priscilla Royal

Satan's Lullaby

A Medieval Mystery

Priscilla Royal

Poisoned Pen Press

Copyright © 2015 by Priscilla Royal

First Edition 2015

10 9 8 7 6 5 4 3 2 1

Library of Congress Catalog Card Number: 2014951261

ISBN: 9781464203541   Hardcover
      9781464203565   Trade Paperback

Poisoned Pen Press
6962 E. First Ave., Ste. 103
Scottsdale, AZ 85251
www.poisonedpenpress.com
info@poisonedpenpress.com

Printed in the United States of America

To MaryAnne and Clarke Johnson
For the pleasure of your friendship

Acknowledgments

Paula Davidon, Christine and Peter Goodhugh, MaryAnne and Clarke Johnson, Henie Lentz, Dianne Levy, Sharon Kay Penman, Barbara Peters (Poisoned Pen Bookstore in Scottsdale, Arizona), Robert Rosenwald and all the staff of Poisoned Pen Press, Marianne and Sharon Silva, Lyn and Michael Speakman, the staff of the University Press Bookstore (Berkeley, California)

It is difficult to fight against anger,
for a man will buy revenge with his soul.
　　　　　　—Heraclitus, quoted in Aristotle's *Politics*
　　　　　　　　　　　(Trans. Benjamin Jowett)

Chapter One

The north wind bit with the sharpness of an angry dog's teeth. The afternoon sun, weary of its summer reign, had grown pale. Although winter would soon besiege this East Anglian coast with glittering ice and deceptively soft snow, all knew that the Prince of Darkness could chill hearts in ways deadlier than a bitter hoarfrost.

Gracia, Prioress Eleanor's young maid, hurried down the path toward the courtyard near the open gate to Tyndal Priory.

The entire religious community, both men and women in this daughter house of the Order of Fontevraud, had assembled there in separate groups. A sea of tan in their clean robes of unbleached cloth, their silence was unsettling.

On the south side near the hospital, Prior Andrew stood in front of his small assembly of monks, their tonsures freshly shaven. Behind them gathered the many lay brothers who did the physical work, freeing the monks to pray.

Opposite the prior, in the northern part of the courtyard, Prioress Eleanor, leader of this double house, held her crosier. The sunbeams struck the silver of the crook and made the color dance with demure grace. Her veiled nuns, no longer accustomed to the world beyond their cloister, lowered their eyes as if confused by the sharp brightness outside a chapel. Clustered at the back, the lay sisters modestly bowed their heads and thought of the tasks they had left unfinished.

Only a few had been excused from this event. Anchoress Juliana and her servant were not expected to leave the enclosure of their anchorage. The sick were allowed to remain in their beds. Gracia, a child who had taken no vows, was exempt as well.

But she was curious.

At a turn in the path, Gracia got down on her knees and wiggled through a small opening she had made in the shrubbery some months ago. This was the place she came when life within the priory overwhelmed her with new experiences and she needed to hide until the fog of her bewilderment lifted. Only Brother Thomas knew of this secret spot. Although she loved her mistress, Prioress Eleanor, she adored this gentle monk who had taught her that not all men were like the one who had raped her.

Settling down on the soft mat of leaves, she reached into her robe and retrieved the portion of mushroom tart that Sister Matilda, the nun who ruled the kitchen, had insisted she take. Most girls her age looked to be on the cusp of womanhood. She still resembled a child, despite eyes that shone with an understanding far exceeding her years. An orphan who had survived on the streets of Walsingham, Gracia might not have yet learned her letters, but she had become skilled in reading the character of most mortals.

Many thought she was so young because of her extreme thinness. When she had first arrived, Sister Matilda cried out in horror. Ever since, the nun had been pressing extra food into the girl's hands, a gesture that Gracia argued against, protesting that she was taking food away from those who prayed for the souls in Purgatory.

Pushing the food back into the girl's hands, Sister Matilda told her that all got *pittances* in addition to the meals, and Gracia would get neither more nor less than anyone else. The girl suspected otherwise, but even Brother Thomas took Sister Matilda's side and said she would hurt the nun's feelings if she didn't eat the food. "Very well," Gracia had replied. "I shall get fat."

She did not, but her teeth no longer hurt as they had in Walsingham when she ate. She now bit into her tart with undiluted pleasure.

Like the monastics, Gracia had been given a woolen robe to protect her against the coming winter. With the wind blowing today, she was especially grateful for the gift and fell to musing over what she had learned about this unusual gathering of the entire priory. An especially buttery mushroom momentarily distracted her from her thoughts.

It was then she heard shouting and bent forward to peer through the branches. Just outside the gate, a band of armed riders had gathered. Instead of entering the priory, they parted and let a black-clad man ride through. Two wagons filled with more men followed.

Prioress Eleanor and Prior Andrew stepped forward.

Even though spoken words were muffled by the wind, Gracia knew that this visitor must be Father Etienne Davoir, priest and youngest brother of Abbess Isabeau Davoir of Fontevraud Abbey in Anjou. She had sent him to review all aspects of Tyndal Priory from roof maintenance to fish ponds, as well as the method of recording income and debts. Even the details of obedience to the Benedictine Rule, under which this Order lived, would be scrutinized by this man of God and his many clerks.

Such visitations were common practice in other Orders, Prioress Eleanor had told Gracia, but the abbess in Anjou rarely ordered them for her far-flung daughter houses. Tyndal had not experienced one in the eight years of Eleanor's rule, even in the early days when she was struggling to lift the priory finances out of their ruinous state.

As far as Gracia knew, there had been little in the message sent by Abbess Isabeau to explain this sudden decision. Such reviews properly included all aspects of priory life, which her mistress knew, but the prioress had found it strange that the abbess had mentioned that her brother would look into whether any impropriety had occurred amongst the religious. According to the prioress' aunt at Amesbury, the few reviews ordered by the abbess in England had concentrated solely on accounting rolls.

If her mistress was concerned, Gracia thought, then she should be as well.

Lay brothers had helped the priest dismount and were leading his horse to the stable. Two other men had ridden in after the priest. One climbed down from his horse with no assistance but some grace. The other slid off but slipped to his knees beside his mount. As that clerk brushed at the dust on his black robe, Gracia was certain that his horse stared at his former rider with an expression of equine amusement.

Father Etienne spoke briefly with Prior Andrew.

The prior turned away and led his charges back to their Chapter House in the monk's side of the priory.

The priest walked over to Prioress Eleanor.

Was it not odd that this priest had chosen to speak first to Prior Andrew, a subordinate to Prioress Eleanor as leader here? Gracia wondered what was happening.

Neither prioress nor priest seemed to greet each other in any expected way, whether by lowered heads or bended knee. Her mistress' face betrayed no emotion, nor could the maid see her lips move.

Suddenly, Prioress Eleanor spun around and led her nuns and lay sisters toward their own Chapter House on the other side of the priory. As a double house, the monks and nuns might live within the same walls, but they remained carefully separated by barriers of stone.

Gracia swallowed the last of her tart. Having known starvation, she never wasted the smallest morsel and carefully licked each bit from her fingers. But the final crumb tasted bitter on her tongue.

Slowly squirming through the opening and back onto the path, she leapt to her feet and ran toward the prioress' residence. She always took pride in serving her beloved mistress well, but, when this priest came to Prioress Eleanor's audience chamber after his formal greetings to the rest of the Tyndal community, Gracia was determined to make sure everything was perfect.

She was convinced that this man had only come to find fault, and she swore she would not be the one to give him any cause to do so. Indeed, she saw the abbess' brother as the snake in Eden, and she feared he would not just harm those she had come to love but also destroy the safety and peace she had found here.

Chapter Two

The sun's warmth coming through the window soothed her. Drifting reluctantly into wakefulness, Gytha refused to open her eyes and did not move from her high-backed chair.

"Just a moment more," she murmured. "Surely the tasks will wait just a little longer." But her weariness was stronger than her will, and she longed to doze for more than a few moments.

Gytha, wife of Crowner Ralf, was heavily pregnant with their first child. Gently she put a hand on her immense belly and felt her babe move. "Why do you wriggle so much at night, my little one?" she whispered. "To let your mother sleep then, so she might tend to her duties when the sun is high, would be a kindness."

Last night in bed, she had lain on her back, the only possible position despite increasing discomfort, and thought of the coming birth. Notwithstanding the anticipated pain and even the risk of death, she knew she would welcome facing these dangers if there was hope that she might lie on her side again, sleep through the night, and see her feet.

As she had stared in the darkness at the ceiling above and mused on the perils of being a woman, her husband emitted a loud snore, his shaggy head resting against her naked shoulder. Gytha had stifled a laugh.

Some wives might resent the ease with which a husband slept while they reenacted the curse of Eve, but she had no quarrel with Ralf. As other wives grew miserable and heavy with child, their men found joy in new bed partners, but Ralf had never left her side.

A few weeks ago, when her body became so unwieldy that she could only waddle with a hand pressed against her aching back, he had brought another woman from the village to take on tasks he felt she should not do. Accustomed to working hard, Gytha had protested but relented when she decided that the help would ease some of his worry about her. In truth, she was grateful for the assistance.

Despite his roughness with others, Ralf was a kind husband. She already knew he was a good father to his child by his first wife, a woman he might not have loved but did honor. He still grieved that the joining of their seed had caused his first wife's death.

"Are you well?"

Jolted out of her current musing, Gytha opened her eyes and reached for her husband's hand. "As well as a woman resembling Jonah's whale can be," she replied with a smile that betrayed the love she felt for this often querulous man.

He knelt and put his hand on her belly, waited, and suddenly grinned. "I feel Jonah himself, eager to escape!"

She laughed. "I shall be more content when he chooses to stretch outside my womb."

A cloud drifted over his face. "What did Annie say yesterday? I came home too late to ask. For once, you were asleep when I came to bed."

And a brief sleep it was, she thought, for she had awakened when he placed a soft kiss on her forehead. An instant later, he fell into a deep sleep. She had struggled to her feet with a desperately urgent need to pass water.

He remained on his knees but began to twitch with restless concern.

"All is well, Ralf! The babe is healthy, as am I. And Sister Anne shall attend the birth. You know her skills. We have nothing to fear."

What neither chose to mention, lest the Devil be tempted to repeat the episode, was the torturous birth Sister Anne had attended when the Jewish family was trapped in the village two years ago. With God's grace and the sub-infirmarian's skill, both woman and child survived, but the young mother was rendered barren.

Ralf never mentioned the need for sons, but Gytha knew her duty was to bear many. Although her husband was the third son of a local lord, Ralf's eldest brother had no heirs and the second had taken vows. So Gytha and Ralf must provide the heirs to title and lands. One living son might be cause for celebration, but in a world where children died too young, more boys were needed.

"I think we should name him Jonah," her husband jested tenderly as he kissed the top of her belly.

"An apt one, my lord husband, but it shall be *Fulke* after your father and brother," Gytha said.

"And if our child is a girl? You must choose that name but have not told me your preference."

"Then it will be *Anne*." She knew that her husband had loved Sister Anne since childhood. When the woman had married another, then followed her husband into holy vows, Ralf fled England to sell his sword in hopes he would die in battle. Instead, he had come home with wealth but with the wound in his heart unhealed.

But the choice of name was an easy decision, for Gytha felt no jealousy over a woman whom she honored herself. Few were allowed to marry as they willed, and Ralf had married another woman solely on the basis of the land she brought to the family. After she died, he gave his heart wholly to Gytha, defied his brother who had other profitable marital plans for him, and married her. She thanked God for the blessing.

"You are a good woman, Mistress Gytha," he whispered into her ear.

"And you a good man, my lord." She ran her hand over his bristling cheek. "It is also time for your weekly shave."

He grinned. "Ah, but first I must tell you that I have just come from the inn, and Signy has sent a present for your birthing. A cup made of jet from which you may drink to chase away fear and lessen pain when labor begins."

"What a generous gift! Sister Anne will be as delighted with this as I. Jet brings a woman in labor good fortune."

"I was unable to tell our good nun the news. She was busy tending to Sub-Prioress Ruth."

Gytha frowned. "Surely she cannot be ill. The Devil would not allow it."

"But God rules in Tyndal Priory, beloved." He laughed. "She suffers from gout."

"Gout? I may not admire the woman, but she does hold fast to the Rule. After our prioress required all in the priory to adhere to the Benedictine diet, no one has eaten red meat or drunk wine unless ill. For all her flaws, Sub-Prioress Ruth does not indulge in secret, luxurious viands. This ailment must be for some other failing."

"Were it for one of her greater sins like unkindness, she would suffer from head to the bottom of her foot. Sadly, it is only her right toe that is inflamed so her affliction must be for a little wickedness. You know her best. What might that be?"

During her years as Prioress Eleanor's maid, Gytha had had many unpleasant dealings with the rancorous older nun. She raised an eyebrow. "Shooing away our prioress' cat, Arthur. She has never approved of him." She pulled at her husband until he rested his head on her swollen breasts. "I commit the sin of uncharitable thoughts," she murmured, feeling comfort in his closeness.

This noble progeny of Norman conquerors, third in line to a title he disdained and confounder of criminals throughout the land around Tyndal, snuggled like a contented pup.

His Saxon wife, sister to a man who brewed ale and bred donkeys, once again thanked God for this husband whom she loved. A woman of lower status, she was deemed worthy only for his bed, but Ralf had wed her in public, before the church door, and granted her the ownership of lands without limitations. Indeed, he had honored her more than most men of his rank did their wives of equal birth. She might have purred in happiness had their child not kicked again. She winced.

Quickly glancing at Ralf, she realized he had nodded off despite his awkward position, and she tried not to laugh. That forceful bump so near her husband's ear suggested the child might resemble his determined and blunt-spoken father, although she hoped the babe would also have his tender heart.

According to Sister Anne, the birth was imminent, and the nun swore she would attend. Signy, the innkeeper and one of Gytha's good friends, would be there to support her on the birthing chair. In the comfort of their encouragement and compassion, Gytha believed she might endure the pain, often described as matching any soldier's suffering from battle wounds. She would need all the strength that her friends could give her to endure because, even if she did survive the birthing, there were dangers for new mothers to face in the days after.

Gytha fought off those grim thoughts. Sister Anne would use all her skill and knowledge to keep her from Death's clutches. Despite her unease, Gytha knew she had every reason to be confident. She prayed she was not being sinfully so.

Without warning, a shiver coursed through her like a malevolent premonition of evil. Had she been so very unkind in her thoughts about Sub-Prioress Ruth? She had not intended malice, only humor, and truly did not wish the woman ill.

Gytha looked heavenward and swore she would seek Brother Thomas on the morrow to confess her sins and seek absolution. No woman entering the perils of birth dared face the trial without cleansing her soul. Perhaps this uneasy feeling was His way of telling her that she had unwittingly erred of late or been insufficiently contrite.

As for her remarks about the sub-prioress, had she not turned her cheek many times when the woman hurled invectives at her or unfairly cursed her? Yet she had just disparaged Ruth to her husband, and that was unkind. If such was her sin, Gytha would perform any penance due. But why not tell God in advance of a proper confession that she recognized her failing?

Sighing, she thought of the walk to Tyndal Priory to see Brother Thomas. Of course she could summon him to the manor house, but Gytha gained no more pride with her elevation in rank than her husband owned in his birthright. And Brother Thomas had always been as much a brother to her in her heart as Tostig was in blood. Although the journey to the priory seemed interminable with her belly so huge and her feet so swollen, she would walk the distance to find the kind monk.

Looking down at her resting husband, she felt more at ease. After confession, and until she had safely delivered this babe, she vowed to avoid the grave errors committed by her foremother Eve.

Her last thought, before she let herself float into a doze, was that she would henceforth let her husband pick his own apples.

Chapter Three

"Abbess Isabeau, my beloved sister, sends her blessing from the mother house at Fontevraud. I know your heart gladdens at my coming, for I am eager to expose the imperfections at Tyndal Priory. Rejoice, my daughter, as well you ought! When your dedication to Him falls short, your prayers reek in His nostrils like rotten meat. But if the errors are corrected, the scent grows sweet, and you please Him once again."

The priest's two attendants mumbled "Amen."

Something in the manner of these dark-robed men filled the room with foreboding. Prioress Eleanor had always been fond of crows with their sailors' walk and raucous cries. But gazing at the man who sat before her, with his young attendants standing on either side of him, she was reminded that the black-feathered birds were considered harbingers of doom for a reason. She was grateful her abbess had sent her blessing. She was in need of it.

"Please be assured that I welcome your inspection," she replied calmly. That the abbess had sent her youngest brother, a priest so favored by the French royal court of Philip the Bold that he would soon be invested with a bishop's miter, was a gesture of respect appropriate for the prioress' status. Not only was Eleanor's own eldest brother a valued companion of the English king, but she was the daughter of a baron. Nonetheless, this man's presence was unsettling.

Father Etienne Davoir smiled but said nothing. He watched her as if waiting for something to happen which inexplicably had not.

Was he expecting to see fear, she wondered. If so, she would not satisfy his longing. Pride might be one of her failings, but she refused to tremble over vague hints.

Although Eleanor knew there had to be a specific purpose for this investigation, she was ignorant of the precise intent. Other religious houses, under the authority of a local bishop, might expect these comprehensive reviews often, but the Order of Fontevraud served only Rome. Because there was no intermediary between the abbess and the papacy, Abbess Isabeau enjoyed an authority over her daughter houses that others of equal ecclesiastical rank in other Orders did not. That included the right to send a representative of her own choosing to examine any house she deemed in need of some correction. In practice, she rarely did this. Eleanor was not pleased that her abbess had decided to make Tyndal Priory the exception.

Davoir remained silent. One of his clerks, thin and of medium height, stared at the ceiling and stifled a yawn. The other, a short and plump youth, glanced with a pained expression in the direction of the priory's garderobe.

When Eleanor received word that Father Etienne Davoir was coming and the approximate date of his arrival, she had talked to Prior Andrew about what might have generated such scrutiny. Neither could come up with a cause. She knew of no moral lapse. Tyndal Priory was financially sound. Soon after her arrival several years ago, she had reinstituted the Rule regarding diet and prayer. There were repairs needed to various buildings, but a few cracks were not worth risking the life of a high-ranking priest by sending him on the dangerous voyage between France and England. An admonitory letter would have sufficed.

The bored young clerk to Davoir's left twitched with ill-disguised impatience. The other also twitched, but, Eleanor suspected, his bowels were the motivation, not apathy.

She ignored the youths and continued to gaze back at Davoir with benign expectation. Of course, she could ask this man why he had been sent, but a flash of anger stopped her. Was she not a competent prioress? Had she not pulled Tyndal back from financial devastation and cleansed its reputation from the taint of dishonor? The abbess owed her the courtesy of greater detail in her missive. Since she had failed to do so, Eleanor resolved that she would not grovel to Abbess Isabeau's younger brother and beg for what she ought to have been given freely.

"I hope your journey was a pleasant one," she said.

"The weather was favorable during the voyage. We thought God had smiled on us." Father Etienne cleared his throat. "When we landed and were met by the armed escort sent by your gracious king to keep us safe on the journey here, we were pleased." He glanced over at the pale clerk on his right. "Yet I fear the ride from the port to your priory was difficult. Jean is unwell."

When Eleanor saw the gentleness with which Davoir put a hand on the plump clerk's arm, she softened. "I grieve that you have been distressed." She looked at the youth more carefully. His soft features had the gray-green pallor of a corpse.

"The world is filled with Satan's minions," Davoir said, turning back to her. "Those who have chosen to serve God outside the walls of religious houses are never far removed from sinful violence." He bent to the young clerk and murmured a question.

Jean swallowed, then shook his head.

Eleanor wondered what might have so shaken the youth that he had taken ill.

Davoir brightened with pride. "But Jean has always found the greatest strength in God."

"What occurred?" The question was not idly asked. Eleanor wanted to establish whether the clerk needed prayer, one of Sister Anne's cures, or both. Fortunately, she thought, this priest will assume I suffer from the wanton curiosity deemed common in women. In fact, it was advantageous for others to assume she was infected with this feminine vice. If it was only curiosity needing satisfaction, mortals were inclined to give details. Crowner Ralf, because he hunted those guilty of crime, had a harder time prying information from the innocent, let alone the guilty.

"I shall be brief. One of the soldiers in our escort quickly became a congenial companion for my clerk. The man was a fine storyteller and entertained Jean on the long journey from the sea. For one disinclined to admire earthly beauty," Davoir smiled at his clerk, "the journey would feel endless." He looked down and twisted the bejeweled ring on his finger. In the sunbeam coming through the window, one of the larger gems flickered with a murky light.

Eleanor folded her hands and patiently waited.

"Last night, there was no religious house to give us beds. We stopped at an inn. This morning, Jean went to the stable to seek his companion." Davoir chewed on his lip. "He found the man's corpse. Someone had cut his throat."

Jean gagged and looked away.

The prioress' eyes opened wide with shock.

Davoir's expression softened with concern over Jean. "When my clerk cried out, the innkeeper ran to his aid as did the captain of the soldiers. The local crowner might have been called, but the captain said there was no need."

Eleanor was surprised, then chose not to interrupt and to let this priest finish his tale.

"The captain swore he knew the cause for the death. Since the soldiers were under his command, he was responsible for rendering the required justice. He gave me his solemn oath, his hand on a crucifix, that we had nothing to fear and were safe from all harm."

"The crowner was not summoned?"

Davoir shook his head.

Perhaps Ralf should be told anyway, Eleanor thought, but saw no purpose in saying anything to the priest. He had made his decision about the matter. She would make her own. "I shall pray for the poor man's soul and that His comfort will ease the pain his death brought you," she said, directing the last words to the clerk.

The lad nodded, but his expression suggested he was not comforted in the slightest.

"It was cruelty born in sin and executed by wicked men," Davoir said. "You may thank God that you will never suffer this kind of violence within the safety of your priory walls."

Eleanor had seen far worse deaths and many more of them since entering the gates of Tyndal Priory but chose not to enlighten the abbess' brother. Instead, she murmured the expected words and changed the subject.

"Your sermon to the nuns was most instructive," she said. The topic had been worldly temptations. She wondered if he preached the same message to the monks and lay brothers. Did the subject hold any clue to the reason he had been sent?

"When we vow ourselves to God's service, much is demanded from our imperfect flesh. It grows weak and eagerly reaches out for the false joys promised in Satan's lullabies. The Devil strikes hardest at those who choose the path to Heaven, and he rejoices most in those he wins back from God."

Eleanor might have been offended at the suggestion that her monastics were lax in honoring their vows, but, as she studied the man seated before her, she felt he meant his words more as commentary than criticism.

Her opinion of this priest remained ill-formed. Had he come dressed in chain mail with a sword by his side, he would not have looked out of place as the warrior son of a French nobleman. That he chose to fight the Prince of Darkness, not the English, was a decision she respected. Yet she had learned from her brother, a returned crusader, that God's knights could be indistinguishable from those who longed less for Heaven and more for land and castles. Each maimed, killed, and tortured with equal ferocity. Did this man follow the gentler God she had discovered in her particular prayers?

As she listened to Davoir elaborate on the theme of his earlier sermon, she noted that he was missing a few teeth but that his hair was still dark blond. If neither young nor old, she wondered if he was in that middle time, one she longed to achieve, when neither the passions of youth nor the fears of age fully ruled. His face bore furrows, which could suggest either worry or humor. His brown eyes were bright with intelligence, perhaps curiosity, maybe zeal. Davoir might be a man inclined to fairness, Eleanor thought, but she had already noted signs that he could harbor a rigid view of human frailty. Uncertain over which had most shaped his reasoning, she prayed it was the kinder mold.

He had paused to take a breath.

"The wisdom you gave us today in your sermon was received by eager souls," she said. "The sisters of Tyndal Priory will benefit greatly from your insights, as will our brothers." She smiled with a hopeful expression. Now, surely, was the time when he would give her the specific message from Abbess Isabeau that would explain the point behind this unusual investigation.

It was in that moment of expectation that Jean turned scarlet and began to cough until he could barely catch his breath.

The other clerk jumped back as if fearing contagion.

Rising quickly, Davoir put his arm around the youth. "I would speak further with you, Prioress Eleanor, but this young man needs prompt care. I insist that the monk in charge of the hospital come immediately and examine him. Jean needs some remedy. I shall offer prayers."

The lad's face was scarlet as he gasped for air.

"Our hospital is run by Sister Christina and her sub-infirmarian, Sister Anne," she replied.

He looked surprised. "No monk is trained in healing?"

"Sister Anne is a physician's daughter. He trained her so well that she became an apothecary with her husband when they were both in the world."

"The husband is nearby, or is he dead?"

"He came first to Tyndal and is now known as Brother John. She followed and also took vows here."

"Then I would have my clerk seen by this brother who is an apothecary."

"He has become a hermit and sees no one, nor has he treated any man since his arrival here. I may assure you that Sister Anne's reputation as a healer is known throughout England."

He twisted his hands with displeased impatience. "No other monk? That is most unusual."

Sensing a criticism of the priory hospital, Eleanor swallowed her indignation. "Brother Thomas has been trained by her in some areas of treatment," she replied with icy calm.

Father Etienne waved that aside. "I will not have Brother Thomas. Send Prior Andrew and this sub-infirmarian to the guest quarters, but she must be properly accompanied and may not touch my clerk. Should an examination of Jean's body be required, including his urine, Prior Andrew must do all that is needed."

"As you will." Eleanor wondered why he had first insisted on a man treating his clerk and then rejected the offer of Brother Thomas' help.

"This shall be done before the next Office." Davoir rose. "I will have the evening meal sent to us in our quarters tonight. Tomorrow, I will discuss my plans for all reviews with you."

Bowing her head with modest concurrence, Eleanor's unexpressed reaction to his commanding tone was less humble.

After Gracia had ushered the men out and firmly shut the chamber door, Eleanor uttered a sigh of relief. "Please go the hospital and bring Sister Anne," she said to her maid. "Then find Prior Andrew and ask him to join us. I pray we will not need a veritable army of monastics to accompany our sub-infirmarian, lest the good priest find some impropriety."

Gracia knew her mistress well enough to chuckle at those words but then chose gravity and a swift departure to carry out the prioress' wishes.

Chapter Four

The lay brother wrapped yellow flowers of arnica around the man's ankle, and then bound it as tightly as he could. Despite the patient's groans, he doubted the injury was serious and bit his tongue to keep from saying so.

He glanced at the ankle again. Even with the wrapping, it didn't look swollen.

If the complaint had been blisters on tender heels, he might have sympathized. These feet, despite the man's claim that he was a poor pilgrim who had walked from London, were as soft as a baby's skin.

"I beg the kindness of a roof and sustenance," the pilgrim said, his accent suggesting he was not of English birth.

The lay brother looked back at the sole of the foot he held. Very tender indeed. "We have no guest accommodations, if that is what you require, nor have we a bed in the monks' dormitory."

The man pulled his foot from the lay brother's hand. "You are refusing charity? A priory? I cannot walk on this..." His lips stretched across his teeth in a well-formed grimace.

Good teeth too, the lay brother noted. "I did not say we were refusing your request, but the only space we have is in this hospital."

"And there will be food for my growling belly?"

"The priory provides simple but nourishing fare," he said. The man was very thin, the lay brother observed with more compassion. Perhaps he had been deathly ill and long enough in bed to soften those feet.

"Why did you not tell me immediately that I was as welcome as Our Lord would have been?"

"Because we normally have room, at least in the dormitory. Few want a bed next to the dying."

"Have so many travelers stopped here?" The pilgrim frowned. "Are any on the way to Canterbury as am I?"

The lay brother shook his head. "Our priory has just welcomed a priest sent by the abbess of Fontevraud Abbey in Anjou. He and his attendants have come to review our lives, our accounts, and our roofs, a common practice in many monastic houses. We are honored to have such a noble visitor." He could not help the note of pride in his voice. "Father Etienne Davoir is not only confessor to a brother of the King of France, he is soon to be invested as a bishop."

"I thought I saw a large party of armed men in the village when I sought directions to your gate."

"The local innkeeper will house the men sent by our king to protect our visitor and his clerks. We accommodate all those men devoted to God's service."

The pilgrim looked thoughtful. "I have been told that the more clerks a priest has, the higher in rank he stands. How many did this man bring?"

"I could not say. Father Etienne and his two senior clerks were given the largest accommodations as is proper for visitors of the highest rank. The others have been lodged with the monks. We are not a large priory and room for guests is limited." He gestured toward the priory. "Our buildings are old. I fear the clerks will be busy over many days checking for cracks, leaks, and mold."

The man nodded with appreciation. "Then I am grateful for the bed and fare you offer me, Brother, and shall stay only as long as it takes my injury to heal. The moans of dying men will remind me that our sins drag our naked souls into the pits of Hell. In return for your charity, I shall add my prayers for those trembling spirits as they anticipate God's judgement."

The lay brother's eyes widened in surprise at this unexpected show of concern for others. After the pilgrim's whining over a minor injury, he would not have expected that. With a nod, the lay brother found a crutch for the man and led the pilgrim to the straw mat that would be his bed.

Philippe was not a pilgrim, although he did come from a town in the region of Picardy and he most certainly had tender feet. His sprain was fabricated, but the pain from walking, when he could not beg a ride in a farmer's cart, was not. Sandals were not his usual footwear, nor was this rough and filthy robe. He scratched at his head and feared he had lice.

When he saw the thin straw mat on which he must sleep, he suspected his smile had resembled the frozen grin on a corpse more than an expression of gratitude, but he was weary of pretending. Not that he truly expected the comfort of a mattress with clean sheets and a coverlet on cold nights; those were for the dying or seriously ill, but he had hoped. Oh, how he had hoped! He ached with hope.

Kneeling, he sniffed at his bedding. At least the straw was clean.

He stretched out and closed his eyes. It had been a long journey, and he was exhausted. For a moment, he must have dozed, but a piercing scream shattered any dreams. He sat up and looked around.

A few yards away, a tall nun was holding a woman back from a bed. The captive was howling like one possessed and flailing her arms as if she were trying to fly. Beside her, a man knelt, his hands pressed to his face. Sobbing loudly, he raised his eyes upward. "My son!" he shouted to the heavens. "Why did you take my son from me?"

Philippe might not have devoted most of his hours to worshiping God, but he deeply felt the grief these two were suffering. Rolling onto his knees, he prayed for the lad's soul and that God would give comfort to the parents. "More than You have given me," he whispered. "Please!"

Finally, the grieving pair were led away, the woman whimpering and straining against the arms of the nun who tried to pull her along as gently as possible.

He lay back on his straw and stared at the high ceiling over his head. Sleep was now impossible. Silently, he uttered a curse.

In a short while, the tall nun returned with a lay brother, and they fell into a hushed discussion over the corpse on the bed. Philippe could not hear their words, but he understood the meaning. The lay brother reached down, picked up the small body, and carried it down the aisle.

As the man passed by, Philippe covered his nose. For such a small corpse, it stank horribly. Trying not to breathe, he glanced back at the nun who was tearing linen off the bed. A lay sister ran to her and bent to pick it up.

"Burn it," the nun said.

Philippe trembled. Priories were not wanton with their hospital linen. If this was so foul, what noxious vapors from the sheets and the corpse had contaminated the air?

He groaned. Might he die too? He would not mind as long as he accomplished his purpose first. Turning onto his side away from the deathbed, he covered his eyes and prayed again. This time his plea was for himself.

"Is this man waiting for a bed?" The woman's voice was very close.

He looked up to see the tall nun standing over him. Her expression was unsettling as her eyes studied him. Had she been a man, he would have feared her. As it was, he still shivered. Despite her habit, he wondered if she might be a servant of the Devil.

The lay brother, who had treated his ankle, appeared at her side. "No, Sister Anne. He came with a sprained ankle and now begs shelter as a poor pilgrim. Since we have no other space for him…"

"I ask for nothing more than the charity of clean straw and food, for which I bless you. Let those in far greater distress have any free beds." Philippe of Picardy sat up, carefully winced, and forced a brave smile. "Are you the leader of this religious house?" He knew better. What noble prioress would tear befouled linen from a bed? But he understood the art of the compliment.

"I am the sub-infirmarian. Prioress Eleanor leads us."

She did not even blush at the flattery, he thought with displeasure. "And the infirmarian?"

As if hesitant to name the person, she was silent for a moment. "Sister Christina. Do you have need of her prayers?"

Philippe shook his head. "If she is so saintly that her pleas to God heal men, I am too unworthy to be in her presence." He lowered his eyes. "I am on my way to Canterbury to expiate grievous sins."

"Are you in pain?"

He grimaced before nodding which, he hoped, suggested brave endurance.

The lay brother snorted and turned away.

"I shall send someone with a soothing potion after I have seen to those who are more gravely ill." She gestured toward the back of the hospital. "We have a chapel there, near the apothecary hut. You may go to pray and ease your soul until you can continue on your pilgrimage."

He brightened with a glow of genuine happiness at her words. Spending time in the chapel would give him a view of the apothecary, but the sub-infirmarian would assume his joy came from a purer motive.

She smiled and walked on. The lay brother went with her, although he glanced back with a puzzled look.

Philippe crawled to his feet. His wince rose from the pain of his abused feet. At least he did not have to feign that soreness. The discomfort should not last long, however. His soles bore no blisters. Not wanting to chance infection, he had made sure of that.

Awkwardly, he bent for the crutch, picked it up, and hobbled off in the direction the sub-infirmarian and lay brother had gone.

He did not have to walk far before he saw an open door across from the chapel and glanced into the hut where, he assumed, this nun kept her baskets of herbs and jars of powders from which she made her potions and ointments.

A girl flew passed him. "Sister Anne!"

Philippe slipped closer to the chapel, hoping the shadows would hide him. If not, he could argue that he wanted to pray but had stopped to rest his foot. He put his hand over his nose. Even at some distance, he could smell the corpse that had been placed near the altar.

The nun came out of the hut to greet the child. "What is it, Gracia? Who is ill?" The sub-infirmarian's tone suggested alarm, but Philippe did not dare move to a spot where he could observe more closely.

"Not my mistress," the girl replied. "One of Father Etienne's clerics is ill and needs your immediate care. Prioress Eleanor has asked that you, Prior Andrew, and a skilled lay brother from the hospital attend our visitor. She will explain what is needed."

Sister Anne told the lay brother that he must accompany her, then asked the child to seek Sister Oliva so she could give directions on specific treatments to administer while she was gone. "As soon as I am done, we will come to the prioress' quarters, as she requests."

Philippe watched the child run back through the hospital aisles. Indeed, he felt like a child himself. There was that much joy filling his heart.

Chapter Five

Brother Thomas had just finished overseeing the care of the horses brought by the visitors. Although others might find horse manure and sweat offensive, he loved the beasts and did not care that he reeked of them. Rubbing down a horse had calmed him. After stroking a munching rouncy on the neck, he walked out of the stables and looked across the priory grounds to the cemetery, orchards, and hidden clearing where the bees were tended.

Father Etienne's interminable sermon and the coming investigation of priory affairs had set him on edge. Perhaps it was unfair to dislike the priest simply because he had been sent on an unpleasant task, but Thomas liked neither the man nor his duty. If horse manure stank, he thought, there was something about this visit that smelled fouler.

Hearing familiar voices nearby, Brother Thomas was surprised to see Prior Andrew, Sister Anne, a lay brother, and Gracia hurrying toward the guest chambers. "Is something amiss?" he called out and hastened along the path to meet them.

When Sister Anne saw him, she raised her hand, her eyes sparkling with relief. "Please come with us, Brother. Prioress Eleanor sent word that one of Father Etienne's clerics is ill. Your observations would be welcome."

Gracia started to say something, then quickly covered her mouth.

Prior Andrew looked down at her with a questioning glance.

"I fought off a sneeze, Prior," she said. "I did not wish to invite the Devil in."

He patted her shoulder and called out to Thomas with a question about the horses.

As soon as the monk joined them, Sister Anne sent the lay brother back to the hospital. "Your skills with cuts, sprains, and blood-letting will be sorely missed there, and Brother Thomas can take your place in this matter," she explained to the man. What she did not say, lest the lay brother be unduly pained, was that this sensitive situation needed the monk's proven knowledge and talent of observation.

"What is the clerk's complaint?" Thomas sniffed at his sleeve. Horse manure might not please a man favored by a king's brother.

"Father Etienne did not tell our prioress," she replied and then dropped her voice to a quieter tone. "I do not like this priest."

"I do not like that Abbess Isabeau sent him," Prior Andrew muttered.

"We have no cause to worry," Thomas said. He might not like this visitation either, but he was trying hard to assume a benevolent motive. "The accounting rolls are current and detailed. Our prioress adheres to the Rule. Perhaps Rome questioned the ability of prioresses to rule their houses with a firm enough hand. If so, what better priory to quell Rome's fears than Tyndal? "

"Why not send Father Etienne to Amesbury? That is the most prominent English daughter house in our Order." Prior Andrew was rarely angry, but his pink face suggested this time was an exception.

"Although Sister Beatrice is not the prioress there, she would be questioned about the novices under her rule." Thomas laughed and looked heavenward. "May God forgive me for saying this, but I fear even He would hesitate to suggest that our prioress' aunt owned any faults in her training or supervision of those young women."

"You have met her, Brother, and I trust your opinion!" The prior's expression relaxed with amusement.

Turning to Sister Anne, the monk asked, "What was the subject of the priest's sermon to you?"

"How the Evil One tempts women. Although he did not accuse us of lust, he said we were most likely to suffer the vice. All women are cursed with that weakness, but he said that Satan tries hardest to lead those women who vow themselves to God into breaking their vows of chastity." Her eyes revealed a flash of sadness.

Thomas noticed it and wondered if her thoughts were of her husband or the doctor from London they had met a few years ago.

"We were told that obedience was a man's usual failure," the prior said. "That message is not new, but I was surprised at his emphasis. Why did he warn us about following sinners and not the righteous?" Prior Andrew stumbled on a raised part of the path but quickly recovered his balance.

Thomas feared his prior's old wound was bothering him but knew better than to offer assistance to the former soldier. As for the sermon, he had been bored by it until the priest warned against following the Devil in the guise of a beautiful angel. Thomas was sure that Davoir was looking directly at him when he said that. Instinctively, he put a hand to his auburn hair. Perhaps this priest believed those many tales that counseled men to be wary of those with red hair.

"A warning against the leadership of a woman?" Sister Anne stopped as they reached the gate to the guest quarters.

"I should not have suggested that, even in jest. Rome has no quarrel with our Order," Brother Thomas replied. "As for Father Etienne, his own sister is the abbess in Anjou. If he were opposed to the leadership of women, which our Order demands, she would not have sent him here."

Prior Andrew called to a servant standing inside the small courtyard behind the gate. "We have been summoned by Father Etienne."

The man nodded, then hurried off to announce them.

◇◇◇

Gracia wished she could escape, but Sister Anne needed her presence in this crowd of men. The maid did not know what to do.

Ought she to have spoken up when Sister Anne invited the monk to accompany them? Was it her place to do so? Her mistress had said nothing about Father Etienne's refusal to include Brother Thomas when she asked that they visit the ill clerk. The prioress had only told them that he asked for Prior Andrew and did not want Sister Anne to touch the youth.

Even though Gracia had wished to tell the sub-infirmarian that the prioress had cause not to include the monk, she did not want to contradict the wishes of Sister Anne. Was she wrong to remain mute, respectful of the nun's decision? Neither choice felt right now, and she longed for guidance but there was no one to ask. How could she tell Brother Thomas of her difficulty when he might be insulted upon learning of the priest's curt dismissal of his skills?

Gracia slipped her hands inside her robe, twisted them with painful indecision, and longed to be anywhere but where she was.

Chapter Six

Father Etienne scowled with displeasure.

Thomas was certain that the man's disapproving glance was the result of the equine stench. Fortunately, he caught himself before laughing at the priest's grimace of distaste.

"We have come to see your sick clerk," Prior Andrew said.

Sister Anne bowed her head and stood meekly behind the prior.

"Jean is resting," the priest replied. "His bowels are loose, his head aches, and he has vomited. Those are his symptoms. I assume you will want to see his urine, Prior Andrew."

The prior glanced at the nun behind him.

She shook her head.

"I am not trained in medicine," Andrew replied.

"Sister Anne is known throughout England for her healing skills," Thomas said, his patience swiftly thinning with this odd conversation when there was a patient to see. "Men of high rank come from the king's court to seek her remedies. A renowned London physician has sought her advice. If your clerk needs healing, you could not ask for…"

"Did I seek your opinion, Brother?" The rebuke was given in a soft tone, but the words possessed sharp edges.

"You did not, but I…"

"Then remember the sermon I have just preached to you in the Chapter House. Obedience demands humility. As the emissary of your abbess in Anjou, I outrank you. You should not speak unless addressed and never give an opinion until asked. Stay humble, my son, and God will embrace you." The priest tilted his head and gave the monk the forced smile of tolerance a father might give his son when the lad had repeated an error for which he had already been scolded.

Thomas knew his face had flushed with anger but bit his tongue and bowed his head.

"Now," the priest said, turning to the prior, "I understand your nun has skills in the healing arts, but my clerk is a modest youth who longs to take full vows. To inflict the presence of a woman on him in his weakened state would be a cruelty and a gift to the Prince of Darkness."

Andrew started to reply.

Davoir raised his hand. "What I propose is this. You shall go into the room and examine my clerk. You need not take a sample of his urine since you do not have the knowledge to interpret the signs in it, and this nun would not have been trained in that. You may then come to the door and present your observations to this nun. She may learn from that what is troubling Jean." He glanced with ill-disguised disdain at Sister Anne.

"I suggest that Brother Thomas take the responsibility," Andrew replied. "He is more observant and better trained in the needed skills than I."

"You shall do this, not he. I had specifically asked for an apothecary monk or the prior because the sub-infirmarian is a woman who may not touch my clerk or even the flask containing his urine. When Prioress Eleanor recommended Brother Thomas, I deemed her choice unacceptable for reasons I need not explain."

Gracia's face reddened with shame.

Despite his sharp words to the adults, the priest looked with gentleness on the girl. "I assume Prioress Eleanor saw fit to contradict my request," he said to her.

Glancing at the frightened girl, Sister Anne said, "It was my decision."

Thomas saw anger dancing in the nun's narrowed eyes.

She stepped forward and looked boldly at Davoir.

He drew back as if afraid she might come too near.

"We met our brother on the path here," she said, "and I asked him to come with us. His observational skills and judgement are respected at the hospital and in the village. Surely I need not mention his reputation and that of our prioress in matters of justice?"

"My sister, the abbess, has fully informed me of these tales, knowing that such news from England is not always of great concern to the French court." Davoir shook his head. "All this may suggest some medical competence, but I remain amazed that there is no monk, fully trained in medicine, in charge of the hospital. How can you manage cures without a doctor who can read the vital signs found in urine?"

Thomas caught himself wondering how a man who had just lectured him on humility could sound so vain. Did this priest really think that he could change a situation, deemed by him to be improper, merely by willing it to do so?

"Since our abbess has made you aware of this fact, you will understand why I called upon his skills in this important matter of your clerk's health." The sub-infirmarian deliberately ignored his remark about an infirmarian monk.

"You and I differ on the issue of what is best for the lad's well-being." Father Etienne turned to the prior. "Since my sister leads the Order of Fontevraud, I both understand and respect the premise of a woman leading men as the earthly representative of Our Lady. This otherwise unnatural situation applies only to the abbess and the prioresses of her daughter houses. It does not apply to the nuns within each priory."

Prior Andrew paled and said nothing.

"They must, as is a woman's lot, follow the rule of men as it is we who represent the higher spirit while women are but lowly flesh." Davoir gestured to the prior. "You will do as I direct, Prior Andrew, and examine my clerk. Sister Anne, you will await his observations and, if required, my further instructions." He spun around and pointed. "Brother Thomas, you may leave the quarters."

"As you wish, Father, but I beg one favor," the prior replied. "Since I must speak with Brother Thomas as soon as we leave about some complex matters, I ask that he remain so I do not have to waste time finding him again." Andrew looked dutifully sheepish. "Such a boon to me would be most kind."

Brother Thomas tried hard not to grin at the prior's cleverness.

Davoir nodded. "As you will." He waved at the monk. "Stand near the door where you will not interfere with the consultation."

Thomas did as he was ordered but was pleased to note that he could still overhear most of what Sister Anne and Prior Andrew discussed.

As expected, the consultation took much longer than needed. In one thing only had Davoir been correct. Not being a physician, Sister Anne rarely examined the color, smell, texture, or taste of a patient's urine, although experience and observation had taught her a little. She had chosen not to mention that detail to Davoir.

But she was a skilled apothecary, and Prior Andrew, a former soldier and untrained in the medical arts, had no idea what he should be looking for. Had the matter been less serious, the back and forth discussions between the pair might have been humorous.

Finally, Sister Anne had had enough and muttered instructions to the prior. The process went much faster. When Prior Andrew next emerged from the clerk's sickroom, Sister Anne whispered some words into his ear, and he turned to address Father Etienne.

"The illness is not dire. Your clerk may have eaten something that did not agree with him. The hospital has a remedy for the humor imbalance, but it must be prepared. We will deliver it to you as soon as that is done. The lay brother will bring instructions on dosage."

Pleased, the priest thanked Prior Andrew, ignored Sister Anne, blessed Gracia, and dismissed the party from his presence. Thomas had already slipped out of the chambers.

◇◇◇

As they walked back to the hospital, Sister Anne laughed. "From what our good prior told me, the youth suffers from too much wine drunk at dinner last night. He almost vomited in our prioress' chambers, coughed to hide the affliction, and swallowed the bile. Then he gagged in the attempt. Poor lad! He denied the excess at first, but his symptoms pointed to a sour stomach and an even more painful head. He confessed all when our prior promised not to tell the clerk's master."

"An ailment most clerks suffer frequently enough," Thomas replied with a grin. "I am sure that Father Etienne sleeps deeply in the arms of righteousness, but his clerks may dance in the embrace of imps while he does."

"Surely he knows this!" Prior Andrew gave an almost accurate imitation of amazement.

"When I was a clerk, my masters either did not or chose not to know." For an instant, a dark cloud from that memory settled over his soul, but it quickly moved away. "'Tis a pity the priest would not let me talk with the youth. I might have given Jean some advice about how to chase away the effects of wine, remedies learned in my own sinful youth."

Sister Anne looked at her friend with gentle amusement. "And for your sins you came to Tyndal and blessed us with your goodness."

Thomas felt his face turn hot with embarrassment.

Gracia looked at him and wanted to weep. Had she spoken to Sister Anne about the prioress' orders, her beloved monk would have been spared the indignity of Davoir's contempt.

Chapter Seven

Ralf drank his ale, rubbed his hand on the edge of the wood table to ease an itch, and stared at nothing in particular.

He had stopped by the inn to tell Signy the latest details of his wife's health. Although he and the innkeeper shared a troubled history, the tension between them eased after his marriage. Signy's close friendship with Gytha tempered the innkeeper's bitterness, and she no longer greeted him with sharp words and mockery as was her wont in times past. She even sat with him willingly now, something she had refused to do before his marriage unless he came with questions in his position as crowner.

But the innkeeper was eager for news of her friend. It was rare that she could take time from the business to walk out to the manor house, although she gave her word that she would be there with Sister Anne for the birth. "And I shall even if the inn is burning to the ground," she had solemnly vowed. Ralf had no doubt she meant it.

When he sat down to drink his ale today, Ralf had commented to Signy about the large number of strange men at the inn tables, and she explained their presence. He had heard that the abbess of the Order of Fontevraud was sending a host of clerks to the priory but not the date of their arrival.

He glanced around and decided the men should be a peaceful enough group. If these soldiers were sent by the king to protect the company of quill-bearing clerks, they would have been warned to behave themselves near the priory. The most he had to fear was drunkenness and a few unwelcome hands on the buttocks of the inn's serving women.

Thinking about the latter, he grinned over his cup of ale. The soldiers would have to seek their pleasures elsewhere. Signy was more than capable of dealing with rude gropings, protecting herself and her women.

Having left him with the finest ale brewed by Tostig, a man who was now the crowner's brother-in-law, the innkeeper walked around the benches of patrons, stopping briefly to chat but never pausing long. Without regret or lingering desire, Ralf watched her.

Signy was a strikingly beautiful woman, despite her somber attire. Had he not known who she was, he might have wondered why a nun or widow dwelled in such a rough place. Although he never quite understood the reason, Signy had chosen not to marry yet expressed no longing to take vows. Instead, she had taken over the inn on her uncle's death and brought two orphans to her home and into her heart as foster children. One of them, Nute, was growing tall and looked more like a man each day. He never saw Nute's younger sister, whom Signy kept away from the eyes of men.

"May I join you?"

Ralf started with unwelcome surprise. It was rare for him to let down his guard. Representatives of the king's justice did not live long if they did, although he was safe enough in Signy's inn. He grunted as he looked up at the man. Had marriage softened him, he asked himself, and then determined that it was just fatigue. Since his wife did not sleep well, he often awoke himself and worried over her health.

The man smiled down at him. "I am the captain of the guard sent by the king to accompany Father Etienne and his clerks from the coast to this priory. Conan is my name."

Ralf gestured to a serving woman for more ale. "A Breton?"

The man laughed. "My forbearer followed the Conqueror, and the family has loyally served the kings since. It has long been the custom to name the first son *William* and the second *Conan* after the one who fought at Hastings."

And this man has swung enough swords himself, Ralf thought, considering the scarred face of the one who now sat across from him at the table. "You have seen a few battles."

"Ah, you see the beauty it has left me with!" Conan rubbed a hand over his scars. "The Welsh fight like demons and little care if a man might want to bed a woman before dark when she might still see his face." He smiled, then looked around. "The only thing that saddens me is that I sometimes frighten the wee ones."

Ralf felt the sorrow and liked the man for that particular regret. "Guarding a priest and a company of clerks must be a relief from battling the Welshmen."

Conan raised the half eyebrow still remaining and bent closer to speak softly. "I'd rather the howls of the Welsh devils. I pray as much as any Christian, but we had to stop every time we heard a church bell toll on the journey here. The ride to this village took twice as long, and we did not always reach decent inns or priories by nightfall. These clerks are not accustomed to sleeping on beds of leaves. Soft creatures, they are, despite the hair shirts they claim to wear."

Ralf raised his cup in agreement.

"Tell me about this inn and the village of Tyndal," Conan took a long drink of ale and nodded with appreciation.

"Yes, the ale is good here, as is the food. You will sleep in clean straw, suffer no flea bites, and get honest value for your coin." Ralf hesitated. "No whores. The innkeeper will not allow her women to offer that comfort to any patrons."

"Are you sure?" Conan tilted his head in the direction of one woman.

"If they do, they find another place to lie with a man."

The captain smiled. "And what pleasure does the village offer?"

Ralf laughed. "If pious talk delights you, there are enough pilgrims stopping at the inn on the way to shrines in Norwich to the east or Walsingham to the west. Many more come to the priory to seek cures for the ills men suffer. The hospital there is known throughout England for successful cures." He winked at Conan. "With the king's invasion of Wales, Tyndal's reputation may have spread to that land as well." He waited but got no response. "Otherwise, there will be a market day soon for entertainment."

Conan briefly looked over his shoulder when someone shouted, then he turned his attention back to Ralf. "Can the hospital cure a man of ugliness?" Lest Ralf think he was serious, Conan laughed.

"If it did," Ralf retorted, "my face would have blinded you with its perfection."

A silence fell as the men drank.

"Tell me more of this famous priory. I have heard that it has a mill and fine guest quarters." He shrugged. "We did not enter the gate. Once we safely delivered the priest and his wagons full of clerks, we were directed to the inn. I was hoping to see more of this unusual place that houses both monks and nuns."

"If you walk back on the road toward the main entrance, you will find a gate in the wall. Those who use the mill take their grain in there, and so the grounds are open. Occasionally, you may see a monk, although it's mostly lay brothers who trim the trees, tend the hives, and serve the needs of the mill. The guest quarters are to the right of that path, across a small bridge over a branch of the stream. You can see the buildings easily enough from the path."

Conan smiled. "I will need exercise. I have been a soldier too long and cannot sit still as merchants can." He reached for the pitcher and poured more ale.

"You still serve the king?" Ralf asked as he also poured himself another cup.

"Aye, and the men under me. To provide this safe passage for these guests from the continent is our reward for battles well fought."

For a while, the two men shared stories of wars and battles, Ralf as a mercenary and Conan as the king's man.

Finally, Conan rose. "I have enjoyed our talk, Crowner. I hope we may meet again. Indeed, I have much time on my hands until those clerks are done, and we can deliver them safely to their ships for France. I'll be glad to see their backs. I do not like the idleness here or fancy the long journey back. The priest and his lead clerks speak enough of our language to offer conversation on the road, but no one else does and we do not understand either Latin or their Frankish tongue. Pity King Edward could not offer us something in the nature of coin or proper land instead of this." He grinned, turning what might be called ingratitude into a jest, then walked off through the inn to the door and disappeared into the village street.

Ralf wondered what this man might do in an isolated East Anglian village with little vice to tempt a man who did not seem inclined to great virtue.

Then he sat back and frowned. The captain had called him *crowner*. How did he know that? Ralf knew he had not mentioned it.

He shrugged. Presumably, someone had told him, but, if so, why had this Conan chosen his company? Few did, even men with no cause to fear one whose work was to seek those who ran afoul of the king's justice.

Chapter Eight

Arthur, the prioress' orange cat and lord of the kitchens, marched through the door and into the audience chamber.

Sister Anne swiftly followed. "He has sired another litter of kittens," she said to the prioress.

Out of the corner of her eye, Prioress Eleanor noted a spark of interest in Gracia's expression. "The hospital will remain free of rodents," she replied, then frowned. "I thought the dam there was still nursing her last litter."

"This one belongs to the anchorage. One of Anchoress Juliana's dams slipped out the window and had a fruitful tryst with Arthur. I have heard some now call him *Lancelot* to honor his many conquests."

Eleanor laughed heartily. "Is she angry?" She tried to give her cat a disapproving look but failed and picked him up instead.

Snuggling into her arms, Arthur half closed his eyes and purred, secure in the belief that his charm could conquer any female heart.

"Our anchoress has been heard cooing over the kittens. Her servant has gotten bits of food from Sister Matilda for the nursing mother. I suspect they would prefer to keep all the kittens, but the anchorage is too small."

"Most will not survive, I fear." Eleanor glanced at Gracia again. The young girl looked sad.

Eleanor instantly looked concerned. "I think I saw a mouse just over there yesterday." She nodded in the general direction of the opposite corner. "Since Arthur spends so much of his time protecting our food in the kitchen from pillaging rodents, we might need more protection in these chambers. Gracia?"

The girl straightened.

"Do you think you could look at the litter and choose a healthy kitten to bring here?" She gestured around the chambers. "I think we might need another cat to keep the vermin out. Have you not seen mice in these rooms?"

"A tail, perhaps." Gracia was smiling. "I would be happy to do your bidding, my lady."

"Then go seek our anchoress' servant. She might be in the kitchen now. Oh, and do you think you might take responsibility for the care of this new charge? Arthur is grown and fends for himself, but a kitten needs special care." She smiled. "Arthur will surely adjust to the new arrival." She looked down at the purring bundle of orange fur in her arms. "It is time you took some responsibility for your progeny, good sir!"

Gracia nodded with enthusiasm.

"The kitten must stay with its dam for a while longer. Look for a sturdy one."

Gracia headed for the door.

"You might want to name the creature and visit often so it will get used to your voice."

The girl agreed and danced out the open door, before running back and shutting it softly behind her.

"You have a problem with vermin?" Anne raised an eyebrow.

"Gracia needs the gift of a creature to love."

"She still does not trust her good fortune?"

"Nor would we if we saw our kin die of fever, learned to survive by our wits through winter, and suffered rape. Oh, and all this before we reached womanhood."

The sub-infirmarian lowered her gaze in sympathy.

Eleanor put the cat down and rubbed the arm that had been broken during her pilgrimage to the Walsingham shrines. Although fully healed, it ached on occasion and reminded her how close she had come to death.

"Would you like some ale?" Sister Anne reached for the jug on the table. "Does your arm still hurt?"

"The memories cause far more pain." The prioress took the offered mazer.

"Then let me distract you with some news!" The nun smiled with mischievous delight.

"Perchance our visiting priest has realized that he should be in Nuneaton instead of Tyndal?"

"Sadly, no, but I wanted to tell you that our beloved and revered sub-prioress has gout."

Eleanor coughed to hide what she knew was unkind amusement. "I am grieved…"

Sister Anne waved aside the need for charitable thought. "She is in pain, but I have shown sympathy enough for us both. When I asked if I could touch the afflicted toe, she stifled a scream and refused. It is very swollen and red, but I have a treatment that might help if taken faithfully and for a long time. That would require patience, a quality our sub-prioress is not known to possess."

"I have never heard of such a remedy."

"It is as old as Jacob and the pharaohs," Anne said. "My father had a recipe for the treatment, which I believe he had gotten from a physician who was very familiar with the work of Alexander of Tralles, and I memorized it as a girl. It is made from autumn crocus, a remedy that can be almost as deadly as monk's hood, if not used properly, and therefore is infrequently applied. But I have used it to help some who suffer the affliction. The dosage requires adjustment for weight and balance of humors, but the sub-prioress is resident here, not a courtier who wants to leave quickly. I can take the time to carefully and slowly make the required modifications."

"Why should she not try it? I have seen men who suffer from this. It often inflames feet until the person can no longer walk." Eleanor grimaced. "Gout is a great affliction."

"To quote our sub-prioress, she will not take 'potions or powders devised by the Devil.'"

"Since when have you offered any remedy that was not a gift from God?" Eleanor shook her head in disgust at her subordinate's obstinacy. "I would counsel her, but I fear she will not listen to me either."

The nun smiled. "I did find a solution!"

Eleanor threw up her hands in mock amazement. "Our subprioress rarely listens to reason. How have you coped with her aversion to logic?"

"I spoke to Sister Christina. Our sub-prioress respects our sweet nun, as we all do, for her gentle saintliness. When I told her Sub-Prioress Ruth's concern, our infirmarian said she would take the remedy and place it on the altar while she prayed. After that, she will take it to our sufferer, explain that it was been cleansed of all evil, and insist she take the blessed potion as instructed." Anne's expression softened. "Sister Christina has a wise heart as well as a kind one. She whispered in my ear that she would warn our sub-prioress about impatience. If God has blessed the cure, the patient must emulate the fortitude of Job."

"Those who think Sister Christina is a saint may not be wrong," Eleanor replied. Despite their differences in approach to healing, the two nuns had always worked together with mutual respect. In truth, having seen them consulting, the prioress concluded that two sisters from the same womb could not love each other more.

Of course Sister Anne prayed for the souls of those who came to her for a cure or relief, but she had been taught by her physician father that remedies were gifts from God for the comfort of men. Sister Christina might prefer prayer as a cure, and knew nothing of *potions and powders,* as Sub-Prioress Ruth called them, but she rejoiced when her sub-infirmarian used them with success and counted the cures as miracles.

"She might have been the better choice to care for Father Etienne's clerk," Anne said. "The priest was very angry when I arrived to diagnose the lad's ailment, but he was even more annoyed when Brother Thomas argued for my involvement and with Prior Andrew's next suggestion that Brother Thomas examine him."

Eleanor started. "Why was our good brother there? Father Etienne specifically refused his help when he told me about young Jean. That is why I had to ask for a lay brother to go with you and not Brother Thomas."

"I fear the error in bringing him with us was mine." Anne bowed her head. "Prior Andrew, Gracia, and I met him on the way to the guest quarters. I was surprised you had not included him in our party so I asked him to come with us." She looked at the shut door. "Poor Gracia knew the priest had refused to let him examine the clerk…"

"And she said nothing? Poor child! She probably believed it was not her right to contradict an adult."

"It was not until later that Gracia confessed that she knew he was not supposed to be there. She was in tears over the matter, believing she could have prevented the rudeness suffered by us all." Anne shook her head and smiled at Eleanor. "She is so much wiser than her years that I often forget she is still a child. I assured her that she owned no fault."

"And I shall tell her again, for it was I who erred in not telling you more than I did." She looked down at her hands. "When Gytha was not much older than she, I explained that I welcomed honesty, although I emphasized that it was usually wiser to speak to me that way in private. I shall repeat those words to Gracia and confirm that you are in agreement."

Anne nodded. She knew how much her friend missed her former maid so was delighted when the young orphan arrived at Tyndal and began to fill the hole in the prioress' heart.

"The priest's restrictions made a diagnosis difficult," the sub-infirmarian continued, "but Prior Andrew gave me enough information from the questions I asked and the observations he made. Growing weary of the awkward method, I suggested he confront Jean about the probable cause of his illness."

"Which is?"

"Too much wine or ale the night before. The youth finally confessed it."

"If Jean is wise, he will confess his sin to someone in this priory and not to his master. Our abbess' brother seems to have little tolerance for weakness or opposition and much faith in the infallibility of his opinions. I fear he may find great fault with the youthful clerk where others might see the need for kind guidance."

Sister Anne shook her head in sympathy. "What is the purpose of this visit? Has he told you why the abbess sent him?"

"No, but I hope to hear soon. If he has offered any clues, they would be in his welcoming sermons."

"The brothers were told they owed obedience to righteous leaders. We were warned against incontinent lust. Prior Andrew, Brother Thomas, and I could find no hint in those sermons that related to our priory."

Eleanor frowned. "Unless someone has suggested to Abbess Isabeau that my leadership is lax and someone is slipping over the walls to whore in the village."

"No one here has a complaint against your rule."

"Sub-Prioress Ruth?"

"She has never forgiven you for taking her place as prioress, but, as you have often noted, she obeys you, albeit with ill-grace."

"Have you heard any rumors about any of our religious breaking their vows?"

Anne looked away. "None except me, my lady. But Brother John has become a hermit, and our meetings were never sinful before my husband left the priory for his hut."

Allowing the pair to meet was a decision Eleanor often regretted, although she never doubted that the pair had remained chaste. "If that is the complaint, I shall have an answer for it and will do penance." When her friend started to protest, Eleanor put a calming hand on her arm. "Fear not. I never questioned your virtue or that of your husband. If there was sin, it was in my judgement, not in your acts."

The two fell silent.

Outside, birds sang to celebrate the last days of autumn warmth.

"If this visitation follows the usual practice for such things," Eleanor said, "he will send out an army of clerks tomorrow to look for foul drains, cracked floor tiles, leaking roofs, and fruit carelessly left unplucked from the trees. Then he shall demand the accounting rolls to review for errors, irregular rent-gathering, the purchase of frivolous baubles, and other horrors expected in any religious house run by a woman."

"How can he think that when his sister is Abbess Isabeau, the head of the Order of Fontevraud?"

"He must bow to Rome's decision that our Order is not heretical, but I suspect he would have concluded otherwise had he been the one to decide."

"He did tell Prior Andrew that he accepted a woman standing in the place of Our Lady as abbess and prioress in our Order, but all other sisters in this priory must obey the natural rule of men. I believe he does expect to find errors which would not exist if Tyndal were led by a prior."

"He will be disappointed." Eleanor shook her head. "I do not fear his review of the accounting rolls, and I know he will find maintenance needed on priory buildings. We have drawn up a list of repairs ourselves, put into the order of importance. He may point these things out. I shall bow my head, thank him profusely, and swear an honest oath that I shall have Prior Andrew attend to these urgent matters."

"You know what you must face. Why are you still worried? And do not deny it. I know your expressions well enough to read unease in them."

"The abbess of Fontevraud would have ordered a visit not long after I was given leadership of this place if there had been concern that I was unable to turn the finances of Tyndal around. She did not. All know this was once a Benedictine priory, converted to a double house in the reign of King John. It is old. Repairs are constant. Unlike other houses, we have had no roof or wall collapse, nor have we begged funds for major repairs. When Prior Andrew last traveled to Anjou after Easter, he gave a full report of what we had done, how we planned to address the remaining issues, and a complete account of expenditures. Abbess Isabeau was satisfied, even complimentary." Eleanor rubbed at her eyes as if longing to see more clearly.

"There is another purpose then."

"And no one has told me what it is. That troubles me."

"He must tell you."

"And he shall, but I do not know what he will do before that. If he believes the priory is guilty of significant wrongdoing, he will not confer with me before he speaks to as many of our religious, choir, and lay, as he deems necessary. In his questioning, he may put my authority and competence in doubt, even if this priory is innocent of any accusations."

"And who would cast such aspersions on the life we lead here?"

"Who knows what enemies we have made or what person of influence found a treatment, a bed, or a meal here to be unacceptable?"

"Surely this will be a small matter and quickly resolved without such damage," Anne replied.

Eleanor walked over and gave her friend a hug. "And, God willing, we shall laugh about it after the dust from the hooves of his departing palfrey has settled."

"In the meantime, I shall go back to my apothecary and prepare the remedy to calm the wine-battered stomach of the clerk, Jean."

"If God is kind, and Jean heals quickly, our abbess' brother may look upon the little faults in our priory with a more benevolent eye. Then we shall honor him with a feast of fish and vegetables from Sister Matilda's kitchen before sending him back to Anjou."

As she watched her friend depart, Prioress Eleanor's brave words dissipated like a morning mist and she was filled again with a sharp dread of what might occur on the morrow.

Chapter Nine

Gracia carefully poured dark ale from a large pitcher into the small mazer held by Father Etienne. Not one errant drop dampened his robe.

He observed that, but his grim expression did not soften.

Catching her maid's eye, Eleanor glanced at the platter of hard cheese and bright apples on the table.

Gracia replaced the pitcher and picked up the heavy platter. When she offered it to Davoir, he waved it away with a gesture commonly used to discourage flies.

Eleanor forced a smile, and then nodded discreetly at the table where her maid put the platter down. Now that the courtesy of offered refreshment was complete, Gracia went to the door and modestly cast her gaze to the rushes covering the stone floor. As inconspicuously as possible, she allowed herself a few glances to follow what was happening.

Savoring the drink, the priest pursed his lips, and then nodded. "Bitter but refreshing," he noted. "I assume there is a purpose for the absence of wine and use of such humble cups?" He raised the small pewter mazer, but his tone suggested curiosity rather than criticism.

"We have wine for the church and the sick," Eleanor replied. "As for the cups and platters, we only use gold and silver to honor God. Man may do with less." She tilted her head, her lips twitching into a brief smile.

"And I agree. Like all men, vowed to God, I have turned aside from the glitter of worldly things."

Without thinking, Eleanor looked at the jewel in his ring, then forced herself to look away as if distracted by the passing cloud that cast a brief shadow in the chambers. To be fair, she thought, the cross around his neck is simple, his robe is plain, and he wears no other adornment.

He waited, then continued. "What shall you do if King Edward visits?"

"Kings are anointed with holy oil, blessed on God's altar. For our king, we would provide a finer chalice, not for the mortal man, but to honor the One who blessed him and granted him the privilege and responsibility of justly ruling a Christian nation."

"My sister told me that you would be clever."

She did not feel clever, and this wordplay was meaningless. Eleanor grew impatient, for she feared that moment would be like the lowering of the hangman's noose over her head. She wished Brother Thomas was here with his calming manner, but Ralf had asked him to visit Gytha and hear her confession. Then, with a mix of dread and relief, she realized that Davoir shared her lack of interest in merry verbal games.

His smile fading, the priest cleared his throat. "My clerks found your accounting rolls to be in excellent order. The entries are done promptly and with adequate detail. They also found no payment for any item deemed inappropriate for a monastic house."

She bit her lip. What did he expect to find? Entries for the cost of falcons? The purchase of arrows so the monks might hunt between the Offices? There were no high-born bishops or abbots here who brought their hawks and falcons to the steps of the altar while they prayed. Some priories and abbeys might allow these luxurious pleasures, but she would never permit them in her priory.

"Abbess Isabeau heard that you had turned the sad state of this priory's assets into a profitable condition after your arrival. She will be pleased to know the tale has been confirmed."

A situation the abbess had learned some time ago after Prior Andrew's visits to the abbey with complete accounts, Eleanor thought, but murmured gratitude for the intended compliment. At least this investigation was not ordered because of some rumor of financial wrongdoing.

"As for the state of the priory buildings, walls, mill, fish ponds, orchards and gardens, I have some questions and a few deficiencies for you to address. Amongst those who accompanied me on this journey is a man who was a stonemason before God called him to a higher craft. I set him to examine the buildings."

Gesturing to Gracia, the prioress indicated that she wished a certain document brought to her. Unrolling it, she waited for him to list his findings.

"There is an unsightly growth of dank moss in the window over the altar in the chapel. It dims the light coming into that place of worship."

"The moss has been deliberately left to remind us that the human spirit must always strive to see the light in the darkness of earthly sin."

Even if he did not acknowledge appreciation of her purpose in words, Davoir's eyes brightened before he went to the next item. "The stones in the wall near the mill gate are loose."

She looked down at her document. "We plan to repair that in late spring. If we did so now, we might have to mend it again after the snows. When the lay brother examined the wall, he found it strong enough to last one more winter."

He mentioned two more items for which she had also planned work. Again he smiled. "Well done. As for the bee skeps, gardens, and orchards, your lay brothers and sisters have tended them with skill. Since these are things for which I have a particular fondness, I chose to examine that aspect of your priory myself."

"Then I am especially honored that you found no neglect." Trying to keep her hands steady, she rolled up her document and gave it back to Gracia for safekeeping.

"I also noted that you seem to adhere to the Rule in matters of diet, silence, Offices, and attire."

"Our nuns, barring needs of family or other assigned duties to God, spend their days in prayer. Our anchoress, Juliana, is known for her pious advice to those who seek it. Our hospital offers spiritual comfort for the dying and cures for those whom God does not yet call…"

He waved his hand to interrupt. "I found no defect in these matters."

"Yet I hear a note of concern in your voice. In what have you found a fault?"

"Your infirmarian is a pious woman and helps the dying turn their thoughts to Heaven with her prayers. As for Sister Anne, I found a lack of humility in her as well as an unwillingness to be directed by those wiser than she." He looked at his mazer.

In an instant, Gracia was at his side and refilled it.

"I am troubled that you have no monk or even lay brother with sufficient training to determine the necessary treatments and potions. While a woman's bodily imperfections are simple and her frailties may be easily understood, the physical ills of God's more intricate creations, Adam's sons, are beyond the comprehension of a woman."

"Since Sister Anne has performed many noteworthy cures, witnessed by physicians and priests alike, I must conclude that God guides her hand." She bowed her head. "How else may we explain this daughter of Eve owning the skills of Adam's sons?" Before he interrupted her, she went on. "But perhaps your investigating clerk did not realize that Brother Thomas has some skill in these matters. He often takes remedies to the village for those who cannot travel to the hospital to receive them." She omitted any mention that the sub-infirmarian made the cures and had done the monk's training.

"Her treatment of my clerk has not been successful. Perhaps God chose this time while I was here to demonstrate His displeasure with her."

Eleanor flushed with outrage. If Sister Anne had improperly diagnosed the clerk, she did so because of the priest's interference. "May I suggest that she and Brother Thomas be allowed to examine the young man together? Prior Andrew is not an apothecary. His skills lie in other areas, such as administering our lands and rents, which you found capably executed."

He stiffened. "I find your stubborn insistence in this matter unseemly, despite my clear objection, and I reject your renewed suggestion. Although I would have preferred to reveal the purpose of my investigation in a gentler manner, you now force me to be blunt. This visit was not something my sister wished to order, nor did she want to send me away from court at the very time when I might be offered a bishop's miter."

Eleanor felt a chill course through her. Had winter come so soon? Trying not to show her fear, she clutched her hands, prayed for strength, and waited.

"It has come to Abbess Isabeau's attention that you and Brother Thomas have an unchaste relationship."

Stunned beyond belief, Eleanor leapt to her feet. "That is a lie! Who has dared to make such a vile accusation?" Her outraged expression of innocence was honest enough. Although she might long for a different union with the handsome and gentle monk than one of brother and sister in God's service, she knew Brother Thomas had never once been accused of sin with any woman since he took vows. Most certainly, he had never shown the slightest carnal interest in her.

"The source of this news shall remain anonymous."

"Ask anyone in this priory or in the village outside our walls. Brother Thomas has never once broken his vows by lying with a woman or even looking at one with lust. And, if he is innocent of that, then you may conclude that he and I are joined only by our love of God."

"I have not yet begun my questioning of the religious in this priory."

"Then start immediately!" Eleanor slammed her staff of office against the floor. All courtesy due this man because of his mission, relationship to the Abbess of Fontevraud, and his stature in the French king's court had just ended.

Davoir blinked in the face of such rage and hesitated before he also rose to his feet. "I shall begin with your sub-prioress."

It was Eleanor's turn to pause. Of all the people he might have queried, he would choose the one who viewed her with much ill-will. But on quick reflection, she believed that even Sub-Prioress Ruth would not stoop so low as to accuse her of bedding Brother Thomas.

"She is an excellent choice," Eleanor replied. "She will answer your questions in a forthright manner and will hide nothing to my discredit. She is an honorable servant of God."

The silence in the chambers grew as heavy as the lead roof over the adjacent chapel.

A loud knocking startled them.

Shocked and outraged over the accusations leveled at her mistress and Brother Thomas, Gracia was red-faced with anger when she ran for the door. Who had dared disobey her mistress' order to be left in peace while she spoke with this priest? If she had had a broom, Gracia would have gladly swept the rude intruder away.

But the lay sister on the other side of the door fell to her knees and reached out in supplication. "Please, my lady!"

Eleanor hurried to the door. "What is it?"

The messenger's face was gray. "The clerk, Jean!"

Davoir stepped forward. "What has happened? Speak!"

"He is dead." The woman buried her face in her hands and wept.

Chapter Ten

Eleanor and the lay sister waited outside the chamber where the corpse rested.

Within, Davoir knelt by the body of his beloved Jean and wailed with unrestrained grief.

"He was like a son to him, my lady," a voice nearby said.

The prioress turned to see the other clerk she had seen with the priest when they arrived. This time, there was no hint of his previous boredom. His thin lips trembled.

"My name is Renaud," he said, opting to remind her of his name as a courtesy lest the tragedy of this moment had chased it from her memory. "I am second in responsibility to my dead companion." A tear wove its way down his cheek.

Eleanor caught herself wondering why only one eye wept, then chastised herself for such a petty thought. "I grieve for you as well. The death of a friend, even one who has surely found God's favor, is a wounding loss," she said. Although compassion required that she honor his grief, her loyalty to Sister Anne equally demanded she probe into this inexplicable death.

"Father Etienne told me that the remedy offered by our healers did nothing for poor Jean," she said. "I did not know of this, nor, I suspect, did our sub-infirmarian. She would have sought an explanation for why her measures were failing before this death took place."

Renaud rubbed the dampness from his cheek. "She must have known, my lady. I told the lay brother, who brought the cure, that Jean failed to thrive. He said the treatment would take time and that he had informed Sister Anne of the symptoms I mentioned."

How odd, the prioress thought. The sub-infirmarian had mentioned none of this, and, if the lad only suffered from a surfeit of ale, he should have been cured by now. "What was this lay brother's name?" If there was blame to cast here, this information was the place to start.

"Brother Imbert."

"Imbert?" The prioress frowned. "Are you certain?"

"I am, my lady. He mentioned his name several times." He flushed. "I cannot be mistaken."

She looked at the lay sister who shook her head. "We have no monk or lay brother bearing that name."

"Someone lies!" Davoir leaned against the door to the dead clerk's room, his eyes swollen from weeping. He gestured to Renaud. "Bring this sub-infirmarian here. Now. She has much to explain."

"Her duties…"

"Now!"

Eleanor flushed at the imperious tone. This was her priory, not his, but she swallowed the insult and chose silence.

Davoir gestured to his clerk and pointed at the main door. Renaud ran from the room.

It did not take long for Sister Anne to arrive. Seeing Eleanor's troubled expression, she knew the summons involved a grave matter.

"Who is Brother Imbert?" Davoir's eyes flashed.

The light in his gaze reminded Eleanor of sermons describing hellfire.

Anne looked at Eleanor, then at the priest. "I am perplexed by the question, Father. There is no such man at Tyndal Priory."

The priest's mouth twisted with contempt. "Tell her what occurred," he said to Renaud. "Let her explain herself."

"But you sent Brother Imbert!" the youth protested. "He brought the remedy for Jean and gave instructions for its use. He insisted that the directions came from you. When I repeatedly told him that my fellow clerk did not improve, he said he had conveyed the news and that you insisted we must be patient. The remedy would take time. Today Jean suffered convulsions and…" He covered his face.

"But I sent no such person to you!" Anne looked around in horror. "A clerk came at your command, Father Etienne. Once only. I did give him the treatment and instructions."

"Name this clerk," Davoir snarled.

"I cannot. He gave me no name. I never saw him again. Might he have been the *Imbert* of whom you speak?"

"Describe the man."

"I am unable to do so with any detail." She clenched her fist and shut her eyes. "Medium height. No distinctive accent or tone of voice." Anne threw her hands up in frustration. "The light was poor. His hood cast his face in shadow…"

Davoir spun around to face Eleanor, his face scarlet with rage. "I sent no one. She lies! Her remedy was useless, and she wants to hide her incompetence by suggesting a strange plot." Tears wended their way down his cheeks again. "Perhaps you are about to claim that this was an imp sent by the Evil One to kill a youth who served God well?" He swiped the moisture from his cheeks and pointed at Anne. "Maybe this fiend is well-known to you, Sister."

"Enough!" Eleanor shouted with outrage. "Why assume there is something evil in a nun who has done much good in God's name? We have no Brother Imbert, but that does not mean my sub-infirmarian has formed a pact with the Devil or is lying." She began to turn toward Renaud and suggest he might have grounds to lie, but his grief-stricken face stopped her and she fell silent. One unjust accusation was one too many.

But Davoir had read her initial intent. "Why look accusingly at my clerk? What cause has he to tell a false tale? Renaud and Jean were like brothers!"

"I do not claim he did," Eleanor replied. As if Satan had passed by, she wrinkled her nose. Something smelled foul, but she could not trace the source. All she knew for certain was that Sister Anne would not lie.

Shaking with anger and grief, the priest glowered at Sister Anne. "I accuse you of murder," he said, his voice rough with emotion. "When I refused to allow you to examine Jean, a godly youth who cringed at the very sight of women, you were resentful and let sin find a welcome in your heart. It was the Prince of Darkness who urged you to poison the devout lad out of wicked spite." Suddenly, he faced Eleanor again. "Or there is another purpose here. You ordered your nun to kill my clerk so that I might flee in fear and not investigate the heinous crimes of which you may be guilty."

Anne staggered in shock. Recovering, she turned red with fury and took one step toward the priest.

Eleanor put a hand on her friend's arm to hold her back. "Beware the temptation to falsely accuse. God deems that a sin," she said to Davoir, biting the end off each word. "If you insist on finding fault without proof, I shall plead my innocence directly to Rome."

His horror was as palpable as his anger. "I never condemn without proof. Nor shall I denounce you until I have concluded my inquiry into the initial foulness of which you remain accused."

Eleanor wanted to argue that he had lost all semblance of objectivity and ought not to continue this absurd investigation at all, but something stopped her. It would be futile, she decided, to attempt to debate with one who was blind to facts.

He raised a hand to command a silence that already existed. "Be grateful that I retain my desire, and that of my sister, for a just examination despite the painful death of my best clerk. I shall not order you to be locked away until I am done, Prioress Eleanor. If you are found innocent, your statements in support of this nun will be given due credence. If not, I shall denounce you both as Satan's whores." He pointed a shaking finger at Sister Anne. "She, however, must be locked away to prevent her from harming anyone else in my party. For that order, I have cause."

Sister Anne gestured to her prioress not to protest on her

behalf. "I accept that confinement, Father, but beg one thing," Anne said, her tone unnaturally meek.

He hesitated, then sighed and agreed.

"Bring what is left of the remedy I am accused of sending so I may examine it. There is no evil in my request. You are here to watch me, and I shall immediately return it into your own hand."

Sketching the sign of the cross to ward off evil, Davoir told Renaud to retrieve it.

When the clerk handed her the open jar, Anne asked what instructions had been given for its use.

He closed his eyes and repeated them slowly.

"Odd," she said. "Those are not what I would have ordered for a drink of powdered ginger root and chamomile. She gazed into the jar, and her eyes grew round with disbelief. "This is autumn crocus," she said in a whisper. "Tell me how he died?"

Renaud described Jean's death agony in great detail.

"This preparation is for gout, not a queasy stomach. Even if Jean had suffered from gout, he would have died from the dosage you said I ordered." Her face the color of chalk, she whispered, "As he has and in the manner described."

"Lock her in a room with the guard I alone provide," Davoir ordered. "If there is a man nearby who represents the king's justice, he must be brought here to see the corpse." He smiled at the infirmarian, his expression not unlike a cat savoring the sight of a doomed mouse. "But the Church will order the punishment you must suffer for this crime, and I promise that you shall long for death."

"I submit to this, my lady," Anne said to her prioress. "As Heaven is my hope, I shall be found innocent."

Chapter Eleven

The tiny cell had no windows. No rushes softened the stone floor. This room had once been used for storage, then converted to a cell to hold a monk accused of murder. One person had died here, and the room thereafter remained empty of all but ghosts. A few claimed there was one in particular, who sometimes hurried through the outside corridor in a stinging mist, wailing for mercy from his place in Hell.

Sister Anne sat on the prickly mat that would be her bed and stared at the lone flickering candle she had been allowed to banish darkness and evil spirits. There was nothing else to give comfort, but if her fortitude had weakened, she did not show it. Hands folded, she stared at the rough walls without blinking.

With no warning, the door squeaked open.

Prioress Eleanor and her maid walked in.

Sister Anne rose to her knees, bowed her head, and only now began to weep.

From the hall outside, a hand reached in and slammed the door shut.

"Forgive me, my lady!"

Eleanor grasped her friend's arm. "Rise! You need not beg forgiveness."

"I have added to your burden!" Anne looked around as if some solution to this nightmare might be found in the trembling shadows. "I swear I sent the right remedy and proper instructions with a clerk who claimed to come from our abbess' brother."

"I know you are telling the truth. We must discover who had motivation to do this thing, why, and how."

"And you have been accused of a vile misdeed by some unknown person? Who would dare do such a thing?"

"There is too much awry," Eleanor said with a thin smile. "You have not asked the nature of my crime, but the word will soon be out. Brother Thomas and I are accused of lying together in lust. That was the purpose for which Father Etienne was sent on this visit."

Anne turned white with horror.

"I do not believe that our abbess sent her brother because she longs to discredit me. She is an honorable woman, and her elevation to abbess brought us great joy. I am convinced they both want facts, not an easy resolution based in half-gathered information."

"Hasn't Abbess Isabeau always found Prior Andrew's reports on Michaelmas or Easter satisfactory?" Anne could barely speak. "How could she give any credence…?"

"She must do so. Recently, she has had cause to fear Rome's displeasure. I heard that some of her abbey monks have grown rebellious under a woman's rule. If Rome learns that one of her prioresses has also broken her vows with a monk, many more bishops will demand intervention, claiming these disciplinary problems prove that a woman's leadership is against God's law. If her brother can satisfactorily resolve the difficulty here, while she quells the restless abbey monks, Rome will be less inclined to interfere with the practices of our Order."

"Someone must want you found guilty and removed from your position," Anne finally said. "Why else damn you for lust and me for killing a young clerk?"

"Perhaps the reasons for the charge of wantonness and the death of Jean are not the same." Eleanor turned thoughtful. Although she had not yet told Ralf of this, she was reminded of the soldier's death on the way to the priory. The guard captain had suggested it was the result of some grievous quarrel between two men, a conclusion Eleanor would not have questioned if the death of Davoir's clerk had not occurred so soon after. Was there another motive that linked the guard's death with Jean's? "To condemn me for unchaste behavior is one thing. That suggests malice. Killing a clerk to add to that accusation is excessive."

"Unless the malice has turned the soul gangrenous, and then murder would not be such an extreme act." Anne looked over at Gracia. The girl's face was wan in the muddy candlelight, and the sub-infirmarian's expression spoke of her grief that this child should hear this and suffer another threat to her security.

Eleanor shivered. She could imagine there were some who would enjoy embarrassing her by claiming she had broken her vows. There was no one she knew who hated her so much that he would kill to force her removal from the leadership of Tyndal. She shook her head to clear it.

Jean's death, the soldier's murder, the accusations against her sub-infirmarian, and the initial claims of her own transgressions could be related. Or not. There were too many coincidences to discount a connection. Yet she had few facts, many paths she might follow, and little time to determine what properly fit together for the most logical conclusion.

If only she could learn who had initiated the original claim of immoral behavior, she might be able to decide if everything had the same foul origin. Regarding the guard's death on the journey here, the event might have been, as Davoir reported, the result of a quarrel between two men. She should leave that matter to Ralf, she thought, but she knew she could not forget about it.

"Dare you investigate this matter at all, my lady?" Anne's voice was soft with concern. "Might you not be accused of tainting evidence or obscuring facts for your own benefit?"

"Nor may Brother Thomas on the same grounds," the prioress replied. "I can only pray that Father Etienne does not conclude he must take over the investigation into his clerk's death since neither Brother Thomas nor I can be trusted to do so."

"Ralf must examine the body."

"But the priory is under the jurisdiction of the Church. All he can do is determine cause of death and help in the investigation. Were he to discover the killer, he could not send him for punishment unless the guilty one is subject to the king's law. Otherwise, the Church decides the penalty."

"I may have been the source of the accusation of murder against you, my lady, but Brother Thomas remains free of that."

Eleanor shrugged. "He is not tainted with the claim of murder, but he remains suspect in breaking his vows and doing so with me. He will be watched. We cannot be seen together."

"How could anyone have accused you both of such acts?"

Eleanor shook her head. "Had this death not occurred, I feel certain that Brother Thomas would emerge from the charge, his virtue untarnished. You know him well. Has there ever been one word spoken against him?"

"Even your sub-prioress has high praise for his piety and goodness."

"Let us hope she will be half as kind to me," Eleanor said. "Father Etienne plans to question her first about my own chastity."

Anne stiffened. "She would not dare…" She stopped, but her tone suggested she thought the sub-prioress capable of doing just that.

"Despite our quarrels over the years, and her justified grievance against me, Sub-Prioress Ruth is a woman of honor."

"She has no justified grievance."

"She was elected Prioress of Tyndal before King Henry over-ruled the priory and sent me to head this place instead. That is grounds for acceptable resentment."

"And you have honored her by placing her in charge during your absences, including her in discussions about the priory businesses, and treating her with respect."

"And I have usually not agreed with her opinions on the way the priory should be run, how best to serve God, or even how to pay our debts."

"You have been proven right in your decisions."

Gracia watched the conversation between the two older women with fascination. Seeing her interest, Eleanor put a hand on the girl's shoulder. "Our sub-prioress owns virtues. Has she not welcomed Gracia to our priory and arranged a fine education for her?"

Anne smiled for the first time. "Even the Devil might accidentally fall into goodness against his will."

Bending forward, Eleanor whispered, "Be careful, Anne! He might hear you." Then she grew serious again. "Despite the difficulties strewn in the path, I shall not remain idle in the matter of Jean's death, even if my involvement must remain secret. Tell me in more detail about the remedy you sent to treat the youth."

Quickly, the nun repeated what she had said before.

After a moment, the prioress asked, "Can you recall anything odd about the person who came to you? A twitch, an odd way of pronouncing a word, some other habit or identifying mark?"

"I did think it strange that the priest would send a clerk when I had promised to deliver the cure by a lay brother who could answer questions, if needed, about the use." She paused. "This clerk spoke very softly. I thought he was shy, but when I asked him to repeat something, he seemed unable to do so in a louder voice. I remember hoping he understood what I was telling him. He did not ask any questions."

"He spoke our tongue well?"

"Yes. But, after I thought more on it, I realize he did have a slight accent. That was why I believed Father Etienne had sent him."

"And you could not see his face?"

"No. He held the hood around his mouth and nose like we do in bitterly cold weather. At the time, I wondered if he was so cold because the climate where he had come from was so much warmer."

"The color of his eyes?"

"I could not see in the shadows."

"Where, I assume, he stayed."

Sister Anne nodded.

"You gave him the container of ground ginger and chamomile with the instructions. Did he leave immediately?"

The nun stared at her prioress. "No! A lay sister came to tell me I was urgently needed. After I resolved the problem, I returned, but the man had left." She shook her head. "I did not think I was gone long and assumed he wanted to hasten back to Jean with the cure and, perhaps, had understood my directions perfectly."

"Was he alone in the apothecary room while you were gone?"

"I thought the lay sister was going to stay with him. When I came back, neither he nor she was there. It is possible that he was alone." She frowned in thought, then shook her head.

Eleanor raised an eyebrow.

"It is nothing. I was thinking that I had been called away so quickly by the lay sister that I wasn't sure I had put the gout remedy back in its place, as is my wont. I must have. It was not on the table when I got back to the hut." Her smile was wan.

"Who would know best about your routines in preparing cures and where you keep the ingredients? I ask because this person might know if more is missing than should be or if something has been moved."

"There is one young nun who is showing promise in the healing art, my lady. She might be able to answer your…" Anne put her hand against her mouth.

"You are right. I cannot go there and ask these questions."

"And Brother Thomas?"

"It would be wise if he did not either."

Anne covered her face.

Prioress Eleanor reached over and hugged her friend. "Weep not," she said. "For every obstruction, there is a path around it." And she turned to Gracia with a warm smile.

The warmth was matched by the eager glow in the maid's eyes. "I would be honored to help in any way you ask, my lady," she said.

Chapter Twelve

Davoir nodded curtly at the nun who admitted him to Sub-Prioress Ruth's empty audience chamber. As he waited to be announced, he gazed at the small room. The few furnishings showed no elegance of form, he thought. Even the prioress owned little that suggested fine craft. How primitive this Tyndal Priory was compared to the abbey in Anjou.

He sighed with annoyance. Perhaps he should have waited until his anger dissipated before meeting with this sub-prioress. Without question, he was a man of good judgement and fairness, with the rectitude expected in one dedicated to God's service, but grief over the death of his favored clerk had scorched his heart until the pain made him lash out in fury. He had been right, of course, to condemn the incompetent sub-infirmarian, but his passionate denunciation of Prioress Eleanor had been unseemly. He would do penance for that. Later he would also apologize to her, but only if she was innocent of the other alleged crimes.

Sadly, he had no choice about continuing this investigation, no matter what grief he suffered over Jean's death. His sorrow would not fade any time soon, despite his efforts to will it away, and his obligation had not changed. He must return as soon as possible with a complete, irrefutable report to Fontevraud Abbey.

The religious of Tyndal must be questioned about their prioress, and it was his duty to do so. Others might peer into fish ponds or test roofs for leaks, but only he had the authority to investigate moral failings of those vowed to God.

Davoir closed his eyes and bent his head in prayer. "May God give me the strength to shake off this womanish frailty of emotion," he murmured. "As a man, objectivity and logic must rule within me."

He looked up. There was still no sound from the other rooms. How long must he wait for this sub-prioress? With growing impatience, he loudly cleared his throat.

How he yearned to be back at court where the world was understandable. Even under better circumstances, he would have found his duty here onerous. His sister might be abbess at Fontevraud, and Rome had given the Order its blessing, but he believed a woman's leadership over men was against the laws of creation. Nonetheless, his disapproval was secondary to the needs of family honor in this undertaking. His sister led this strange Order, and he was obliged to do anything for her that would keep the name of Davoir from disgrace.

If the arrogant Prioress Eleanor, her assertive monk, and her incompetent sub-infirmarian were innocent of the alleged wrongs, the findings would cleanse his sister of any hint of misrule. If the trio were as guilty as he believed, he would make sure their punishment was harsh enough to turn dishonor into praise for his family name.

A voice interrupted his thoughts.

Casting his musing aside, he turned to see a stocky woman lumbering painfully into the room, assisted by the younger and vacant-eyed nun who had admitted him.

The presumed sub-prioress fell into her high-backed chair with an inelegant grunt.

Despite the sub-prioress' modest veil, he noticed a forehead creased with scowls and eyes narrowed as if in perpetual disapproval. Perhaps she had as much cause as he to be angry against the rule in this priory. Or, glancing at her foot now resting on a stool, was she simply in pain?

He was annoyed that this nun did nothing to honor his standing before God and his position as the representative of Fontevraud Abbey. He waited while the attendant nun settled the sub-prioress into a more comfortable position and then took her own place against the wall by the door.

"I beg for your pardon, Father," the sub-prioress said, gesturing at her foot. "I suffer from gout and cannot stand."

He forgave the fault and quickly gave the blessing she begged. As a man honored in the court of his own king, and soon be named one of the Church's bishops, he concluded she would be especially grateful for his benevolence. Indeed, she flushed with evident thankfulness. He was content.

"Were you present for my opening sermon?" He did not remember this square-bodied woman, but he might not have noticed her.

"I fear my affliction did not permit it, Father, but Sister Christina repeated as much as she could remember of your words." With a fleeting smile, even more briefly warmed with a hint of affection, she gestured at the nun who kept her eyes lowered.

He caught himself resenting the sub-prioress for having a cherished attendant when his own had just died. Stiffening his back, he attempted to expel the imp-inspired jealousy with a sharp cough.

"I do know that your purpose here is to review all aspects of our life, recommend improvements, and order punishments for any lapses that offend God." She put her hands together in an attitude of prayer. "We are all sinners," she murmured, "and each of us suffers some vice."

His brief moment of sinful imperfection defeated, Davoir studied the sub-prioress with his accustomed objectivity. Gruff as this woman looked, he suspected she possessed as much intellect as any woman could honestly own while still retaining a proper meekness. His sister also had a more manly sagacity, but she had preserved a modest demeanor. In this priory, however, he had found at least two women who lacked that essential feminine virtue of humility. He bestowed a benevolent smile on Sub-Prioress Ruth, who had not lost the attribute.

"How may I assist in your investigation, Father?" She winced and reached to touch her foot, then drew back with an expression of horror at the pain she had almost caused.

He understood, having known men at court who suffered this disease. It was rare for a woman. Davoir wondered if the prioress had lied to him about the simple fare offered here, and others did the same out of fear of her chastisement. Perhaps she had only provided him with food and drink according to the Rule, while the monastics drank fine wines and the flesh of four-footed beasts when no one was here to see them.

It would please him if that were true, and he could point to this woman's gout as proof of a rich diet. But this sub-prioress' sternness suggested honesty to him, and he suspected she would speak only of facts. He would confirm with her what others of lower rank in the priory had said about diet.

"It is indeed my duty, as decreed by your abbess in Anjou, to look into the practices of Tyndal and the virtue of all inhabitants here." Davoir was encouraged by the sight of a scowl so deep that the sub-prioress' eyebrows collided. "My first questions are whether the Hours for prayer are honored, if the diet prescribed by the Rule of Saint Benedict is practiced, and whether the nuns keep their vows and remain sequestered."

"And it is my responsibility to make sure our nuns honor the canonical hours, their vows, do not communicate with the world unless family concerns or God demands it, and spend their waking hours in prayer or other holy work. In these matters, I can confirm strict obedience. If any have said otherwise, I shall explain or provide proof of their error."

Her demeanor pleased him, and her brevity was refreshing. According to his sister, this sub-prioress also had no cause to love Prioress Eleanor since she had been supplanted by the younger woman at the will of the English king. For this reason, he had chosen the sub-prioress to interrogate first. If anyone would tell the truth about the leadership here, it would be she. Even Prioress Eleanor did not dare say otherwise. "And diet?"

"Sister Matilda is in charge of the kitchens. Although our beloved Prioress Felicia expected each nun to take on new responsibilities after a certain period of time, Prioress Eleanor has chosen to retain nuns in positions when she finds them well-suited."

Ah, he thought with a shiver of excitement, a criticism of the woman who led here. "This practice might promote unacceptable pride amongst the few."

"I would have chosen to follow the direction taken by our former prioress in that matter." She gnawed on her lip. "Yet our adherence to a strict diet grew lax during her last years. When Prioress Eleanor arrived, she ordered a return to a more careful observance of the Benedictine Rule on food. Only the sick and aged are allowed wine and meat. There are other exceptions but all within the Rule. Some say she follows a more austere interpretation than most, but I cannot fault her for that. The blessed Robert, our founder, believed that even the sick should abstain from meat."

Davoir nodded. Then the monastics had not lied to him. The young prioress had certainly given him unremarkable refreshment, although she had not stinted on the quantity of fruit and cheese. The ale had actually been of good quality, and there were no worms in the fruit. "Pride in accomplishment still troubles me. If this nun in charge of the kitchens does well..."

"Sister Matilda performs her duties with joy, a form of prayer that God accepts. Sister Edith, who has remained in charge of directing the lay sisters in the gardens, does the same. God has blessed us with abundant vegetables and fruit from our orchard." She raised her chin in defiance. "If I believed either nun owned sinful pride, I would have admonished her in Chapter."

He agreed there was no fault in pious joy and went on to another concern. "Why are there only nuns in charge of the hospital?"

Ruth flushed behind her veil. "Sister Christina is our infirmarian, a nun whose virtue is exemplary and whose prayers have healed many." Discreetly, she indicated the woman by the door.

"Prayers are worthy," he said. "I was more troubled by the sub-infirmarian, a woman who uses herbs and roots more than prayer." He grew solemn. "Her forceful manner is also troubling in a woman who has taken vows."

"Prioress Felicia would have agreed with you. She feared that Sister Anne's potions gave ease to men whose sharp pain might otherwise bring about repentance of their grave sins." She shook her head. "Still, God has not punished us for wickedness. The sub-infirmarian's skills have cured many, and their gratitude has brought us gifts of land, rents, and flocks. I still have doubts, but God has shown no sign of His." She smiled at the silent nun nearby. "Perhaps it is Sister Christina's prayers that please so much, and, for that, He has forgiven any other fault?"

As anger stabbed at his heart, Davoir failed to acknowledge her question. My clerk died due to Sister Anne's remedies, he thought. Perhaps that was a sign that God had lost patience with the arrogant sub-infirmarian.

He cleared his throat. "I must now ask an especially troubling question, one that will try your loyalty to your prioress but which must be answered honestly. God demands it. Your abbess does as well."

Ruth's face turned pale, but she assented firmly. "Prioress Eleanor knows that I do not often agree with her and that I will speak my mind. She has always allowed me to give my opinion without fear of public rebuke."

"Abbess Isabeau has been informed that Prioress Eleanor and the monk, Thomas, have an unchaste relationship, that they lie together to satisfy their unholy lusts, and that their wickedness is well-known."

The sub-prioress' head snapped back as if she had been struck. Her mouth opened, but all she could utter was inarticulate sound.

Sister Christina rushed to her side.

"Please bring me a cup of ale," Ruth managed to gasp. She closed her eyes and covered her face. "A mazer for our guest as well," she whispered.

Davoir shook his head at the offer and stared at this woman he expected to rejoice in the accusation against her prioress. If proven, the sub-prioress would be the likely choice to replace the disgraced leader. Not knowing what to say, he waited for her to finish her ale and recover her composure.

She sipped at the drink, and her complexion regained a more uniform color. "Forgive me, Father, but those particular charges were so unexpected…"

He tried not to show his disappointment.

"As I said, Prioress Eleanor and I have had many disagreements. For years, I resented the manner in which I was set aside from the position she now holds, not because of God's will but rather the wish of our earthly king." She gave the cup to Sister Christina who remained by her side. "Indeed, I admit my failure to cast this sin from my heart each time I see my confessor."

"Is the claimed offense against the prioress correct?" The priest in charge of this woman's sins could deal with her soul, he thought. He wanted an answer to his question.

Sub-Prioress Ruth sat up in her chair and stared at him. "Brother Thomas is known by all, in the priory and including those he serves outside, as a virtuous and kind man. Never has anyone claimed that he has broken his vows of chastity. Like our blessed founder, he has walked into the midst of wickedness and emerged shining and victorious because of his goodness. You may ask anyone."

"And Prioress Eleanor? Has she remained chaste?"

"Most certainly she has never lain with Brother Thomas!" She gazed at the ceiling, swallowed several times, and fell silent, then looked back at Davoir with an inscrutable expression. "Nor has anyone questioned her chastity. A prioress must step outside the priory walls to serve God and talk with wicked mortals, a duty that puts her resolve on trial. As proof of her virtue, many here believe that the Virgin blessed her with a vision, yet our prioress claims she could never be worthy of such a thing and went on pilgrimage last year to expiate any sin of pride she might own. That speaks to her humility."

He had hoped for another response and was surprised by the sub-prioress' defense of a woman she despised.

"On my hope that Heaven shall welcome my soul as it flies to God's judgement, I swear to you that I believe Prioress Eleanor is innocent and that the accusation against her is not only without any basis but was spoken with foul intent."

Even though he detected an element of sorrow in her tone, Davoir found no good cause to argue against her forceful oath.

With minimal courtesy, he stood and abruptly left the chambers.

Chapter Thirteen

As that hour approached when God tints the sky with blues and lavenders, the time when weary creatures long for the blessing of rest after their labors have ended, Philippe of Picardy slipped out of the hospital grounds and found the path that led to the guest quarters.

Lest someone look curiously at him, he slowly hobbled on his crutch. If anyone chose to question why he was walking that particular way, he could honestly say that he was healing and the easy path let him strengthen the ankle before he traveled on. One look at his ragged attire would confirm that Philippe was too poor to pay for a horse or a ride in a cart and needed two sturdy feet for any journey.

As the sun slipped into its bed below the earth's edge, the air swiftly cooled and he shivered. Briefly, he wondered if the world was flat, like some claimed, or round, as others averred, but quickly decided it was a question too immense for any flawed mortal to answer. All he knew for sure was that the earth was the center of God's universe and the sun must be obedient to it. He thought it regrettable that the orb had not retained that submission a bit longer so he need not suffer this nighttime chill.

As he approached the quarters, he looked around. In that moment, there were no others to see him. He slipped to his knees and crawled into the shrubbery where he had previously found a comfortable clearing with a nice mat of leaves on which to sit and view the place where the hated priest stayed.

It was regrettable that the clerk had died, he thought. The lad was innocent, but Philippe did not overly grieve. Anything that hurt Davoir gladdened his heart, and Jean was as beloved as a son to the man. "Of which he has had many," he muttered with sharp bitterness. Jean was but one of those the priest had begun to prepare for a career in the Church that would complement the stellar heights Davoir hoped he himself would eventually obtain. Or perhaps Jean would have been cast aside to suffer the oblivion of poverty no matter what his talent.

This time Philippe shivered for a reason besides the chilly air. Then his eyes filled with hot tears. He rubbed them away, but the pain lingered, for the heat was born of hatred. Only one thing would purify his heart of this rage, and he was feeling more confident that he could soon achieve it.

His one fear in coming to this place was the knowledge that Prioress Eleanor and Brother Thomas were blessed by God with uncanny abilities to ferret out guilty souls. Although he might be willing to die if he could make sure Father Etienne suffered agony enough to pay for his cruelties, Philippe preferred to escape back to France and live with the sweet peace he believed revenge would bring him.

Now that Jean was dead and a rumor was spreading that Sister Anne was accused of murder, perhaps under the direction of her prioress, he felt more certain of survival.

Even before he met her at the hospital, Philippe had heard of this sub-infirmarian's reputation for healing and her keen eye for a suspicious death. That she had been cast into a cell was good news. And the prioress herself was under enough suspicion that she dared not investigate lest she be charged with unlawful meddling.

His heart beat with increasing joy. As for the monk, Brother Thomas had been accused of bedding his prioress, information he learned from his informant who had alerted him to Davoir's journey here. Anything the monk did to look into the clerk's death would also be deemed questionable. As for the local king's man, Philippe assumed he would be as ignorant as any other without medical skills when it came to death by something other than a sword or rock.

"God wills it!" Philippe caught himself before he spoke above a dangerous whisper, but his self-assurance was growing rapidly.

With the sub-infirmarian safely locked away, another death would cast more blame on the prioress and perhaps on the monk as well. The resultant commotion would also allow him to escape, or so Philippe hoped. If any subsequent investigation proved all three innocent, so much time would have passed that he would be far away. Why should anyone suspect a poor pilgrim with an injured ankle to have any part in heinous crimes? All he had to do was discover the perfect way to achieve his desire.

He looked back toward the hospital. The darkness was now growing like a malignant shadow. Philippe knew he must return or leave himself open to questions by people who might remember that he had been gone far too long for brief exercise.

Crawling out of his hiding spot, he pretended he had fallen and dragged himself to his feet with appropriate grunts. With the sub-infirmarian gone, others might take her place in the apothecary, but he counted on them being less skilled than Sister Anne and unaccustomed to careful practices with the herbs and poisonous roots. If God truly blessed his efforts, Philippe hoped to slip into the apothecary and steal an especially fine poison to slip into Father Etienne's food. Although he was no apothecary, he knew enough to recognize monk's hood and make a lethal dosage.

"My mother taught me well enough," he muttered with grim appreciation for the woman who had raised him with little love and a much-callused hand. If not monk's hood, he thought with a smile, he would find something equally deadly.

Carefully limping back down the path to the hospital, completely distracted by his plans for another untimely death, Philippe did not see the person who stepped into the path behind him.

After briefly following the man from Picardy, the shadow stopped to watch until the purported invalid disappeared into the hospital grounds. Then the figure turned back and faded into the darkness.

Satan's hour had come.

Chapter Fourteen

Gracia hurried to keep up with the long-legged woman who accompanied her to the hospital that next morning.

Although she said she did not need the assistance of Anchoress Juliana's servant to get the information, Gracia suspected that Prioress Eleanor was right to involve the woman. Hiding the real purpose of visiting the apothecary with an alleged request from the anchoress was a good stratagem, and Juliana had agreed she might need a toothache cure. "If not now," the anchoress had said to the prioress, briefly considering whether this qualified as a lie, "then surely someday."

Nor would anyone question why Gracia had to come with the servant. The woman never spoke, although there was a rumor that she was not mute but stammered so badly she had given up all attempts to speak. The story might be accurate, for the woman bore a scar across her mouth. Pressing hot metal against the lips was a common attempt to cure the affliction.

When the anchoress' servant visited Sister Anne, the sub-infirmarian understood the signs that the anchoress and her maid used to communicate between them. Their language was mostly gestures often employed by monastics during periods of silence, but some had been devised to meet the special needs of the anchorage. Because of the differences, others had not learned to read the meanings. Some did not want to.

Many, including a few who worked in the hospital, found the silent woman unsettling and avoided her when they saw her coming. Had she not served the unquestionably holy anchoress, they might have whispered that the Prince of Darkness lived inside her and that was why she was unable to utter words. Knowing that some villagers had already concluded this and that marriage for their daughter would be out of the question, her parents were grateful that the priory took her to serve the anchoress, a duty that seemed to please the daughter well.

The servant looked behind her and slowed her pace, realizing that Gracia's legs were not as long as hers. Smiling at the young girl, she stopped and waited.

Although there were several years between their ages, they both lived on the edge of acceptance in a world that feared the different and deemed it evil. A growing sense of affinity was developing between the abused orphan girl, too knowing for her years, and the woman whose unsettling eyes, the color of a winter sky, and lack of speech caused many to sniff the air for the sulphurous reek of hellfire.

The servant took Gracia by the hand and they walked together down the path to the priory hospital.

The hospital was a formidable place, not because of the rough stone walls black with damp, but for the cries and stench that filled it. Most came here to die, comforted by the religious attendants and the symbols of their faith. But for the living, not yet ready to surrender their souls to eternity, the process of dying was a fearful thing, even for the most faithful.

It was not a place where Gracia went often. When she was sent to summon Sister Anne for her mistress, she ran through the aisles lined with the sick. Never once did she stop, as some did, to stare at cancer-eaten faces or other disfigurements suffered by mortals. Sometimes she put her hands over her ears to blunt the moaning and rattling breath. The latter reminded her too much of the sounds her own mother had made as she slipped into death from a fever.

On one occasion, a girl, not much younger than she, grabbed her robe, forcing her to stop. Instead of tearing her robe from the child's grasp, Gracia knelt by her side and held her hand while the girl fought to pull breath into her useless lungs. After the girl had died, Gracia looked at her own hand and found the palm bloody from the dead girl's nails. For the first time since her parents had died, Gracia prayed.

As was her wont, Gracia and the anchoress' servant now hurried down the aisle and past the chapel to the door leading to the apothecary. When they reached the hut, they saw a young nun inside, busily grinding something with mortar and pestle.

Hearing a sound, Sister Oliva looked up, saw the servant with the maid, and smiled. "How may I serve?"

Gracia explained what had been troubling the anchoress.

The servant walked back toward the chapel.

With a mildly curious expression, the young nun watched the woman leave, then walked to the shelves lined with jars, woven baskets, and sealed, glazed bottles. She pulled down a large earthenware container, pried off the wooden stopper, and began to weight out what would be used in the simple cure.

"I am grateful you are here, Sister, but grieve over the burden laid upon you due to the absence of Sister Anne," Gracia said, gazing at the markings on the stored items. She had just begun to read, a skill for which she found both aptitude and interest, and used every chance to hone her knowledge.

"No one at Tyndal questions her innocence," Sister Oliva replied, securing the seal back on the jar with a thump of her fist.

Gracia tilted her head and frowned as she pretended not to be able to read the label attached to one woven basket. "Sister, would you mind telling me what that is? I can see a 'b' and a 'k'…"

"That contains blackthorn flowers. As an infusion in wine, it opens the bowels for those who suffer a binding thereof." She put the jar she had just used back on the shelf, ran her finger along the shelf, and selected another.

"This all is so tidy." Gracia gazed at the articles before her. "Different colored and shaped jars. Metal and wooden containers. All labeled, it seems."

Dumping a pinch of a pale green powder into a mortar with the measured amount of the other herb, the nun began to grind and mix. "Sister Anne did not want us to accidentally use the wrong ingredient. A few items can be dangerous if used incorrectly, and many look the same to the untrained eye. Although she makes the majority of the remedies, she had trained a few of us to prepare the most common cures."

"So she would let you mix a cure for an uneasy stomach?"

The nun stopped grinding and gave the maid a sharp look.

"I do not suggest that you or anyone else here mixed the wrong things together for Father Etienne's clerk, Sister!" Gracia decided to trust the nun. After all, Sister Anne did, having found the young woman reliable and worthy of more advanced training. "I ask so I can better comprehend what might have happened and thus find a way to prove our sub-infirmarian's innocence."

Sister Oliva nodded, bent toward the maid, and whispered, "Do you know what Sister Anne believed to be the cause of the clerk's illness?"

Gracia glanced around. She and the nun were alone. "A surfeit of ale," she murmured.

With a grin, Sister Oliva gestured to the maid. "Come and I will show you."

Gracia followed her to the other side of the hut.

"The remedy would consist of one of two preparations," Sister Oliva said. "A drink of chamomile with ginger is often used to ease the symptoms as well as one of mixed yarrow and elder-flower to balance the humors." She pointed to a basket. "Here is the container of elderflowers, for instance." She dropped her hand to a lower shelf and put a finger on a basket. "Here is the one filled with yarrow leaves." Stepping back she gestured at the entire wall of shelving. "If one cannot read, one can learn the jar shape, color, and size. As for baskets, Sister Anne attached a colored cloth in the lid of each."

Gracia studied the items. "It would be easy to memorize the position of each ingredient as well?"

"Yes, and she insisted that every item be put back immediately after use and in the space allotted for it. For those who could read, Sister Anne preferred to keep everything in alphabetic order. Other than the most needed remedies, and the simplest to make, only she and I made the cures. And lest you fear that a truly lethal item might be used accidentally, let me assure you that this was not possible. The toxic roots, seeds, leaves, and flowers are kept over here, well out of the way."

The nun led Gracia to a large covered chest and raised the lid.

Gracia peered in. There was a strange smell coming from the chest. It made her uneasy. She drew back.

"You can see that a poison could not be sent by accident, even by one of us. We were not allowed to touch the dangerous ingredients, not even I, although Sister Anne had promised to train me in those skills." Sister Oliva flushed with pride. In an older woman, this might be called a sin. In one of the nun's youth, it was an innocent display of joy.

Gracia clapped her hands with pleasure. "How wonderful to be chosen by Sister Anne to learn from her!"

The nun bowed her head. "I am humbled by her confidence," she said, "and have atoned for my conceit."

"Surely it is no sin to be grateful that God gave you the ability to learn this astonishing craft, Sister. Since I have taken no vows, I shall be proud for you!"

Laughing, the nun kissed the girl on the cheek. "You are good to say so," she said.

As the pair went back to the place where the nun had been working, Gracia considered what she should ask next. "Poor Sister Anne," she said, "but surely her tale that someone was sent by the priest can be proven."

Sister Oliva shook her head as she picked up the pestle and ground away at the toothache treatment. "None of us saw anyone. We have discussed it. It grieves us all that we cannot offer proof that she told the truth."

Gracia gestured to the hospital. "None of the healthier patients witnessed a hooded man near the hut?"

"Most look only to God, my child. One pilgrim with a sprained ankle was questioned. He sleeps on a mat near the chapel. After he asked many questions to aid his memory, he still denied seeing anyone."

"I was there when Sister Anne told Father Etienne that she would send the remedy with a lay brother who could give instructions. After we had left, she told Brother Thomas that the cure was a simple thing." Gracia blinked with a suggestion of confusion.

"It is. And I was here soon after she was arrested. Nothing had been mislaid. Everything was put back on the shelf. All looks as it should."

"I have heard a rumor that what killed the clerk was autumn crocus." She pointed to the large chest. "I assume it would be in that?"

"It is a noxious thing. Most certainly it would be there."

"Was it often used?"

The nun ran her finger through the mixture she had been grinding to check the consistency. "Rarely. Sister Anne was using it to treat our sub-prioress' gout. A few courtiers come here with the complaint, and she has used it on some, but not all." She laughed. "Courtiers do not always wish to remain out of the king's sight long enough for that cure to work, and it is too dangerous for them to use without close observation."

"Will you show it to me?" Gracia's eyes sparkled with interest. "I am curious to see this extraordinary thing."

They went back to the chest. Lifting the lid, the nun reached in, then hesitated. With a puzzled expression, she bent to look deeper into the chest. After a moment, she straightened with a frown. "It isn't here."

Gracia walked to her side and stared inside at the stored jars and boxes. "There are not many in there. It cannot have fallen into some hidden place."

Now the nun's face was pale. "It could not." She rushed back and carefully looked at every item on the shelves. "I cannot find it!" Her voice rose in panic.

Looking around, Gracia knew that the room was too small for something to be easily hidden. All looked neat. It would be hard to lose a container, and the nun had checked to see if it had been placed in the wrong spot.

"Has anyone come here asking for autumn crocus?" Gracia asked.

"Sister Christina," Sister Oliva said, her voice hoarse. "But all know she is close to God. She would never harm that clerk!"

"Why did she ask for it?"

"Sister Anne had given her a few, carefully measured packets for our sub-prioress. Sister Christina was the only one who could get her to take it. After Sister Anne was arrested, the infirmarian ran out of her supply and came back for more. I could not give her any because I am not trained in this treatment, nor could anyone else." The nun glanced back at the chest. "And because there was nothing we could do to help our infirmarian without Sister Anne's help, I did not even look for the item in the chest."

Gracia had been in the priory long enough to know that Sister Christina was too saintly to bring harm to anyone. Sub-Prioress Ruth, although known for her dislike of Prioress Eleanor, might own a murderous tongue, but she would never poison someone. "Fear not," she said to the nun. "You are not to blame for this missing item. It will be found. I am confident of it."

Indeed, it had been found, or at least some of it, in the dead clerk's room, but this was not information Gracia believed she had any right to divulge. She asked no more questions, and let Sister Oliva finish the preparation for the anchoress.

Taking the packet she had allegedly come for, she thanked the still-troubled nun, hurried out of the apothecary, and found the anchoress' servant praying alone in the chapel.

As they left the hospital, Gracia tried to think how she could question Sub-Prioress Ruth about her supplies of the gout remedy without offending her. Perhaps Prioress Eleanor would think it was wiser for another to do that. If need be, Gracia knew she could talk to Sister Christina.

Glancing at the packet in her hand, Gracia decided that her teeth still troubled her on occasion, and she would keep this cure for herself.

Chapter Fifteen

Brother Thomas paced up and down the path near the hospital, unable to dampen his anger. How dare that arrogant priest accuse Sister Anne of murder?

Proving her innocence should be simple, he thought with bitter sarcasm. All he had to do was find the hooded and unidentifiable messenger who had come for the remedy, and do so without offending Davoir, who seemed to dislike him anyway.

Thomas knew the elusive one could not be a lay brother or monk from the priory. He must be one of the clerks, slipped like a venomous snake into Tyndal by that accursed priest. Or, he thought, he was one of the soldiers who had accompanied the band of investigators here. If he found a man he suspected, he wondered how he could arrange a meeting between the suspect and Sister Anne with the hope she would recognize the voice if she heard it again.

"Brother!"

Thomas turned to see a gray-faced crowner behind him. "You have finally been summoned?" He had tried to keep his sour mood out of his tone but failed.

"Only after a miscarriage of justice and much reluctance by that priest." Ralf threw his hands up in despair. "The man may have the unquestionable right to do as he wishes with those vowed to God on priory grounds, but I tried to argue on Sister Anne's behalf, believing my long acquaintance with her was useful. He silenced me with a churlishness not even a confessed thief deserves." Ralf swallowed a curse. "If God dared to disagree with him, I doubt this Davoir would even listen."

Despite the crowner's sharp words, Thomas thought Ralf looked both weary and distraught. "You have examined the body?" he quickly asked. His own anger fleeing in the face of his friend's unease, the monk's voice grew gentle.

"That I have, for all the good it did me. My conclusion is that the clerk, Jean, is dead." He flashed a scornful smile. "Beyond that, I can say little with any certainty. He bears no stab wounds, signs of a crushed skull or garroting. Has he been murdered? I fear he has. That other fool of a clerk whimpered about convulsions and wild visions but claimed the lad never had a fever."

"Was that the clerk called *Renaud*?"

Ralf nodded in disgust. "But, when I tried to question him further, all he did was blubber like my brother, Odo, when he was a boy and I yanked his hair."

Thomas tried not to smile. Ralf's ill-loved and second-oldest brother had since taken vows, become an abbot, and grown fat on the king's frequent gifts of venison.

"I need Annie's opinion just like I did when Martin Cooper was killed. Poison is not a weapon I know well, and that seems the most likely explanation for the death."

"Jean had no enemies?"

"After I yelled at Renaud to stop whining, I asked. According to him, the clerk was the saintly beloved of this pest from your abbey. The worst Renaud could say about him was that he was unsure whether Jean was wrestling with a demon in bed, having visions from God, or was sick." Ralf ran a hand under his nose, and then sneezed. "Don't bless me, Brother. The Devil and I meet with such frequency over villainous deaths that we have become like kin."

"You are not only a father once but soon to be twice. You need a blessing, Crowner." And he gave him one to keep evil from filling the space left by the sneeze.

Now that his contempt of clerics was vented, Ralf sank into unhappy silence.

"You have learned from Davoir or his clerk about the accusations against Sister Anne?"

"From that vermin sent by your abbess. How could he be trusted to review anything when he is blind to all facts?" He spat. "I swear I saw ears on Davoir. If he owns them, why can he not hear when those with knowledge of Annie's virtue speak so eloquently on her behalf?"

"I do not understand how he could insist on her arrest and confinement either. Father Etienne may have the authority to examine the state of Tyndal Priory, but Prioress Eleanor still rules here."

Ralf hit the monk on the shoulder. "Have you not heard the rest of the foul news? This I learned from the sniveling clerk."

The monk stared at him as if unable to comprehend that something even worse than the arrest of the sub-infirmarian could have happened.

"Davoir also threw suspicion on Prioress Eleanor regarding his clerk's death. And do you know why?" His voice had risen to a shout.

The force of his friend's outrage was so numbing, Thomas found he had lost the ability to ask for an explanation.

"That tonsured louse claims that our good prioress may have ordered Annie to kill the clerk." His face flushed red, and he turned away. "The priest accused her of doing this to make him flee, lest he discover the truth about…"

"The purpose he was sent here? He finally said why this visit was ordered?"

"You and Prioress Eleanor have been accused of lying together in unholy lust." Ralf could not face the monk as he said that. Instead, he stared back at the guest quarters as if willing them to spontaneously combust.

Thomas' mouth dropped open.

Ralf spun around and shook his fist. "Swear you will defend yourself against this vile accusation!"

Thomas stared at him. "I have heard many lies, Ralf, but this is one of the most abominable. As for defense, I must rely on the strength of the truth. "

"Who could have accused you both of such a thing?" Ralf laid a hand on his sword hilt. "Since your vows preclude you from doing violence, tell me the name. I shall render the justice due the lying fiend." He lifted and dropped the sword back into its scabbard.

Thomas fell silent as he thought, then shook his head. "I do not know, Ralf. Our prioress owns great virtue and ably serves God. She feeds and clothes us all well. The poor are given food. The sick receive the finest care in England. The mill grinds the village grain at no profit. And, when she is not running this priory with an integrity and skill most men would envy, she brings murderers to justice. The reason for this condemnation is not based in any fault she owns. Someone has grown jealous of her virtues."

"She may run the priory with the aid of others, but it is you who stands by her side in matters of unlawful bloodshed. Someone hates you with equal fervor."

"I do little enough, Crowner. It is she who leads me to the truth, just as she leads all at Tyndal to God. The insult is against her, not me." Thomas shuddered. "Sinner though I may be, and God knows best what frailties I own, I am not guilty of lying with our prioress nor is she, virtuous woman that she is, guilty of breaking her vows with any man."

Although he had once suspected her of suffering lust, he had also seen her battle with the evil spirit of desire until it fled and she saw the wicked heart the man possessed. For her valor and fortitude in that struggle, he respected her even more. He often told others in confession, that it was not the temptation God abhorred. It was the succumbing He loathed. As for his own sinning, he had surrendered only once to his greatest weakness. Yet it was an act he could not fully repent and one still debated with God.

"The accusation against you both remains unaddressed," Ralf said, "and most probably will until this clerk's death is solved. The resolution will be difficult. Annie is locked away. Prioress Eleanor cannot help prove her innocence. If she tries, she will be accused of tainting the evidence to protect herself. And you..."

Thomas felt ill. "And I am hobbled like a horse because I am accused of being our prioress' lover."

Ralf nodded. "Someone has been fiendishly clever. Those most able to solve this problem have been rendered impotent."

"You are left to do it. Alone." Thomas might be frustrated over his inability to act, but he had no doubt about his friend's competence.

"I cannot do it all, Brother. Although I may investigate a suspicious death, I am treading on God's earth at the priory. There are people I cannot question without a witness present. If Davoir chooses that person, the monk or nun might hesitate to give an honest statement out of fear of the priest's retaliation. If I find the culprit, and he falls under God's law, I cannot take that person into custody. Church justice outranks the king's here, as does the final questioning. And it is hard to imagine that the killer slipped over the walls to administer a lethal dose of some poison to a clerk in the company of Father Etienne. I fear the man is one of yours, not mine."

"You must still ask the priest questions."

"Which he can refuse to answer because he denies my authority to do so. Not only is he vowed to God, he is the brother of your noble abbess, and he is the confessor to one of the French king's brothers."

"If nothing can be resolved quickly about the clerk's death," Thomas said, "the accusation against our prioress festers. Prioress Eleanor will not meekly submit to the injustice rendered against her. The matter will go to Rome."

"And we may all be dead by the time Pope Nicholas III renders judgement. After the roof fell and killed his predecessor, he might be leery of making decisions without long consultations with God." The crowner turned pale. "And my wife needs our Annie with her at the birth. Gytha is a brave woman, but this is her first babe. If anything goes wrong…"

"Has Sister Anne said there was any possibility of a problem?"

"Would she?" Ralf covered his face. "Remember the horrible

birthing of that young mother when the Jews were almost murdered by the mob here?"

Thomas put his hand on his friend's shoulder. "Not all women suffer so. If our sub-infirmarian is confident this late in Gytha's pregnancy that all is well…"

"Women have died after being told they had no cause to fear the birth." Ralf's voice grew hoarse. "My first wife was given no grounds to doubt her survival. Sibley was born healthy, but my wife died a few days later. Gytha resides where my heart lives, Brother. Without Annie's care, she might die and so shall I."

Ralf turned his back on his friend, but Thomas saw the tears. "Then we must prove Sister Anne innocent and free her in time for the birthing."

As he spun around, the crowner's face was scarlet with rage. His fist clenched as if he longed to strike the monk, but he wilted in an instant and fell to his knees on the path. "Were Gytha to die, I will leave this world. I swear it."

Thomas dragged his friend to his feet. "You would be a most troublesome monk, Crowner. And if you meant you would commit self-murder, I advise against it. Your wife, a good woman and a loving spouse, would be in Paradise while you spent an eternity far away from her in Hell for your crime. I suggest we set our minds to figuring out how to get across the moat the wicked and the fools have dug around us. We shall find the truth."

Ralf glared at his friend, then burst out laughing. "You are right, monk. I have no calling for chastity or obedience, although poverty might suit me well enough. But should I fall into Hell, I think even God would pity Satan, for I would surely make the Devil as miserable as I."

"I fear even I might feel some sympathy for the Prince of Darkness!" Thomas grinned, then took Ralf by the arm and whispered in his ear. "Let us consider our choices." He looked around, but no one was close enough to hear.

"Do we have any?"

Someone called out to them. Looking up, they saw Gracia running toward them.

"Come!" she said, skidding to a stop and panting from the exertion. She looked over her shoulder, then lowered her voice. "Prioress Eleanor calls you both to attend her. She has something to discuss. But you must arrive without being seen, lest a wandering clerk report the meeting to a certain high-ranking guest. I see none on this path. Hurry!"

"If our prioress has joined our conspiracy, Crowner, I begin to hope," Thomas said to Ralf.

As the trio hurried down the path to the prioress' chambers, Ralf glanced back and saw Conan walking toward the guest quarters. Fearing the man had seen the three of them together, the crowner raised his hand in greeting as if he wished to tarry with the guard captain. In fact, he only hoped to distract Conan lest the man see Thomas walking toward Prioress Eleanor's quarters.

But Conan ignored the gesture and continued on his way.

Chapter Sixteen

Gracia poured each of the men ale, and then offered warm bread and a white goat cheese.

The usually ravenous crowner glanced at the food and refused it.

"You have now heard everything Gracia has discovered from Sister Oliva," Eleanor said.

Thomas smiled at the maid. "God gave you good wits," he said, "and you apply them well."

The girl flushed with pleasure. "It was my lady who thought to send me, Brother. If I have shrewdness, it is she who directed the use of it."

Silent and melancholy, Ralf stared into his mazer.

"Something troubles you, old friend," Eleanor said. "What is it?"

"I beg pardon, my lady. The moment I heard that Ann..." He glanced at Gracia and cleared his throat before rephrasing his concern. "Now that I know no one can identify the man sent to Sister Anne by the priest, it is hard to chase away my fears. As you know, I honor her and refuse to give up hope that she will be released. But that time seems even further off now, and my wife is near her term. Gytha must bear our firstborn in terrible pain without Sister Anne's comfort and skill. I can only hope God listens to my wife's prayers and shows mercy..."

"Sister Anne will attend your wife's birth if I have to take our sub-infirmarian from that cell myself and stand guard outside the birth chamber like the cherubim at the gates of Eden." Eleanor knew he was terrified for Gytha's safety, a woman he cherished more than his own soul. Nor was Ralf the only one worried. Gytha had been her maid for several years before she married the crowner. The entire priory loved her, and the woman was as dear to the prioress as a younger sister.

Thomas watched his prioress' hand form into a fist. Although she might otherwise tread carefully in this sensitive matter that could wound the tender pride of God's anointed kings, Davoir and his army of clerks could not stop her from freeing Sister Anne when Gytha's birth pains began. His spirits rose. Prioress Eleanor was no novice in the clash of wills and usually won the jousts.

"My lady, neither my wife nor I want to put the outcome of this ill-considered investigation, ordered by your abbess, at risk…" Tears trickled down the crowner's cheeks. There were many in Tyndal village who would be shocked to see this often rough man weeping.

Eleanor shook her head. "Until Abbess Isabeau orders otherwise, Ralf, I rule this priory, not Father Etienne. I shall not allow the health and comfort of a new mother and her child to be set aside because one man has made a bad decision, one he shall soon rue. Sister Anne has been unjustly accused. She shall be at your wife's side and bring both Gytha and the babe safely through their ordeals."

"Your kindness is beyond measure," Ralf murmured. "I shall reassure my wife."

"And no matter what malicious lies have been spewed forth against us with unknown but foul intent, the God we serve at Tyndal Priory is loving and compassionate." Eleanor's face was white with fury. "He will vindicate the honor of us all, but the matter of Sister Anne's innocence comes first."

Thomas had rarely seen his prioress this angry or determined. "How to do so remains a mystery to me," he said.

Ralf swallowed the last of his ale, and, his fears for his wife abated, he glanced at the food with renewed interest.

Gracia filled his cup and brought him the bread and cheese.

He thanked her with a smile.

"Neither you nor I can investigate without casting doubt on the validity of any evidence we find," Thomas said to his prioress. "And Ralf's authority here is limited."

"You and I have always worked together in perfect accord, my lady, but Davoir will not allow me that freedom of consultation or investigation." The crowner raised a fistful of food and then bit into his cheese.

"The precedent of cooperation has been set, Ralf. If Davoir questions it, any at this priory can confirm the practice and the respect you have always shown God's law. In order to determine if this death is murder…"

"Davoir has already decided Sister Anne killed his clerk." Fighting a resurgence of despair, Ralf waved a diminished handful of food at the ceiling. "May God curse him," he muttered.

"And no matter how firmly Father Etienne holds that conclusion, he is in error. If he cannot be wooed by logic, I shall exercise my right to override any attempt by him to supersede my commands." Her smile was as cold as a north wind on the feast of All Saints.

"What if he orders his clerks to lock you into a cell?" Ralf's face turned gray.

"He has his clerks. I have loyal lay brothers under the command of Brother Beorn, all of whom wield pitchforks with the same skill clerks use quills."

There was absolute stillness in the room as they all stared at her.

Thomas broke it with a laugh. "Brother Beorn might be army enough by himself, my lady. Even our crowner gives way to our lay brother on the path when they meet each other." Glancing around, he was relieved to see that the mood had lightened. Even Ralf was grinning.

"At times I pity God that the lay brother serves Him," Ralf said, then took more cheese when Gracia quickly offered it to him.

"If God has compassion for our guest, we may not need to use the lay brother, our greatest weapon. I can debate for hours with Father Etienne. By the time the priest and I have stopped quarrelling, Crowner, you will have done everything needed to prove our sub-infirmarian innocent or at least raise a reasonable doubt in Father Etienne's mind." Eleanor sat back in her chair and fingered her staff of office. The time for jests was over.

Ralf rose and began to pace. "Whom may I approach?"

"Begin with Sister Anne while you may," she replied. "I will send someone with you for proper attendance. Ask for her version of the events, seek any clarification you need, and present your observations of the corpse. You have seen, touched, and smelled the body. From your questions and comments, our sub-infirmarian may have enough information to give you her firm opinion on the cause of Jean's death." She thought for a moment. "If God is kind, she may be able to help with timing of the death. Perhaps the beginning of the symptoms will provide a new clue, although I fear this elusive Brother Imbert remains the key to the locked chest where the solution lies."

"But will Davoir allow this?"

"We shall invite his participation. Ask him for one of his best clerks to record and witness the interrogation. For all I care in this matter, you can leave the door to the cell open so everyone can hear what is said. There is no purpose in hiding anything if you phrase your questions cleverly." Her smile was mischievous. "And I know just how clever you can be, Crowner. After all, you stole my maid from me."

He flushed.

"Sister Anne must be made aware of this plan," Thomas said. "How can that be done?"

The prioress gestured to her maid. "Gracia shall take our nun her meal from the kitchen and give her a brief message to alert her."

"Won't Davoir be suspicious if your maid appears so often, my lady?" Ralf asked.

Eleanor stood and gestured to the girl to come closer. Putting an arm around her, the prioress said to the crowner, "Look upon her. Do you see a child or a woman?"

"When you first came to Tyndal, Gytha was only a little older but had a woman's form," Ralf said after a moment. "Gracia does not."

"Exactly. If Father Etienne notices her at all, he will dismiss her competence due to her perceived youth. Perhaps he thinks I selected a babe to serve me out of simple charity and will soon rue my choice. He most certainly does not see her as a messenger, nor one who observes and reasons far better than most owning many more years on this earth. Brother Thomas and I learned just how clever Gracia was in Walsingham. I am grateful she chose to come back with us and bring those skills."

Gracia flushed with pleasure.

Thomas winked at her. "More fools they. Look at how effectively she questioned Sister Oliva in the hospital apothecary hut."

"I did nothing except obey my lady," Gracia said softly.

Eleanor gave her a hug. "And I take no credit for the gifts God has bestowed on you, my child."

"Then let us plan what I must ask," Ralf said eagerly.

Eleanor began to sit, then changed her mind and walked to the table to pour herself a cup of ale. "Forgive me, Ralf, but there is information I learned from Father Etienne that I should have sent to you long before now. I fear the clerk's death and the arrest of Sister Anne chased the news from my memory."

The chamber door creaked open, and the prioress' cat entered. Contemplating all in the assembled group, he chose to favor Gracia with his attentions and rubbed against her legs.

She knelt to pet him.

"On the journey here," Eleanor said, "one of the soldiers assigned to protecting our guests was killed. The captain of the guard insisted that he was aware of the circumstances and would render the appropriate justice. No crowner or sheriff was called. Perhaps the captain was correct, but I believe you should know about this."

Ralf raised an eyebrow.

"Father Etienne did not say if any soldier was punished or executed for the crime. He was more concerned about the health of his clerk." She sipped her ale. "Nor have I concluded there is any link between that death and Jean's. Nonetheless, I did not want you to remain in ignorance, lest there be some connection or error in failing to alert you to the crime."

Indeed I should know, Ralf thought, recalling the badly scarred man who sat with him at Signy's inn and exhibited a rare curiosity about the village and the priory. Conan had made him uneasy. Now he had more cause to investigate this guard captain further.

Chapter Seventeen

Davoir looked at Conan with contempt. "Why should I fear for the safety of my clerks or myself when the one who killed Jean is imprisoned?"

"She has not yet been found guilty, Father." The pale light from the window only deepened the furrows and ridges of the captain's scars.

"She shall be! If I can keep Prioress Eleanor and Brother Thomas away from the investigation into her guilt, the verdict against the nun will be fair and untainted. If necessary, I will insist the sub-infirmarian be taken from their undue influence to Fontevraud Abbey where my sister can render an objective judgement."

A peculiar light flickered in Conan's eyes. "You believe there is that much wickedness in this place consecrated to God? If you are so uneasy about the role of Satan in the priory, you should welcome my suggestion that I examine the security of these quarters."

Davoir laughed. "You think your sword is strong enough to keep the Devil at bay? Who taught you about faith, soldier? It was no priest."

Conan's face became spotted as if he had a pox, but he said nothing.

"Father, may I express some thoughts in this matter?"

Sighing, the priest turned to his pale-faced clerk but barely hid his annoyance. "You have my permission, Renaud, but keep your speech brief."

"The captain and his men have protected us from the moment we set foot in England. On the way here, no bandits attacked us. No harm came to us." He waved his hand. "Other than that matter about the dead guard, but he was not of our…"

"Our safety was their purpose, my son." The priest's voice was rough with impatience. "Your meaning, if you please."

"If Sister Anne has wicked friends in this priory, and the leadership is directed by the Prince of Darkness, might there not be other liegemen of the Evil One who wish you ill? If the poisoning of Jean was a failed attempt to frighten you away before uncovering the inequities here, another imp might try a direct attack since your resolve has not weakened."

Davoir looked surprised. "You speak well, Renaud."

"Thank you, Father."

"I may have always found Jean superior to you in learning, perception, and quickness of analysis, but this concern for my well-being and your reasons for same are well-expressed and well-considered."

Renaud's face flushed with joy.

Conan stood as still as a statue in a church.

Davoir flicked a hand at the man. "Very well, Captain, tell me what you propose."

"Perhaps your clerk will take me around the guest quarters so I might examine the various entrances to your chambers. Like a castle under siege, Father, those entrances should be guarded by a patrol for the duration of your stay here."

"Guards in a house shielded by God? I will not permit armed men in this priory."

"Prayer is useful, Father, but God has often shown that He approves of soldiers, depending on their intent," Conan replied. "He did travel with those who took arms against the Infidel to regain Jerusalem."

Shaking a finger at the captain, Davoir growled. "Do not preach to me or claim to know more than a priest about the reading of God's holy will."

For a moment, Conan looked like he might laugh. He bowed his head quickly.

"If I may be so bold as to make a suggestion, Father?" Renaud was wringing his hands.

Raising both eyebrows as if awed by a minor miracle, Davoir gave permission.

"We need not have armed men. If I show the captain around our quarters here, he can advise on the places where someone with wicked motives might enter. Day should not be as difficult a time to keep watch. Perhaps one clerk might walk around the buildings, but I could assign several clerks to do so at night." He puffed out his thin chest. "I would take over for the weariest clerks. Our prayers will be our swords."

A brisk knock at the door interrupted his argument. Renaud rushed to open it.

Gracia stood outside with hands meekly folded and head bowed.

"What do you want?" Davoir barked at her.

She stepped back, visibly trembling.

"Speak! I do not have all day."

"Crowner Ralf asks permission to question Sister Anne, Father. He wants one of your clerks with him to witness the procedure. If you approve, he asks that this clerk record the meeting so there can be no doubt of fairness or propriety." She pronounced each word like a child repeating a memorized passage.

Davoir opened his mouth, then rethought what he was about to say. "His proposal is fair. I shall allow it. Tell him to meet me here before the next Office." He glanced at Renaud. "Surely you and the captain will have finished by then."

Renaud flushed and looked at Conan.

The captain nodded.

Gracia fidgeted in the doorway.

Davoir glared at her. "Go! Tell the crowner of my decision."

As directed, Gracia fled.

"Annoying girl," Davoir muttered. "Having such a wit-less child as a maid does not reflect well on Prioress Eleanor's judgement. She ought to have chosen a lay sister or even a nun of more mature years." He shook his head. "Shut the door and get on with your plan," he said to Renaud. "You will also record the meeting between the king's man and this vicious nun."

As Conan and Renaud walked around the guest quarters, Renaud said to the captain in a low voice, "I agree with your fears and plan, Captain, even if Father Etienne does not. He may be close to God's ear, as well as that of our king's brother, but he often forgets that evil men do not respect the armor of prayer and do violence against the virtuous. I fear for his safety."

Conan nodded, then pointed out a window which was just big enough to allow a small person to climb through. "Your eyes are red with weeping," the captain said as they continued on. "You and the dead clerk must have been friends."

"We were as boys, Captain, but Jean rose above me in so many things. Father Etienne saw his quick intellect and deep understanding of godly matters. He promised him a fine benefice or the position of secretary to a man of high ecclesiastical rank. Jean served him with great love and devotion. Rarely was he absent from Father Etienne's side."

Conan turned and studied the clerk for a moment. "And now you stand in that place of honor."

Renaud flushed. "Do you think so? I am not sure. Father Etienne often criticized my writing and my ability to both learn and reason. My Latin is faulty as well."

"I am only a rough soldier, clerk, but I think you misjudge his respect for you. Did you not hear his praise for you today?"

Renaud modestly lowered his gaze and walked on.

The captain followed, his expression a mix of pity and amusement.

As they circled the quarters, Renaud began to indicate other low windows and one door.

Conan said little more until they reached the main entrance to the priest's quarters.

"I see the crowner coming," Renaud said with a nervous quiver in his voice. "I must leave you and accompany him to the sub-infirmarian's cell."

"I will not keep you, clerk. Since I cannot send my men to protect your priest, you and some of the other clerks should patrol during the night. You know the dangerous entrance areas. If you see anything untoward, call out. Make a great noise. Awaken those who sleep. That should be enough to frighten off any man who wishes your master ill. If it does not, the shouting will bring help. Not all the lay brothers in this place are corrupt. And send word to me at the inn. Your master may not want armed men on holy ground, but we will come quickly if nothing else deters the wicked."

Pleased, Renaud thanked the captain for the confidence he had shown in him.

"One thing more, lad," the captain said, "I would take the darkest part of the night patrol yourself and alone. Perhaps between the last Office and the rising sun. Let the other clerks sleep. You know the perils best and what signs to look for. I think that deed will please your priest." He winked.

Renaud glowed with hope and promised Conan he would do as suggested. "It is my joy to serve my master and take the greater responsibility on myself," he said.

"Go meet the crowner," Conan replied.

Renaud smiled and left.

Slipping around the quarters to another path, Conan found the way to the mill and carefully avoided the king's man. He had accomplished what he desired and had no wish for any conversation with Crowner Ralf.

Chapter Eighteen

Seeing those gathered in her chambers, Eleanor struggled with envy, the child of her thwarted longing for action. Unable to participate in the investigation into the clerk's death, she sat in these rooms, surrounded by accounting rolls, left only with the right to pray for justice. This galled her. As a consequence, she feared she spent too much time beseeching God for patience when she should be begging mercy for a long list of tormented souls in Purgatory.

As she glanced at Gracia, Ralf, and Thomas, she smiled with forced calm. I must stop whining and use what is left to me, she decided. If I am banned from the inquiry, I most certainly can direct others to do what I dare not. Do I not have the wits to circumvent these restrictions? She sat just a little straighter with renewed purpose, eager to hear what they had discovered.

"Ale for all," Eleanor said. "Then let us discuss what we know and must do next."

Gracia hurriedly served each, then ran to her place by the chamber door.

Ralf grinned at the girl. "Thanks to your maid's forewarning," the crowner said, "Sister Anne was very precise in her replies. Most of what she said was a repetition of her prior testimony as you described it, but she very carefully went over what Prior Andrew had observed and gave well-considered conclusions." He drank from his mazer with obvious enjoyment.

Eleanor briefly wondered if the priory's ale brewer ever gave the crowner and his wife the occasional gift of the beverage. Ale was considered calming for a pregnant woman, although she thought Ralf might need it more than Gytha when the time came for the birthing.

"I had already talked with the prior about what he had seen," Ralf said. "The details were the same as those reported by Sister Anne. Then I confirmed all with Brother Thomas."

The monk concurred.

"The clerk, Jean, had no fever, and his symptoms were no different from anyone else who has had too much to drink the night before." The crowner laughed. "I know the signs well myself." He blushed and looked away. "Or did before my marriage."

"Did our sub-infirmarian know that the lad had not improved with the treatment she sent with this unidentified clerk?"

"No, but she was uneasy when she heard nothing. She knew she was not welcome at the guest quarters but did send a lay brother to offer advice or answer questions. He was refused admittance, told that all the clerks were busy with the investigation of the priory, and promised his message would be relayed." Ralf shrugged. "I talked with the French servant who guards the priest's gate. He didn't welcome my questions, but a coin with an English king's head serves as well as one engraved *PHILIPVS REX*. After payment for his time, he confirmed that a lay brother had come from the hospital and was sent away with the excuse reported."

Eleanor waited, then asked, "To whom did this man give the message?"

"He gave it to one of the clerks but could not recall which one." Ralf scowled.

Brother Thomas turned to his friend. "Might the man's testimony be suspect? You paid him for the truth. Someone else might have paid him more to lie to you."

For a long moment, Ralf stared at the wooden crossbeams in the ceiling. "It matters not if he was asked to lie about the clerk to whom he gave the message. It only matters that his story about the hospital lay brother confirms that of Sister Anne."

"Now we have evidence that Sister Anne acted responsibly within the limits imposed upon her by the priest." Eleanor gestured for Gracia to refill the mazers. "You also spoke with the lay brother who went to the priest with her message?"

Ralf nodded.

Putting down the pitcher and almost dancing with enthusiasm, the maid turned to her mistress.

Eleanor smiled. "Do you have something to add, Gracia?" How like a child and yet how unlike one, the prioress thought. She never knew which aspect of the maid would manifest itself.

"While the crowner was questioning Sister Anne, the clerk, Renaud, was very displeased when she offered an analysis of the cause of death."

"Was he now?" Eleanor folded her arms.

"Until that moment, he had remained silent and busy writing down the testimony," the girl added.

"Well noted," Ralf said. "Sister Anne had had time to think about the presence of autumn crocus in the clerk's room. From what she was able to learn about the symptoms, and what I told her about the corpse, she is convinced that Jean was poisoned with it. There are other lethal herbs that exhibit similar symptoms and cause death in the same number of days, but she saw no reason to think another method had been used when the autumn crocus was inexplicably found at the bedside. Once again, she confirmed that she had sent only chamomile and ginger with the elusive, hooded clerk. When she said that, Renaud stopped writing and insisted that she was lying."

Gracia enthusiastically nodded.

"He demanded that her opinion be deleted from his record for he believed it was only an attempt to hide either her murderous intent or her incompetence and carelessness." The crowner snorted. "Careless? Incompetent? Ignorant whelp!"

Knowing Ralf had more to say, Eleanor said nothing, raised an eyebrow, and waited.

The crowner leaned forward to continue. "I asked him what experience he brought to the matter of solving crimes. He confessed he had none as such, but he was knowledgeable in debate over higher matters pertaining to Heaven. I told him to use those skills when he took vows and let me deal with more worldly problems. I am crowner here. Heaven may be the Church's realm, but murder is mine."

Eleanor laughed.

"That did silence him," Gracia said, her eyes twinkling.

Ralf's eyes shifted to look at a fat loaf of bread, fresh from Sister Matilda's oven and sitting on the nearby table.

"What was your opinion after you heard Sister Anne's answers to your questions, Ralf?" Eleanor tilted her head toward the crusty bread, smiled at her maid, and looked back at the crowner.

Gracia brought the warm loaf to the crowner, who eagerly tore off a large piece and gave the maid a wide smile.

Chomping down on his fistful of bread, the crowner continued. "When have I ever doubted Sister Anne's conclusions in these matters? She had no doubt that it was murder. Neither do I. The problem is how to convince that thick-skulled priest…" He turned aside and coughed in an effort to keep from insulting the other representatives of God in the room whom he considered friends.

Eleanor covered her mouth to hide her amusement.

"The use of autumn crocus as a treatment for gout is not widely known, but Sister Anne said its use as a poison has been recognized for centuries. What she did not understand was how it got to the clerk's room. When I told her that the remedy had disappeared from the chest in the apothecary hut, she was horrified."

"Nor was Renaud pleased when he heard this, my lady," Gracia added.

"Why do you say that?" Ralf looked with curiosity at this maid. "I did not see anything to suggest such a reaction, nor did he voice any concerns."

"Did you not smell him, my lord?" Gracia wrinkled her nose. "He stank of fear."

Ralf eyes widened in surprise. Although he was an observant man, body odor was not something to which he paid much attention, other than the flowery scent his wife gave off when he held her. Knowing he had flushed with the thought, he lowered his head and muttered, "No, child, but then I was concentrating on what Sister Anne was saying." He glanced up at the prioress.

"You are keen," Eleanor said to the girl. "What else did you notice about the clerk?"

"He twitched a lot as soon as Sister Anne began discussing the effects of autumn crocus. The more she explained, the more his face lost color." She paused, then noticed the crowner seemed eager for her to continue. "When you finished questioning our sub-infirmarian, and he began packing up his writing instruments, I think I saw him weeping. I am not certain about that, but I would swear his cheeks glistened in the candlelight."

"His tears are consistent with his grief over the death of his fellow clerk." Eleanor shook her head. "His protest that her conclusions were as faulty as her cure might have been a loyal repetition of his master's own assumption. What I do not understand is why he showed fear, not bewilderment or even anger, over the theft of the autumn crocus. Does he know who Brother Imbert is, or is he afraid he knows who is involved in this death, someone he wishes were not?"

"We have never asked him for the name of the person who administered the remedy to Jean. Was Renaud really the one to give Jean the medicine? Perhaps he is taking the blame, for reasons he has not told anyone, when he truly had no part at all in his companion's death," Thomas said.

"So many questions," Eleanor said. "We have yet to identify this Brother Imbert. Renaud must be questioned further. I suspect he does know far more than he has said. Maybe Father Etienne ordered the lad to keep silent."

The three were briefly interrupted when a lay sister brought a tray from the kitchen.

Ralf's eyes widened in delight when he saw Sister Matilda's vegetable pie.

Gracia served the company but gave the crowner an especially large slice.

Ralf took an equally huge bite, then continued. "I would like to hear your opinion," he said to Eleanor. "Is it possible that the priest had a hand in this death?"

The prioress was relieved to see her friend's legendary appetite had returned. "I doubt it, Crowner," she replied, her expression grown serious. "I believe Father Etienne is devoted to his family honor and to his sister, our abbess. He left the French court to investigate our priory with the sole purpose of protecting her reputation in Rome, and I am certain he intended to resolve the accusation hurled at us in a manner that would give the most credit to the Davoir name. An untoward death in one of Abbess Isabeau's daughter houses is scandalous and only sullies her reputation further. In addition, why would he kill his own clerk, especially one he favored?" She looked down at her uneaten food, then gestured for her maid to take it away. "No, Ralf, I do not believe he is a killer."

"Yet he has no love for our Order, my lady." Gracia had that solemn look the young often do when allowed to speak freely in the company of adults.

But Eleanor was most taken by the girl calling the Order of Fontevraud *our Order*. Although she would never force Gracia to take vows, she was touched by these hints of fondness for the priory and its rules. "He may not approve of women ruling men, but Rome has sanctioned the Order and his sister has been placed in charge of it, a high honor for a noble family. With these circumstances, he will set aside his personal opinion for the authorized one."

"Then I should question Renaud further," Ralf said.

The prioress nodded. "Have you spoken to the guard captain about the death on the journey here?"

"Not yet, my lady, but he is staying at the inn, and I shall delay no further."

"Did you ask our sub-infirmarian if the container she saw was the same one stolen from her apothecary?"

"I did not," Ralf replied.

"I would like to see that container in which the autumn

crocus was held." Eleanor stopped and shook her head with annoyance. "Someone else must do that. I cannot, nor should I chance the discovery that it was brought to me in secret."

"I could slip into the room, look, and describe it to you and to Sister Anne!" Zeal for the game glowed in Gracia's eyes.

"I shall not ask that of you," Eleanor replied. "Searching through Jean's room without clear purpose would endanger the safety of my best spy."

Initially disappointed, Gracia frowned at first, then her smile indicated she had chosen to be content with the intended compliment.

"Ralf, you may ask to see it," Eleanor said. "Look at it well, and we shall get the description to Sister Anne." Gesturing to her maid, she smiled. "Since you take her meals to the cell, you can whisper the description in her ear, and she can tell us if it is the original container or if there is something noteworthy about it. My hope may be slim, but if the jar comes from the hospital, that may suggest the man named Brother Imbert stole it. If it is not, the owner of the jar might be found or suggest the identity of the killer."

The girl eagerly agreed.

"I shall insist on examining the dead clerk's room," the crowner said. "Davoir can threaten hellfire on me all he wants. I shall remind him that no detail should be overlooked, for I wish to protect his sister's reputation just as much as he." He grinned at the prioress. "I promise to be more subtle than that, but he will be made to believe that I wish him no ill."

"And question Renaud."

"That too. I can tell him I want to go over his written report. In so doing, I can pose questions. When he grows uneasy, I shall press him on it."

"At last I feel more confident that we will resolve this crime without giving Father Etienne cause to cast the discoveries aside," Eleanor said.

"You have every reason to hope, my lady," Gracia said, then pointed to Ralf and herself. "You have us."

Chapter Nineteen

Gytha winced and pressed a hand against her belly.

"Is it time?" Signy stood up, a worried expression on her face.

"No, but he kicked hard enough to make me wish it were so." Gytha started to grin but winced again. "Nor shall I ever forgive our mother, Eve, for bringing this upon us all."

Signy sat down again and smiled. "Your child shall come soon enough."

Looking at the bowl of chicken and vegetable soup set before her, Gytha dipped her spoon to take a sip, then set it down and sighed. "Without Sister Anne to assist, my husband will be terrified."

"And you?" Signy reached out and squeezed her friend's arm.

"I fear this less than he, although birthing is a perilous time. Even if I do not have Sister Anne in attendance, I will have you to support me, and the comfort of your gift of the jet cup. Surely Sister Oliva, whom our beloved nun is training, will be a good midwife." She watched the fragrant steam rise from her bowl for a long moment. "Should I die, Signy, take care of Ralf and Sibley. And if I can bear a living babe before my death, will you..."

"I swear all of that, but I have prayed much to God and am confident that He has no wish that you suffer more than any woman must in birth." Signy grasped her friend's hands and held them tight as if she could keep Death from Gytha's side by sheer force of will. "You served Prioress Eleanor well before you married. Ralf, for all his faults, honors our prioress and serves justice fairly. God has grounds to bless you with a safe delivery and a healthy child."

"Ralf's last wife did not deserve her death."

"We do not know what cause God might have had for allowing that sorrow. After my prayers on your behalf last night, I rose to my feet with a heart lightened of fear. I take that to be a sign that those pleas have been heard with favor by Him."

Her tension dissipating, Gytha decided that God was most likely to listen to Signy, a woman of quiet charity and honorable spirit. "You have given me courage," the young wife said.

Signy released her iron grip on Gytha's hands, and the two women smiled at each other with deep affection.

Resting her chin on her hand, the innkeeper said, "Although I do not wish to ask too much of God, do you think this babe might be the son both Ralf and his brother desire?"

"I have no doubt of it," Gytha said with a laugh. "He kicks like one of my brother's donkeys, refuses to be born until he wishes it, and, I fear, will have a ravenous appetite like his father when I put him to my breast. This is no trembling daughter of Eve that I carry, but one who thinks he is the master of the world around him."

"From that description, I believe you will most certainly give birth to a Norman son in the image of his father's kin," Signy said with dutiful solemnity.

Gytha sat as close to the table as she could. "But Ralf is distraught, as am I, over the injustice bestowed on our beloved Sister Anne."

"Has he found anything to help prove her innocence?"

"Nothing except his knowledge that she would never kill the clerk."

"So her version of events cannot be proven."

"Nor disproved. The other clerk says a certain Brother Imbert brought the remedy and gave instructions for its use. Sister Anne says Father Davoir sent a clerk, whose face she could not see.

The brother named is not one of our priory's religious, lay or choir, nor has he ever been."

"Then the clerk's story truly cannot be proven any more than hers." Signy shrugged. "Sister Anne cannot be condemned on such thin evidence."

"But who had motive? The priest believes that our sub-infirmarian killed the clerk out of spite because her request to question and treat the lad was denied. The worst accusation is that Prioress Eleanor ordered her to kill the clerk, frighten the priest, and make him flee before he discovered the evils hidden in the priory."

"What wickedness?" Signy snorted. "The mill does not make a profit?"

Gytha smiled but quickly moved away from that subject lest she be asked for more detail. "Ralf cannot find a reason for anyone to kill the clerk."

After gazing over her shoulder and around the inn, Signy cupped her hands around her mouth to further muffle her softly spoken question. "Did Ralf not mention a man named *Conan*?"

Gytha thought for a moment, and then shook her head.

"He is the captain of the guard that brought Father Etienne and his group of clerks from the port. When Ralf was last here, he approached your husband for company, or so he said, and seemed quite curious about the priory and village."

"He did mention that but not the man's name. I told my husband that any stranger might look for amusement and ask about the village and priory. I saw nothing odd about the questioning, but my husband was troubled."

Signy nodded. "After Conan left his table, Ralf asked me if anyone had told the captain that he was the crowner here, for the man had called him by the title. I had not and, when I questioned the serving maids, I learned that none of them had either, nor had they seen him asking any of the other townsmen. Indeed, this Conan is a solitary man and habitually sits apart from the usual customers and even his own soldiers. Do you not think it odd that such a man would seek your husband's companionship? "

"Is he here now?"

Signy subtly indicated a man sitting alone in the far corner of the inn near the entrance.

"A soldier, from the scars I can even see," Gytha said. "As my husband has told me, a man accustomed to battle does not sit apart from his men if he has shared the company of Death with them. He may lead them, but he eats what they eat and endures the same hardships. I do not understand why he remains aloof, and Ralf may not have noticed this."

"Then tell your husband that I find Conan odd as well. He does not spend the night in his bed either. Since I live near my inn, I can see the entrance and have witnessed him slipping away after I have gone to seek my own rest."

"In which direction?"

"Night swallows his shadow before I have had a chance to see if he walks toward the priory or simply into the village."

"A woman?"

Signy chuckled. "There is a serving maid here whom I saw flirting with him. When I questioned her, she confessed that the coin he flashed to pay for extra ale had tempted her to find out if he might tuck another into her hand for lying with him, despite his terrible face, but he has done no more than smile at her."

"She is fortunate he did not take her to the hayloft. You do not countenance whoring."

"As she well knows! She already has one babe born after accepting a pretty coin. I reminded her of this." Signy shook her head. "But I fear there may be many babes born after these men leave. I see their eyes following any woman they see and know that they will seek bedmates because they have nothing else to do."

Gytha wondered if any had dared approach her friend, then decided that few would try. She had seen the look Signy gave those so bold. Castration might be less painful. "Ralf told him that the inn did not allow whoring, and he seemed to accept it. To have so quickly found a woman from the village willing to lie with him seems unlikely."

"The cause of this man's strange habit may prove to be dreams of war that drive away sleep." Signy looked pensive. "That is the most harmless conclusion. In truth, I do not like the man and trust him less."

"You say he leaves the inn every night?" Gytha thought for a moment. "'Tis a pity we cannot have him followed. It might be helpful to know what he does."

"Your husband's sergeant?"

"He is some distance away, helping Tostig build a shelter for my brother's new flock of sheep."

Signy frowned in thought, and then looked up with a grin. "My Nute is small enough to go after this man for just long enough to see where he goes. If fortunate, we may even learn why the guard captain leaves every night."

"Would that be safe? What if this Conan is an evil man?" Gytha reached around and rubbed her back. "Or fears the discovery of some secret and would do harm to protect it?"

"Your husband has taught my lad how to stalk animals in the hunt, and he can take his slingshot with him as protection. I will explain that all we need know is where Conan goes and perhaps why. Nute is sensible and will not seek further if I explain there might be unnecessary danger and I forbid him to do so. If the crowner supports my cautioning, he will listen." She smiled. "He would do anything for your husband and will be overjoyed to learn he is helping Ralf out."

"Tonight then?"

Signy nodded.

"I will tell Ralf as soon as I see him." Gytha struggled to drag herself to her feet. She did not need to see her feet to know her ankles were swollen. "I do wish this child would decide he is curious to see the world."

Signy put her arm around her friend as they walked to the door. Neither noticed that Conan had been watching them.

Chapter Twenty

The night air was as soft as a lover's kiss, but Nute was not yet old enough to know of these things and instead stood trembling in the shadows. Touching the sling tucked into his belt, he gained confidence and was determined to make Crowner Ralf proud of him before this night was over. He held that thought close to his heart, and it warmed him a little.

Stalking a man would surely prove to be little different from hunting game for the table, he thought, and threw his thin shoulders back. But a man was far larger than a rabbit and much more dangerous. Casting that thought from his mind, he hardened his resolve and waited.

It did not take long for the man to emerge from the inn. Despite the darkness, Nute knew he was the one to follow. His foster mother had made sure he served the man his ale and pie at supper so he could study the soldier's shape. With no moon, Nute could not see the deep scars across the guard captain's face, but this man's walk and build matched the one the boy had been waiting for.

Although Conan was not tall, he walked at a pace that forced Nute to run. Fortunately, the road out of the village toward the priory was one the lad knew well or he might have tripped in the ruts and injured himself. That the man he followed did not know the road yet walked swiftly and with self-assurance astonished the boy. Perhaps he was one of those who saw well in diminished light. Some men did and were better soldiers for it.

When Conan reached the mill entrance gate to the priory, he hesitated, pressed himself against the stone wall, and peered around.

Nute rushed into the shrubbery by the road side as quietly as possible and felt certain that he remained undetected, even if the captain was sharp-eyed in the night. He held his breath.

Conan slowly opened the gate and disappeared inside.

Creeping up to the entrance, Nute peered around the gate.

Suddenly, the thick clouds above slipped aside to reveal a full moon.

Nute groaned. With the cloak of darkness lost, he would not find it easy to follow anyone on that open path to the mill. He forcefully reminded himself that the crowner had entrusted him with a man's job this night. Clenching his teeth, he swore he would not disappoint Ralf.

He looked down and gripped the sling for courage, then entered the priory.

Once inside, Nute noticed that Conan had slowed his pace. The man looked neither right nor left but seemed intent on getting to some planned destination. The boy tried to keep his step light so the soldier would not hear the distinctive crunch of gravel behind him.

Other than the cries of scurrying night creatures, the rhythmic thump of the mill wheel, and the soft whisper of a gentle wind brushing through the trees, Tyndal Priory was quiet. The evening prayer done, the religious were asleep, although it would not be many more hours before they rose to greet the morning with orisons. Other than the moon, the only light came from the hospital where lay brothers remained awake and carried flickering candles as they tended the sick and dying. In that moment, the priory seemed as devoid of iniquity as Eden.

Suddenly, Conan veered off the path and down into the clearing where the bees dozed in their woven skeps.

There was no place for Nute to hide. Falling to the ground, he wiggled into deep grass and hoped that it would hide him well enough. A sudden chill wind blew across his back. He tensed and willed himself not to shiver.

Cautiously lifting his head, he saw a shadow crossing the bridge over the branch of the stream that ran alongside the guest quarters. At this distance, Nute could not say whether the shape was a man or a woman, but the figure was moving quickly in this direction.

Trembling more from fear than any cold, he desperately tried to control his breathing so no one could hear him. To his own ears, each breath sounded like a drum beat.

Nute waited.

The shadow turned down the path leading to the main gate and hospital, merged into the darkness, and disappeared.

Conan reemerged on the path and began to run to the bridge.

Nute jumped to his feet and tried to keep up. In his ears, he could hear his foster mother cautioning him not to take chances. It was a warning echoed by the crowner when he agreed to let Nute follow Conan.

He slowed his pace. Was it enough to have seen this man entering the priory? Dare he follow him further?

The choice was a hard one, and he had little time to make it. Finally, he stopped, asking himself what would be most helpful to the crowner while also keeping his word not to be foolish. "I must learn exactly where the soldier is going," he muttered and continued to follow but at a safe distance.

Conan crossed the bridge and hurried to the guest quarters.

Halfway across the bridge, Nute halted and watched the man open the gate and slip into the courtyard leading to Davoir's chambers.

Nute knew he should go no further. If he followed the man into the quarters, he would probably be caught. How could he explain why he was following the soldier? And even if he succeeded in hiding, would he be able to see anything of significance should the soldier enter the priest's chambers? That was one place Nute most certainly dare not go.

On one hand, the boy longed to prove his courage. On the other, he feared breaking an oath he had been required to make while touching the crowner's sword hilt. Even if he was willing to disobey his foster mother and Ralf, Nute knew he could not defy God.

Spinning around, the boy fled back to the inn where Signy and Crowner Ralf waited for his report.

Chapter Twenty-one

Renaud pulled his cloak tighter around his thin body, bent his head, and willed himself to walk another circle around the guest quarters. Although the breeze had been soft when he first toured the lodgings, this sudden northern blast was as jagged as Satan's claws and ripped at him until he was sure he bled. When would they leave this cursed priory, he wondered as he pushed himself against the merciless wind.

The gust began to whistle an obscene tune in his ears, and shadows mocked his terror as he felt evil beings crowding ever closer. He began to shake so hard he feared he would piss on himself for this was the hour owned by the Prince of Darkness when ghosts, fiends, and the damned ruled the earth. All god-fearing men were wise to look over their shoulders for hellish creatures that lurked with malign intent in the gloom.

From a frail part of his soul, a wicked voice whispered that God slept during these bleak hours and would do nothing to help any mortal foolish enough to walk alone where some imp could drag him into Hell. Renaud would never confess to any man about this weakness in his conviction that God was all-knowing and all-caring. Indeed, he dared not. His confessor was Father Etienne, a man most intolerant of delicate faith.

Like a fool, Renaud thought, I took the captain's advice and sent the other clerks off to their beds. I should have kept a companion. He longed to fly to the monk's dormitory and shake one of his fellows awake so he would not be alone in this darkness replete with frolicking hell spawn. It took every ounce of resolve and pride not to do just that.

Suddenly, he stopped, his mouth opening in fear. What was that sound?

He froze, held his breath, and then spun around with the cross, worn on a rope around his neck, held high.

Nothing.

Surely the howling is only from the wind, he assured himself, and those twisting shadows will be born again in the morning sun as shrubs.

Bending to lift his robe, he determined that the cloth and his legs were dry, and then sighed with relief that he had not suffered complete humiliation by losing control of his bladder. That was enough to give him sufficient courage to lower his head and continue marching through the brush and grass behind the guest quarters.

As he turned the corner of the building, that tiny reserve of strength vanished. He again whimpered with longing for the companionship of a fellow soul. Even the servant, who usually sat near the gate, had gone to his bed soon after the last Office was sung. If Renaud had dared, he would have cursed, but even an innocent oath took on a more sinister meaning in the night where the creatures from Hell found cheer in any hint of blasphemy.

As he resumed his patrol into the small garden near the entrance gate, he slid to another stop, put a hand to his mouth, and bit back a horrified cry.

Something was in the shadows. Not a shrub. Not a wild creature. The twisting shape resembled a man, featureless and hooded.

Renaud wanted to scream, but his tongue froze with terror. He wanted to flee, but his feet were bound to the earth. All he could do was gape with an awful fascination. This shape had not been there before. He was certain of it. As the shade writhed, the clerk suddenly recognized the creature.

"Jean?"

The only response was the wind's high-pitched shriek.

Renaud staggered backward. "Surely it is not your spirit that has come to haunt me," he sobbed. "Your soul must be in Heaven."

There was no answer. The wind now calmed, but the shape continued to writhe, one long arm raised in a beckoning gesture.

He slipped to his knees. "Father Etienne swears that you died pure in body and soul. He never knew a man so worthy of Paradise."

The shadow appeared to reach out to him as if longing to draw him into an embrace, doomed and eternal.

"No!" Renaud scrabbled backward. A stone cut into his knee, but he did not notice. "I did nothing to endanger your soul," he howled. "I swear it, Jean. I meant only to get you drunk in jest. If that tainted you with sin, you committed the transgression in ignorance. Surely God knows that."

He was certain the spirit had begun to approach, its gait heavy with the weight of damnation.

Again opening his mouth to scream, he could only moan. Now he feared no one could hear him except this menacing phantom. "I was jealous of you. I wanted to prove to our master that you were imperfect like other mortals. Just one failing, nothing grave!" He stretched forth a pleading hand. "Anything to show him that you were no better than I!" He put his hands over his eyes and wept.

Blinded by tears and weak with terror, he began to sway. What had he done to cause this horror? How could Jean's soul have gone to perdition because of a silly prank? No matter what he had tricked Jean into doing, Renaud believed that his fellow clerk was cleansed of all sin when he died. No matter how much he longed for Jean to show flaws in the eyes of the priest, he had never wanted him to lose all chance for Heaven.

"Forgive me!" he cried out, then stared into the infinite darkness above him. "It was I who sinned, Lord, not Jean!"

Those were the last words he spoke before the blow fell.

Chapter Twenty-two

Ralf eyed the man next to him. His fingers itched to truss him up like a chicken and lock him away so he could not endanger another man.

Innocent of his companion's thoughts, Conan stared down at the still form of Renaud, the clerk. The deep scars in the guard captain's forehead darkened with concern.

The lay brother rose to his feet. "I think he will live. The blow left a bloody welt on this side of his head, but the bone seems intact. His breathing is steady, and I bound a poultice of comfrey and marsh mallow against the cut." Looking at Ralf, he sighed. "I would feel more confident if Sister Anne could examine him. God has blessed her hands with the healing touch." He looked back down at the youth who seemed to stir. "But I shall pray that God have mercy on this lad and not condemn him for my ignorance of earthly remedies." Then he begged leave to treat another patient and hurried off.

Ralf laid a heavy hand on the guard's shoulder. "I expect the miracle of Renaud's recovery, don't you? Is it not a matter for wonder that you were so near the guest quarters? Did He whisper in your ear that you would find the wounded clerk if you walked through the unlocked gate into the place where the priory guests slept? I stand awestruck by the marvel of these circumstances."

Conan stepped away from the crowner's touch.

Ralf's expression resembled that of a hangman about to perform the duty for which he was justly proud.

Conan's mirthless smile matched the crowner's. "If you arrest me, must you wait to see if an angel frees me from prison like one did Saint Peter from the dungeons of Herod?" He grunted in contempt. "Such proof of innocence is not required. I may be a wicked man, Crowner, but I did not attack this youth."

"And why should I believe that?"

"Had I been the one to strike Renaud, I would have killed him. I am not a man who wastes time on trifling blows."

With reluctance, Ralf nodded and some of his anger dissipated. He had no proof that Conan was lying, but the man's blunt response suggested innocence. Having been a soldier himself, one paid for his killing skills, Ralf knew men like this captain well. They did not bother with the simple wounding of their prey.

When Nute told Ralf that he had followed Conan to the priory grounds and watched him go through the unlocked gate of the guest quarters, the crowner raced there with a speed that impressed the boy who tried to follow lest there be need for a messenger. By the time the crowner arrived, he met Conan, with Renaud in his arms, on the path to the hospital.

Conan might be innocent of this attack, Ralf thought, but he had not explained why he was on priory land and within the guest area when there was no known purpose for him to be there.

Renaud groaned and put a hand to his head.

Ralf shouted for the lay brother who ran back and knelt by the youth.

After a swift examination of the clerk, the lay brother said, "He may be recovering his wits." Then before the crowner could speak, the man looked up at Ralf and added, "He needs rest, not probing by the king's man. Tomorrow, perhaps, he will have strength enough to answer your questions."

"By your leave, Brother, I shall ask but one question now, and then I will leave him in peace until the morrow." He gestured at Conan beside him. "You will see neither of us until then, and this one may not visit without me."

Conan seemed not to have heard the crowner. With an odd expression, he stared down at the clerk.

Ralf slammed his palm on the man's shoulder.

Startled, the captain put a hand to his sword and stepped back.

"Did you hear me?" the crowner growled.

The lay brother shook his fist at the two men. "Hush!" he ordered. "The clerk is awakening." Then he gestured to the crowner. "You are allowed one question, and then you must leave."

Both Ralf and Conan knelt by Renaud's side and watched the youth open his eyes.

"Am I dead?" The clerk tried to sit up, his eyes wild with terror.

The lay brother gently pushed him back. "You are in the priory hospital, in this world, and still bound by your mortal body."

Renaud's eyes widened as if this news did nothing to diminish his fear, then he rubbed at them and winced. "I am in pain."

"You were struck by a mighty blow on the side of your head," the lay brother said.

The clerk dropped his hands and blinked. "Who…?"

"We don't know," the crowner said.

Suddenly, Renaud recognized the guard captain. "I failed!" he cried.

Reaching out to touch the clerk's arm with more gentleness than might be expected of this soldier, Conan replied. "You did your best. I came to see how you were faring in your patrol and found you lying on the path near the gate."

All this sounds so reasonable, Ralf thought, but he remained uneasy. "What do you remember?" he asked, and then raised one finger at the lay brother.

The man raised his own finger in acknowledgement.

"The quarters were haunted," Renaud replied and began to shiver.

The lay brother took off his own cloak and tucked it around the youth.

Ralf glanced at the guard captain. Conan looked as bewildered as he.

"Jean was in the shadows. I swear it!"

"Jean? You mean the dead clerk?"

"His soul is damned for eternity! It was lurking in the shrub-bery, waiting to drag me away to burn in perdition's fires with him. He was stretching out his arms to grab me when I…"

"You were struck from behind."

"Cannot the Devil do extraordinary things? Surely Jean's ghost could reach out to me, as I believe he did, and then fell me with a blow from behind. Or else it came from Satan's hand." He squeezed his eyes shut, either from pain or the fear of Hell.

Were there two men involved? Ralf scowled at the possibility of a more tangled crime.

The lay brother was now giving him a warning shake of his head.

The crowner truly did not want to tire the wounded youth with too many questions. Renaud seemed obsessed with his belief that he had been attacked by a malevolent spirit, a con-clusion that might weaken with a good night's sleep. As far as the crowner was concerned, demons were as unlikely as guard captains to waste energy on feckless blows.

The crowner raised another finger to the lay brother and mouthed his promise that this question would be his last. "Other than the ghost that was urging you forward, did you hear any-thing else? Any sound at all?"

"Only the wind." Renaud's voice was weak.

"Enough," the lay brother said and waved the men away. "You will have time after the sun rises to ask more. The lad needs rest."

Ralf agreed and turned away. As he passed by Conan, he grabbed him by the arm and pulled him along beside him.

Together and in silence, the two men left the hospital.

As they entered the courtyard leading to the priory main entrance, Ralf stopped and loosened his grip on the captain's arm.

Conan turned to face him, his lips curled in a sneer. "You are fortunate that I respect the king's men, Crowner. Were it otherwise, you would be missing a hand by now."

Ralf ignored that. "Why were you at the guest quarters and not in your bed at the inn?"

"Because it is my duty to safeguard this French priest and his mewling clerks. Davoir believes that God will protect him from all evil. Being a man most likely destined to entertain the Prince of Darkness for all eternity instead of the Prince of Peace, I put my faith in a sharp sword rather than wafting prayers. If this man, destined for a bishopric and beloved by the French king's brother, were harmed, our English king might have a war on his hands. I doubt he fancies that idea while he is away, taming the Welsh." His laugh resembled a growl.

"You have gone there every night?"

"Every night, Crowner." Conan bent forward and murmured. "And why have you had me followed? Are you really the king's man or in league with another?"

Ralf came within a heartbeat of striking the man but drew back. It would not help matters if he lost his temper. If Conan was involved in Jean's death and responsible for Renaud's attack, Ralf needed indisputable proof. If the man were honest, he could help the crowner solve Jean's murder. Either way, there was no doubt the captain was clever and not an easy man to trick into confession.

But the crowner had one more issue to resolve and laid his hand back on his sword hilt when he asked the question. "Why did you not report the death of the one of your men on the journey to Tyndal?"

Conan looked surprised, then shook his head. "It was not a matter worthy of your interest, Crowner."

"I should be the judge of that."

Noticing Ralf's hand on his sword hilt, Conan raised his own hand and placed it against his heart. "The explanation is a long one, but I pray that the simple version will satisfy you. Need I remind you that I command this company of military guards under the authority of the king, and, as such, I determine the action required if a crime is committed?"

"I understand."

"When I was in Wales, this particular soldier was accused of the mutilation and rape of several young women." Conan shrugged. "There were probably witnesses to his crimes, but those men may have joined him in his acts or else feared his wrath if they spoke against him. Only the Welsh kin of the women gave testimony. The man's commander decided that the charges against the soldier could not be proved. When I was chosen to lead the company on this journey, I discovered that this soldier would be under my command. I objected, but my plea was rejected. The man had friends."

"Hell spawn," Ralf said, his voice low with fury.

"On the way to this priory, I noticed that the soldier often rode beside the clerk, Jean, but I found no cause to intervene. When we arrived at an inn, I overheard him tell the youth to meet him in the stable early the following morning and he would show him something wondrous. Noting the youth's feminine face and soft body, I feared ill intent."

Ralf nodded.

"I have given my oath to protect this company of French liegemen so rose early myself lest the clerk need assistance." He stopped and studied the crowner for a moment before continuing. "Imagine my surprise, indeed my relief, when I found the soldier dead."

"And who killed him?" Ralf asked, then wondered if he truly wanted to know.

"One, it seems, who wished justice rendered. The soldier's crimes were known to many, even if no one had spoken in support of the violated and tortured Welshwomen. We fight against their men in honorable combat, Crowner. What he did made angels and saints weep."

For a long moment, both men looked at each other without speaking.

"Are you finished questioning me?' Conan finally said and gestured toward the entrance gate.

With only a slight hesitation, Ralf stepped aside.

Conan walked out of the priory and back toward the village.

Chapter Twenty-three

Gracia opened the door to the prioress' audience chamber.

Davoir strode in.

Seated in her carved wooden chair, Eleanor held her staff of office, an unequivocal symbol of her leadership over Tyndal Priory.

On her right side stood Brother Thomas, on the left Crowner Ralf.

"We have just received word that your clerk, Renaud, has regained consciousness," she announced in a gentle voice, "and has suffered no significant harm."

The priest nodded once, his body rigid and his expression replete with disapproval over the presence of the two men. The news of his clerk's recovery did not merit even a blink of interest.

Eleanor tried not to judge him for his lack of compassion, but, to her knowledge, he had neither gone to his clerk's side nor sent anyone on his behalf. She suspected that the first positive word he had received about the condition of his wounded clerk was what she had just relayed. As hard as she struggled not to condemn, she could not completely set aside her conclusion that he owned a stone heart.

His expression almost luminous with disdain, the priest folded his hands into a prayerful attitude, raised his chin, and cleared his throat. "I have decided that you are not fit to rule this priory," he announced. "Although you will be treated with courtesy, I shall now take your place." He stepped forward with his hand outstretched to take the staff from her hands.

"Indeed?" Eleanor swallowed her fury at his presumption and kept her tone even. "Although I choose to believe you spoke those words without malice or intent to defame the king who appointed me to my position here, I find your words offensive and, of course, refuse to comply."

He reddened. "You have no right to contradict me. My clerks, if needed, will lock you away as we have your wicked sub-infirmarian."

Ralf stepped forward.

Eleanor murmured something, and he stopped. She turned back to the priest. "Your authority in this investigation lies in discovery of wrongdoing and the offering of recommendations to our abbess in Anjou. When we last spoke, you said you had found no fault with Tyndal, other than some minor repairs, all of which we had planned to correct. Apart from your conviction that Sister Anne killed Jean, an unproven accusation, you have given me no reason to believe that Tyndal is in such fearful peril that you must take extraordinary measures beyond your authority." She tilted her head and smiled. That expression might have been benign, but her eyes flashed with contempt for his arrogance.

He stiffened. "You allowed an incompetent woman to treat my clerk. She killed him out of ignorance or spite."

"Unproven and thus irrelevant," Thomas said.

"Silence!" the priest roared.

"I have given him permission to speak, and he shall." Eleanor voice remained calm.

"You both are the Devil's creatures, filthy with lust and rotten with sin!"

"Other than an allegation from an unnamed source, have you any proof that this tale is true?" Eleanor held her breath for just a moment and silently prayed.

The room filled with a silence that was as heavy as the air before a summer storm.

Davoir began to sway as if suddenly faint, and he put a hand over his face.

At a sign from the prioress, Thomas brought a chair for the priest and helped him to sit.

"Jean is dead. Renaud was attacked trying to protect me. My life is surely in danger. You cannot protect me. No woman could," he mumbled.

"Again, Father, I ask whether or not the accusation against Brother Thomas and me has been proven."

"No," he muttered. "All hold you both in the highest regard."

Briefly, Eleanor shut her eyes in gratitude. "Then you have no cause to remove me from the leadership of this priory."

He slammed his fist down on the chair arm. "You have failed to safeguard my clerks!"

"You have failed to allow anyone to properly protect you," Ralf snapped.

"This is God's earth! Armed men have no right to be here," the priest replied, half rising to his feet.

"And your clerks failed when they tried to use prayer as you insisted," Ralf said. "Tell me how that proves you should wrest the priory from its proper leader and take over yourself."

Davoir's face turned blood red.

Eleanor bent toward the crowner, said something only the two of them could hear, and again faced the priest. "Father Etienne, you and I agree that the Church rules over this priory. We also agree that your two clerks have suffered violence, one fatal and one not." She studied him for an instant and noted that his high color was fading. "You have also exonerated Brother Thomas and me from the vile accusations hurled at us." She waited.

"I have found no evidence that the allegations are true, but I have not yet questioned everyone…"

"Have you spoken with Sub-Prioress Ruth?"

He nodded with evident reluctance.

"Surely you know that King Henry, as a boon to my father for his loyalty, sent me to lead this priory, although Tyndal had

already chosen Sister Ruth, as she was then, to be their prioress."
Surely he did, she thought, but it was a fact that bore repeating.

He mumbled concurrence.

"She has good cause to resent that decision by our king, but
Sub-Prioress Ruth is God's most devoted servant." She smiled.
"She and I rarely agree, but I chose her as my sub-prioress over
all others because of her competence and honor. If anyone would
tell you of my failings, including the breaking of my vows, she
would be honest enough to do so."

"And she has not," the priest replied, once again slumping
in his chair. The admission had obviously and deeply distressed
him. "She defended your virtue and that of Brother Thomas with
fervor." Unable to look at either monk or prioress, he turned
his face away.

"Then let us agree that you have no cause to remove me from
my position as head of Tyndal…"

"That statement in support of your innocence aside, I still
do! You are a weak woman…"

She raised her hand. "Please let me finish, Father. You have
not questioned all those whom you would like. That is understood, but you have yet to discover any proof that would suggest
my guilt." She hesitated for a moment, then continued. "Regarding the attacks against your clerks, I am obliged to protect all
guests here from assault. We may debate which of us was the
most negligent in this tragedy, but such an argument is futile
when swift action is needed to catch a killer."

"Action is what I require," Davoir growled.

She ignored his tone. "I believe we agree that we must find
a method to do this without the use of swords."

The priest blinked.

"I wish to make the situation perfectly clear," Ralf said,
returning the prioress' subtle nod at him. "Jean was murdered.
You accused Sister Anne of this. Renaud was subsequently
struck down. This attack could not have been done by the sub-
infirmarian. It is my suspicion that you are the ultimate target
for this violence. Even if you are not, you could still be in danger.

Your other clerks have not been troubled in their duties, and they sleep in the monks' dormitory where they are far safer. You, however…" He shrugged as if suggesting the final conclusion was obvious.

"This sub-infirmarian may have a host of imps under her control, those who are eager to turn suspicion away from her." The priest's voice shook.

"According to the lay brother who treated Renaud, the blow was a heavy one, not a woman's light tap. For that reason, we can eliminate the possibility that the assailant was a nun or lay sister," Ralf said. "When I questioned your clerk, he believed he had seen a ghost beckoning him, a shade that bore a man's shape. I spoke with Prior Andrew. He knows his monks and lay brothers. He did not see any empty dormitory beds or notice anyone missing at an Office. Although this is not absolute proof that no monk or lay brother could be guilty of attacking Renaud, Prior Andrew's testimony suggests that the men in Tyndal are innocent."

Davoir's eyes still flashed with annoyance, but his hot fury had muted. "Then what do you suggest?"

Ralf did not hesitate. "Allow the priory to free Sister Anne."

Seeing the high color return to the priest's cheeks, Eleanor winced. Although she longed to release her friend from her narrow cell, she knew she had to lead this reluctant priest to that decision slowly. Patience came hard, but the desire for a complete victory over this man made it easier. She asked the crowner to remain silent.

"You are probably safe in the company of your many clerks during the day," she said to Davoir in a conciliatory tone. "At night, we must provide you with a proper guard and preferably set a trap for the guilty man. If we can catch him, we will end this chain of tragedies and bring justice to the dead and injured."

"No weapons," Davoir replied.

Eleanor was pleased that he had accepted the basic plan. "I agree in principle," she said, "and believe the plan would not require several armed guards. I do fear that one sharp sword is advisable, lest the killer be armed himself or the man fall under the jurisdiction of the king's law."

Davoir scowled. "God will protect us here."

"And He often does that by urging us to use the sagacity He gave us. Although I would not want more than one sword, two at most, I have learned that our crowner only uses his when God gives him no other choice. He would be the one chosen to carry the weapon, a sword which was once blessed on our altar."

Ralf instantly stared at his feet with apparent humility. Only the prioress knew how shocked he was to learn that anything of his had been on the priory altar.

Davoir's eyes shifted unhappily as he tried to find grounds to reject this idea. Finally, he sighed. "Very well."

Eleanor tried not to betray her joy. "You may, of course, continue to question all whom you wish during the day in the continuation of your investigation. I would advise you to keep several of your clerks with you at all times."

He nodded.

Ralf whispered a request to the prioress. When she agreed, he asked, "Do your clerks have any enemies? I apologize for this next question, but I must know. Is there anyone who might wish you ill?"

For the first time since his initial roars of outrage, Father Etienne gave some indication of cooperation. "My clerks are virtuous and have no enemies, other than some who might envy them. But I can think of no one who would let resentment morph into murder." He looked up at the ceiling for a moment. "As for myself, I have been shown great favor by King Philip and his brother. Even more honor awaits me on my return home. As all men are sinners, there will be those who wish me ill. But I can think of none who so hate me that they would endanger their souls by killing me."

Ralf was not confident about that. He found the man reprehensible, an opinion he was wise enough not to express.

"Do you agree to set a trap for this creature that has killed one of your clerks and injured another?" Prioress Eleanor opted for a mollifying tone. Her own position and authority once again secure, she believed it tactful to offer the priest a choice. "It will be done at night."

"I do, if I must," Davoir replied, but his gaze remained on the ceiling as if hoping God might offer a better option.

With a sideways glance at Brother Thomas, she said, "Then let us plan it now."

Chapter Twenty-four

Gracia stood outside the hospital trying to decide how to help her mistress in this matter of the autumn crocus jar without actually disobeying her commands. Were she still dwelling on the streets of Walsingham, she would have done whatever she deemed necessary, but she had a home again, different concerns, and others to consider. Dwelling in a priory was no different from residing with any family. There were rules.

But after her family had died and she was left to subsist by her own wits, she could no longer afford the habits or practices that the well-fed and warmly clothed deemed immutable. Survival demanded different precepts, and those lessons remained useful, even if they must be modified. In this matter of the clerk's murder, all she had to do was look beyond the obvious, recognize the perfect opportunity to assist Prioress Eleanor, and not do anything foolish.

That opportunity presented itself.

"Sister Christina," Gracia cried out and quickly rushed to the infirmarian's side. "You look troubled. May I help in some way?"

The nun stopped and squinted. "Gracia," she said, her face softening as she recognized the girl's voice.

Gracia took Christina's arm. Although Sister Anne was kind, the girl sometimes felt intimidated by her gravity and well-honed intelligence. With the gentle, extremely near-sighted infirmarian, Gracia felt only affection. "I was going to the hospital. If you were as well, may I accompany you?" While she would willingly take the nun wherever she wished, Gracia fervently hoped the planned destination was the apothecary hut.

"Sub-Prioress Ruth sent me to seek Sister Oliva, my child. Do you know where I might find her?"

Gracia almost skipped for joy. "I do, and we shall go together for I wished to ask her a question." Truth enough, she thought, and was pleased she did not have to lie to this good woman.

The journey through the hospital was slow. The infirmarian's eyes were weak, but her ears never missed the weakest sigh or softest groan of anguish.

Several times, Sister Christina stopped to kneel and pray by a bedside, not caring what rotting flesh her hand grasped. Once she spoke with a woman sitting in a hot bath, violets drifting in the water, and expressed joy that the patient had gotten relief from the horrible pain of bladder stone. When a heavy, red-faced man cried out in fear when told he must suffer blood-letting between his finger and thumb for his severe headaches, Sister Christina knelt with him and distracted him with pleas to God while the lay brother made the cut. With kind touch and tenderly spoken prayers, she brought peace to the dying and those in unspeakable pain.

Although the sight of so much agony was difficult for Gracia, she waited while the infirmarian gave consolation. Tears for the suffering stung the maid's eyes, and she admired Sister Christina for her compassion. Like so many at Tyndal Priory, she was certain the nun was a saint. Some claimed to have been cured by Sister Christina. Gracia had never witnessed this herself, but Sister Anne had confirmed the stories and this convinced the girl that they must be true.

At last, the pair reached the door leading to the hut where the medicines were stored.

"It was Sister Anne who had this place built," the infirmarian whispered to Gracia. "She believed the suffering had too long to wait for what little ease we can give them and begged permission to have all remedies here, rather than in the tiny hut on the other side of the priory near the gardens."

Gracia saw tears in the infirmarian's eyes and loved her more for that.

"She is a godly woman, my child. Everyone at Tyndal knows she is innocent."

Gracia looked through the door and saw Sister Oliva in the hut. "The nun we seek is there," she said and lightly pressed the infirmarian's arm to guide her in that direction. As she did, something caught her eye, and she turned to glance into the chapel just opposite.

A man quickly turned his head and covered his face with his hands as if lost in prayer.

For an instant, the girl hesitated. She would have sworn he had been staring at them. His body remained twisted at an awkward angle. He might wish for an observer to assume his soul looked to Heaven, but Gracia was convinced he was far more curious about what was happening on earth.

Yet there was a crutch lying next to him, Gracia noted. Surely he was just one of many who came here for healing and had been distracted from his orisons for a moment by their arrival. But she remained troubled and did not set her uneasiness aside. The instinct honed for survival is never lost or wisely dismissed.

"Is something wrong?" Sister Christina squinted.

"No, Sister," Gracia replied. "I thought I saw one of the lay brothers approaching, but he did not need your assistance. Let us go to the hut."

Sister Oliva brightened when she saw her visitors. "I pray you have come with news that Sister Anne has been sent back to us," she said.

"I fear not," the infirmarian said.

Gracia shook her head in confirmation.

"I have come on behalf of our sub-prioress who prays that some way has been found to make more of the medicine for her gout." The infirmarian smiled hopefully.

But Gracia wondered if the smile also suggested that even the kind Sister Christina could find gentle amusement in the sub-prioress' change of mind after discovering that Sister Anne's earthly remedy took away her great pain.

Sister Oliva frowned. "I fear there has been no alteration in what I said before. There is nothing left of the preparation."

"The redness on her toe has brightened, and the throbbing returns." Sister Christina frowned, but the expression never meant anger with the infirmarian. She was worried.

"Only Sister Anne has the skill," the young nun replied. "She may have promised to train me in some of the more complex treatments, but the one for gout is both difficult and dangerous. Not even her former husband knew how to balance the ingredients. I would not even try to do this."

Sister Christina stepped closer. "If we were to smuggle all she needed to make the medicine into her cell…"

"And chance the great anger of Father Etienne, Infirmarian? I do not know what she would need even if we could."

"Might there be just a little left?" Gracia smiled eagerly.

Sister Oliva stared at the girl with surprise.

Gracia quickly put a finger up to her lips and shook her head.

Sister Oliva raised an eyebrow but remained silent.

"Do you remember the color of the container, Sister Christina?" Gracia asked. "Perhaps our sister can look for it." A foolish remark, the girl thought. Sister Oliva would surely know where it was and what it looked like. She only hoped the infirmarian knew less than she did about how much this nun had been taught.

The infirmarian shook her head. "It was dark and round, I think, and about this large." She drew a circle in the air, and then gestured toward the area where the chest of poisonous herbs sat. "When Sister Anne made up the pouches for me to take to our sub-prioress, she went in that direction."

Sister Oliva tilted her head, looked at Gracia, and pressed one hand against her mouth.

Gracia nodded, relieved that the woman grasped the need to pretend. Deciding she liked the young nun for her sensitivity, she also appreciated her cleverness and understood why Sister Anne had chosen her to learn the apothecary art.

"Your description has helped me recall the item," the nun said. "It was a dark brown pot with an ill-fitting lid." She made a rough circle with her hands but carefully watched the size she was indicating. "Round as you described, Infirmarian." She made a show of checking the chest and glancing around the shelves. "I fear I see nothing like that here." Looking down at Gracia, she smiled, knowing the infirmarian was too near-sighted to note it. "I suspect our sub-infirmarian may have sent the pot away for a better-fitting lid after the last dose was used."

The prioress' maid grinned back.

"I fear we have absolutely nothing left of the remedy, Infirmarian. I shall ask God to give our sub-prioress more strength to endure her pain."

"I shall as well and also pray for the swift return of our good Sister Anne," Sister Christina said, bowing her head. "Until then, many will suffer." She looked up in the general direction of the young nun, her expression benevolent. "I know God has blessed your hands with skill…"

"As we both know, Infirmarian," Sister Oliva said in a low voice, "God has endowed Sister Anne with the skills of a great healer. Although those of us working under her direction do so with dedication and prayer, we are not as honored with those same gifts."

With that, Sister Christina turned to leave. Gracia once again took her arm and guided her through the hospital where the suffering reached out to receive the relief she gave.

As for the penitent with the crutch in the chapel, he was nowhere to be seen.

Folding her arms and with a thoughtful air, Sister Oliva watched the pair depart, then went back to the table where she had been crushing rotten apples used to treat sore eyes.

◇◇◇

After accompanying the infirmarian to the sub-prioress' chambers, Gracia hurried away.

If there was no other reason for thinking Sister Christina was at least *Blessed* if not quite a saint, her tolerance of Sub-Prioress

Ruth's faults would be enough. All knew that the infirmarian was much loved by the sub-prioress, but, as the raised voice of pained outrage from the chambers suggested, even Sister Christina was not completely safe from the sharp rebukes for which the sub-prioress was known.

Safely on the path back to her mistress, Gracia saw two men coming toward her. One was Brother Thomas and the other Crowner Ralf. She waved with enthusiasm and ran to meet them.

Seeing the girl's happy expression, Thomas called out to her. "Do you bear good tidings?"

"I wish better, Brother, but I do have some news." She nodded at the crowner with a friendly smile but reserved her highest regard for the auburn-haired monk.

"The missing pot containing autumn crocus was about this big." She studiously replicated the young nun's estimation. "It was dark brown and had an ill-fitting lid." She hesitated and looked hopefully at her favored monk before adding, "Sister Christina could not see the pot well but said it was round, dark, and about this big." She frowned and drew a bigger circle with her hands.

"Well done!" Thomas grinned.

"Hearing this news from you is fortunate," the crowner added. "I have just searched Jean's room and found no pot there."

Gracia's enthusiasm vanished like the flame on a snuffed candle.

Ralf reached into his pouch and pulled forth a brown pottery lid. Holding it out to Gracia, he said, "But I did find this just outside the guest quarters in the tall grass close to the stables."

She took it in her hand and studied it. "Sister Oliva said the pot had an ill-fitting lid." Running a finger around the edge, she grinned. "This would be ill-fitting," she said. "It turns up just here." She pointed out the flaw and handed it back to the crowner. "That lid would not sit firmly on any jar."

Thomas thanked her for her observations.

Gracia blushed.

"I questioned Renaud," the crowner said, "but he could not recall anything about the pot. It was he who was given the responsibility to administer the required dosage to Jean. He was outraged over my questions and swore he did not care about the shape of any container, only that it held a cure. He did remember how much he had been instructed to mete out by the elusive Brother Imbert. After Jean's death, he paid even less attention to the pot because he saw no cause to do so. When I noticed the absence, he said he did not know when he last saw it." Ralf snorted. "Davoir claims he never saw the jar or the monk who brought it."

"I share your disdain for this priest, Ralf, and know what you are thinking," Thomas said. "But I agree with our prioress in this matter. No matter how unkind and unobservant he seems, Father Etienne has excellent motives not to have killed his clerk."

"I more than dislike him, Brother," Ralf replied. "I despise the man for his vindictive treatment of Sister Anne and his irrational refusal to disallow the obvious lies told about you and our prioress. Yet I reluctantly concur with your opinion."

"He loved his dead clerk," Thomas said, "although that might not be one of the best reasons to conclude his innocence."

"Love? That requires a heart, and, if the man had one, I'd agree that affection precluded violence. Family honor? I accept this as justification not to murder Jean. In addition, my court-loving brother says that King Philip has been negotiating for peace with our king for years. This would argue against any conclusion that Davoir was sent from the French court to trouble the sister of one of King Edward's favored knights by committing murder in her priory in addition to the slander from an unnamed source." He took a deep breath. "That would not be politic."

"Although he accused Prioress Eleanor of ordering Sister Anne to kill Jean, he did so in anger and has not pursued that matter with any vigor," Thomas said.

Ralf shrugged. "And this man will go home to receive a miter?" He chuckled. "The French claim we are governed by kings so raving mad they chew the rushes on the floor, yet they choose bishops who condemn the innocent with no better cause than spite. If these are the men the French believe to be holy, they shall soon burn saints and praise God when the bishops excommunicate angels!"

Gracia listened with fascination to the two men. Although she had rarely heard any good spoken of the French, she did not know much about them, except that they were not English. Once, when she asked her mistress about these strange people, she learned that Prioress Eleanor's maternal family had come to England from the Aquitaine with King Edward's great-grand-mother and had spent some time at the French court. "When we speak of French kings descended from King Louis VII," the prioress had said, "we do so with sympathy, my child. Those ruled by these kings deserve our compassion, not contempt." What her mistress did not explain was why she had smiled when she spoke those words.

"I think we better tell Prioress Eleanor what Gracia and I have found," Ralf said.

Thomas agreed, but his expression became thoughtful. "While you are doing that, I will go to the hospital and ask questions. I cannot believe that no one saw this Brother Imbert. Any detail might prove useful in our efforts to release Sister Anne, if not find the clerk's killer."

"Go, Brother!" Ralf said, turning pale. "Annie must be freed. My wife will give birth any day!"

Chapter Twenty-five

Thomas hastened down the path to the hospital.

The tale of Brother Imbert troubled him. The name was uncommon in East Anglia, which suggested he was not a local man. Prior Andrew certainly knew nothing of him, but Father Etienne had not recognized the name as belonging to one of his clerks either. Was the hooded one, who had visited Sister Anne, Brother Imbert? If his existence wasn't a complete lie, the mysterious monk owned a corporal body.

Although many claimed to have seen ghosts, Thomas never had and often doubted there were such creatures. Even if this Imbert was a damned soul, condemned to restless wandering and the tormenting of wayward mortals, he was more likely to inhabit dreams than steal a lethal dose of autumn crocus for a clerk who, by all accounts, was a gentle lad.

Sensible as this sounded, it was also the case that *reason* has always been a matter for debate amongst those with differing interpretations. After Thomas had spent much time at the hospital, engaged in lengthy questioning of lay brothers, lay sisters, and even a few of the patients, he begin to question how sensible his beliefs were about the character and existence of the wandering damned. Brother Imbert was very elusive indeed.

One patient said he might have seen a shadowy figure come from the direction of the apothecary hut and pass by his bed on the night in question. But he had had a fever and also swore that a fiend danced around his bed, forked tail twitching in response to an unheard melody.

Another man thought for a moment and then recalled that he had seen a hooded man rush by his cousin's cot. He remembered because he called out to him to pray for the soul of his dying kin. When the figure did not stop, he screamed at him, for he knew no lay brother would ever deny prayer to a soul about to face God. The hooded one disappeared, but another lay brother had come to his aid and his cousin was able to die a good death. The man was now convinced the hooded creature was no man at all but rather Satan, fleeing the sight of the cross.

Just as Thomas was about to give up, a lay brother suggested that he might ask the pilgrim who had come here with a twisted ankle. Although the injury was not severe, the lay brother noted with a hint of sarcasm, the pilgrim had been given a place to sleep near the apothecary hut. "He is well enough to see and hear as clearly as you or I, Brother. He was in the right place to notice a hooded man holding a pot too large to put in a pouch." He rubbed his chin as if wondering whether it was time for his shave. "I asked him about this matter once before, and he claimed to know nothing." He grinned. "Looking up at you as you ask stern questions might brighten his memory."

But the straw mattress where the pilgrim slept was unoccupied, and Thomas decided to talk with Sister Oliva lest some detail had come to mind after Gracia last talked with her. As he reached the passageway leading to the apothecary, he glanced into the chapel. Only an elderly woman was there, kneeling in front of the altar. Her back was bent so severely that her nose almost touched her breasts.

He hurried down the walkway to the apothecary hut.

As he grew near, Thomas froze, and then slipped to one side so he would not be too visible from the hut's open door.

A man was standing in front of the shelves. A crutch was leaning against the wall. He was taking items down from the shelves, studying the labels, lifting the lids of some and peering at the contents.

Thomas watched just long enough to make sure this was not just idle curiosity, then walked in. "Are you searching for something?" His question was not asked in a kindly tone.

The man started, almost dropped a jar, and spun around. His face was pale and his eyes wide with terror.

The monk stepped closer and put his hand on the crutch to keep the man from using it as a weapon. "Did I startle you?"

"My lord…"

"I am a monk of Tyndal Priory."

"Brother," he croaked. The man's expression suggested that he did not believe a man of Thomas' height and breadth of shoulder was anything but a knight with a sword by his side. As one who stood no taller than most, the man obviously feared this monk who loomed over him.

"Neither our sub-infirmarian nor her assistant is here." The monk slowly looked at the man from head to foot. "You are in no distress. Why are you riffling through the shelves instead of waiting for another to bring whatever you think you need?"

Trying to recover some dignity, the man puffed out his chest. "I am in pain, although you may not have noticed that. I do not like to whine about my ills." He hesitated, then winced as if deciding it would be wise.

Noticing the man's accent, Thomas smiled. "You are not English," he said, knowing he was stating the obvious and carefully not asking more. With luck, the man might believe the monk was not overly concerned with details beyond the apparent.

The man exhaled with relief. "I am from Picardy," he said. "On pilgrimage to your shrine at Canterbury for my sins."

"Surely there are shrines closer to home, Pilgrim. Why Canterbury?"

"Blood," the man stuttered. "My penance involves blood."

Thomas raised an eyebrow.

"I am not fleeing the hangman."

Had the man been telling the complete truth, he would not be squirming like a boy trying to hide a stolen pastry behind his back. On the other hand, Thomas doubted he was escaping execution or was even the elusive Imbert. The monk smelled fear issuing from the man but no malice. Watching him twitch, Thomas doubted this alleged pilgrim had enough composure to hide his identity and pretend to be a clerk sent by Davoir.

But he is from Picardy, the monk thought. Davoir was from Anjou. The priest came from a noble family, and this pilgrim was not of great worldly rank, although his body suggested he was not accustomed to hunger or to hard labor. There was no cause to see a link between priest and pilgrim. Surely this man had not traveled all the way from Picardy to kill a clerk.

Reluctantly, Thomas concluded that the pilgrim must be trying to pilfer medicines, hoping to sell nostrums on the road to Canterbury to those who did not object to some earthly help while waiting for the miracle of healing from the sainted Becket.

The monk gestured for the man to sit on a nearby bench.

Dutifully, the pilgrim obeyed.

"Explain more fully what you are doing here."

"I am in pain. My ankle needs to be rewrapped. I know something of herbs, and all the lay brothers are busy. I came here to find the remedy myself."

Thomas asked him to raise the foot so he could exam it, then he undid the binding. Not only were the herbs fresh, the ankle was not discolored with bruising. There was no sign of any swelling to suggest a recent injury. No wonder the lay brother had been skeptical of the tale told about a sprain.

He looked up at the man. "This foot?" He pressed his thumb against the ankle bone.

The man cried out.

Thomas knew he had not caused any pain but became more firmly convinced that this man was just a thief while the prey he sought was a murderer. "I will treat you," he said but refused to apologize for the pain he had supposedly produced.

As he went over to the shelf that held a small basket of arnica, he asked, "Do you sleep on the straw mat near the chapel?"

"That I do," the pilgrim replied. His tone was hesitant.

Thomas mentioned a night. "Did you happen to see a hooded

man leave this hut and go through the hospital with something in his hand?" He turned around.

The man's expression suggested genuine surprise—with a hint of relief. He took time to consider the question. "I was asked before, Brother, and swore I had not. But you just said that he was carrying something, and that makes me think I did see a man, although he may not be the one you seek." He looked sheepish as if embarrassed by the poor excuse for the sudden recollection. "He was of medium height, as are most men, I fear. Nor did I see his face. He had a hood and kept his head down, and I thought he held something against his chest. He seemed to be in a great hurry. I remember him only because a man called out to him to stop and bring succor to his dying cousin, but this hooded creature did not even slow his pace, nor did he call for a lay brother." He drew a deep breath and frowned. "I thought that odd, so grabbed my crutch and went to seek a man of God myself."

Thomas waited, then asked, "You did not see where the hooded man went or hear his voice?"

"Neither, Brother. That is all I know."

Thomas tried to decide if he believed the pilgrim or suspected he had been the man he was seeking. Either the guilty man or an innocent one could have mentioned these details.

Yet this pilgrim had been upset enough to seek a lay brother for the dying man after the hooded figure so callously rushed by. And, he suddenly remembered, this matched the story told by the cousin of the one whose soul was facing God. No matter what this pilgrim's real crimes might be, he did not strike Thomas as an especially cunning man. He wasn't even good at telling a plausible lie. Twisted ankle indeed!

After a brief pause, the monk concluded that this man from Picardy could not be Brother Imbert. He thanked him for his help and finished wrapping the ankle, then gave him his crutch.

As Thomas stood there hoping he had not made a mistake in judging the man innocent of murder, he blinked at what he just noticed. Was he wrong or had this pilgrim gone several steps out of the hut, hobbling on the wrong foot?

Chapter Twenty-six

Renaud struggled to keep up with Father Etienne, wishing the priest would slow his pace. His head ached from the blow, and his shoulder hurt where it was bruised by his fall.

Indeed, the clerk felt more wretched than he ever had in his life. If only his master would turn, smile lovingly, and say something kind. That was all he truly longed for.

"Father!"

Davoir spun around and frowned as if his pondering over the shades of meaning in a significant theological problem had been rudely interrupted.

Renaud stared. Did his master not recognize him? Might he have forgotten he was beside him?

The priest blinked, his eyes slowly focusing on his clerk. "Ah." His lips twitched upward. "Yes?"

A thin-lipped gesture for sure, but it warmed the clerk's heart and eased a bit of his pain. This pause also let Renaud catch his breath.

"Your plan for the protection of our quarters addressed the problem," the priest said, a statement related to nothing he had said since leaving the hospital. His expression also suggested the comment was less a compliment than a problem requiring analysis.

Renaud humbly bowed his head, but his heart beat faster with a stirring of pride.

"Your suggestion was wiser than the Captain's. I fear he is a godless man."

"Why else would he have suggested bringing armed men to stand on holy ground?" the clerk murmured, head still lowered. It was a gesture often used by Jean, he recalled. Although he had not meant to imitate the dead youth, Renaud found it so easy to slip into Jean's habits. Surely this was an omen that he was meant to take the favored one's place in his master's heart. He stole a glance over his shoulder to make sure the dead clerk's spirit was not hovering.

"Although the man was correct on one point. God blesses the swords of those who fight the Infidel."

Renaud blinked. Did the priest mean he saw some virtue in the captain? How should he respond to this? He raised his eyes to look at Father Etienne and reassured himself that his wits must be agile enough to keep up with his master's unexpected twists and turns of thought. Jean's always were. "Without doubt," he replied.

"Without doubt?" Davoir's eyes narrowed.

The clerk began to sweat. Why was the priest testing him now of all times? He had just suffered a blow to his head by one of the damned. He felt dizzy. "Dare one say otherwise about those who seek to recover Jerusalem?" That was a good response, he thought.

"And if those pilgrims turn their swords against other Christians? Does God also bless that deed?"

Burning sweat from his forehead dripped into his eyes. "Perhaps the Christians have been wicked and deserve the attack." He was stammering, and he hated himself for it. Jean would have presented his opinion in a confident tone.

Davoir laughed, his tone mocking. "Poor reasoning. I had hoped to hear better from you after your solution to the guard problem." He sighed. "But, having considered that apparent spark of competence more thoroughly, I can see that your plan held the same flaws as the rest of your work."

Renaud began to tremble. He wanted to shout that he was still weak from his injuries. The priest ought not to press him so hard on these difficult questions. But he did not cry out or beg for mercy. Instead, he stood like a child, gaze bound to the earth and hands folded. Although the tears sliding down his cheeks were caused by sweat in his eyes, not sorrow, he felt humiliated as he always did when Father Etienne chided him. At least Jean was not there to witness this.

Or was he? Renaud had not told the priest that he believed the dead clerk had attacked him for sending his spirit to Hell. Maybe Jean, reeking of burnt souls, had come to Father Etienne in a dream and told him of Renaud's sin. He longed to look over his shoulder again but did not, lest the priest ask him why.

"You chose to take the darkest hours to patrol alone instead of assigning more clerks to do so. I would have praised your judgement if you had taken a daylight tour by yourself when there was less danger of attack. At night, the Devil brings all his minions with him, and the fellowship of more clerks, chanting prayers as they circled the quarters, would have kept the Evil One at bay."

The clerk wanted to blame the guard captain who had suggested he take the night watch alone. But Renaud had still accepted the plan although he could now see the faulty logic of his choice. Why had he listened to that soldier? Maybe the captain was not just weak of faith but a servant of evil. His ugly, scarred face suggested that for there was no beauty unless God was present. Yes, he had been duped, but it was not something he could confess or he would suffer even greater admonishment from Father Etienne.

"Jean would not have made that mistake."

This was too much! Renaud whimpered like a mongrel facing a wild boar.

"Stop whining!"

"Yes, master," the youth mumbled.

"Jean made errors too, but he never acted like a witless babe when shown his mistakes." Davoir waved his hand in disgust at the clerk and strode away.

Renaud ran after him. He wanted to shout that the priest's beloved clerk had been no saint. He had gotten drunk, admittedly with Renaud's help, and had behaved like a feckless girl over the attentions of one of the guards on the way from the coast.

But he knew Davoir would not care. When he once told the priest about seeing Jean commit a secret sin, Davoir had scolded him for tattling and said that his favored clerk had already come to him for penance. Even when Jean sinned, he always did the right thing in the priest's mind.

"Father!" Renaud fell to his knees.

"What is it?" Davoir turned around and glared with repugnance at the squirming clerk.

"Have I not served you well and dutifully?"

Father Etienne folded his arms and stared at the miserable youth. "You meant well with the planned defense, and I grieve that you were injured in that duty. Yes, Renaud, you do the best you can to serve me, although you rarely do anything ably."

Reaching out his hands in supplication, the clerk did not even know what more he wanted from his master, but these words of little comfort bore into his ears like hot iron from the smith's fire. He heard screams, as if from a tortured man, but those sounds came from inside his own head.

"Despite your ambition, you can never hope to replace Jean. Indeed, that is something even you must have known would be unreasonable."

Jean! Jean! It was always *Jean*. Even with his soul in Hell, he was keeping Renaud out of favor. The clerk's heart beat painfully against his chest.

"You are incompetent. You always have been, lad. For your father's sake, I wished it otherwise. He was a good and loyal steward to my father, and so I kept you by my side longer than I ought. Your Latin is abysmal. Your debate lacks force of logic. I cannot read your writing, nor can the other clerks."

"You will keep me with you, surely!" Renaud crawled on his knees, grabbed the priest's robe, and pressed his face against the man's feet.

Davoir pulled himself free and stepped back. "Get up! This display is unseemly!"

"You will keep me with you!" Renaud wailed.

"On your feet, lad," the priest replied with unexpected gentleness. "I will not cast you aside without finding a place for you that is suited to your skills. You have chosen to serve God, and that is what He wishes most from us." Then he turned his back and briskly walked down the path to the quarters.

Renaud scrabbled to his feet and stared at the man who had the power to lift him into prominence or dash him into oblivion. He wiped his hand across his dusty cheek and under his dripping nose. He knew the kind of service Father Etienne would find for a discarded clerk. The last one got a small parish that could barely feed and clothe him while he preached to whores and beggars. Davoir might believe God would find this suitable, but Renaud did not.

As he trailed behind his master along a path that felt like the road to his own Golgotha, Renaud no longer suffered grief, nor had his misery been replaced by anger.

His heart had turned to ice.

Chapter Twenty-seven

Eleanor sat in the cloister garth and closed her eyes.

Bees hummed love songs to the flowers. A gentle breeze caressed her cheek. In the distance, a seagull called out its pride in the successful hunt for food. Even the autumn sun gave what vigor it had left to warm her.

This peace should have cheered and strengthened. Instead, like a prisoner granted one final glance of the bright world, she felt the heaviness of despondency.

"Oh, you are a foolish creature," she muttered aloud.

"May I help, my lady?"

The prioress had forgotten that Gracia was so close. She had brought her maid along so the child might have a few moments for simple play, something the girl rarely had time to do.

I have burdened her too much with tasks involving this murder, Eleanor thought. Yet she noticed that Gracia was delighted with those challenges and even suggested clever ways she could do more. This was not a girl happiest when clutching her cloth poppet, the prioress decided, and now she wondered if the education offered at Tyndal Priory could match the quality of the child's wits.

Yet there was a problem.

As the descendant of one who had served and entertained Eleanor, Duchess of Aquitaine and Queen of England, the prioress was not inclined to let a woman's ability to learn go fallow. But, intelligent as Gracia was, the girl's family still belonged to the lowest rank of free men. How should Eleanor best teach her maid while also preparing her for the place she would have to take in the world outside Tyndal Priory?

Her former maid, Gytha, had come from a line of Anglo-Saxon thegns, even though Norman rule had reduced that family's position to breeders of donkeys and brewers of ale. Before the marriage to Ralf, Eleanor knew Gytha would marry at least a merchant. Gracia had little hope of such a high union.

I need guidance, the prioress thought, and she resolved to write Sister Beatrice, her aunt at Amesbury, to seek advice.

"It is nothing momentous, my child," Eleanor said. "I had just forgotten to look at an entry in another accounting roll that would answer a question I had."

Gracia nodded, but her deep set blue eyes shifted color to gray.

Eleanor had learned to identify this as a sign that the maid recognized a lie. It was a trait that troubled some but not her. She reached out a hand and touched the girl's thin shoulder with affection. If she were to win Gracia's complete trust, she must not utter even innocuous falsehoods.

"Very well, but my complaint truly meant nothing," she said gently. "I was pondering a dilemma that requires more patience and understanding than I am wont to own." Then the prioress clapped her hands together with amusement. "I shall tell you a secret. Reaching womanhood does not mean we have learned all we need to know of life, but we often believe we have, then rue our ignorance. It is a common failing."

As Gracia carefully memorized this bit of wisdom, her eyes regained their color of a bright spring sky.

Standing, Eleanor took the child by the hand and proceeded along the path, pointing out various plants, giving their names, and an interesting detail about each.

Gracia touched them all and repeated the name, adding her observations on color and form.

What a truly clever girl she is, the prioress thought with pleasure. "Are you happy here, my child?"

"Yes, my lady!"

"You have done well in this matter of Sister Anne and Father Etienne. I am proud of you."

The girl blushed.

"You have been my eyes and ears and blunted my impatience with the restrictions placed on me. Were it not for your efforts, I would have little hope."

"You have Brother Thomas and Crowner Ralf," the maid replied with honest modesty.

"Brother Thomas can do little more than I, and our crowner serves the king's justice, which does not rule here. He is limited in what he can do to seek the truth. You have helped where they and I cannot."

Gracia turned pale and fiercely grasped the prioress' hand. "You will not be sent from here, will you?" Her voice was so soft it was almost inaudible.

"There is no reason for that to happen. I am innocent of all accusations as is Sister Anne. Once the intent behind these vile charges and crimes is revealed, Father Etienne can declare us blameless, go back to Anjou, and Sister Anne may return to her hospital."

Squeezing the child's hand, she realized that she had not reassured Gracia as she should have. The girl had been present when Davoir accused Eleanor of breaking her vows, yet Gracia had remained steadfast in her loyalty despite fearing she would lose the home she had just found. The prioress wished she had immediately told her maid that the child's world would not be upended again.

"I must confess something." Gracia looked up but did not let go of Eleanor's hand.

"And what is that?"

"I have not liked this priest from the moment he arrived."

Neither had Eleanor, but she hid her concurrence and encouraged Gracia to explain.

"When he spoke to you and Prior Andrew, after you had first greeted him, his manner reminded me of the men who walked past me when I was begging at the inn in Walsingham. Not all were so cruel that they would push me to the side with a boot, but some wished they had not been faced with a child who sat begging. The sight was unpleasant, yet they had no solution for my need, and thus passed by, pretending they had not seen me."

Something in these words caused a dim light to flicker in a dark recess of her mind. The prioress urged her to continue.

"Perhaps Father Etienne brings us grief, not because he wants to do so, but because he believes he has no other choice?"

Or does not wish to see, Eleanor realized, and drew Gracia into a warm hug. "Well said, my child!"

The crunching of the gravel caused them both to look up.

Sister Christina appeared at the bend in the path. "My lady?"

Noting the infirmarian's pale cheeks and eyes widened with distress, Eleanor called out to swiftly reassure the nearsighted nun. "I am here. What has happened?"

The nun looked nervously over her shoulder and began to twist her hands.

Panting with effort, Sub-Prioress Ruth came into sight. Despite the aid of two sticks, she struggled to walk. Her teeth were clenched, and her breath came in short gasps. The woman was in much pain.

Eleanor sent Gracia to help Sister Christina ease the older nun onto the stone bench.

The sub-prioress waved them back. "My lady, I am unworthy of your kindness. Let me stand on these wretched feet and beg forgiveness. Even to kneel and kiss your feet, as I ought to beg for mercy, would bring a relief I do not deserve."

"You may not stand," Eleanor replied and sternly pointed to the bench. "I command you to sit and tell me what you have come to say."

Rejecting assistance, the sub-prioress struggled to sit down on the rough stone, then put her arms around her knees and groaned before she could speak further.

Eleanor waited, banishing all compassion from her expression. Sub-Prioress Ruth would expect nothing else from the leader of Tyndal Priory.

"My lady, I have a terrible sin to confess. And after I have told you of my wickedness, I will resign my position and, with true repentance, accept whatever punishment you deem appropriate." She began to sob, a sound as dreadful to hear as it was rare to behold in this proud woman.

Eleanor felt a deep chill course through her and stiffened her back to banish any overt tremor of fear. "Leave us," she said to Sister Christina and Gracia.

The pair quickly went to seek a far corner of the garth.

Then Prioress Eleanor sat down next to this woman who had always hated her and waited for her to speak.

Chapter Twenty-eight

With the stride of one confident of God's favor, Davoir entered the audience chamber. When he saw those who had gathered to greet him, he hesitated. The surprise displeased him.

Brother Thomas and Crowner Ralf stood on either side of Prioress Eleanor. To her left sat Sister Ruth. Her hands clasped and head bowed, the elder nun failed to greet the priest, mumbling instead a long prayer. Standing beside the troubled woman was Sister Christina, forehead creased as she gazed down with concern.

Gracia approached the priest, bobbed with courtesy, and offered him a mazer.

When Davoir looked into it, he was astonished to see red wine. He looked at the prioress and raised an eyebrow

"When souls or bodies need healing, Father," she said without the trace of a smile, "we may drink wine." Then she gestured for him to sit.

He did. Not knowing how to respond to that statement, he remained silent and sipped at his mazer. The wine was of good enough quality, he thought, but not as fine as the offerings at the French court.

"I shall be brief," the prioress said. "I have called you here because Sister Ruth has information you must hear. I believe her news will be quite enlightening, especially about the reason you were sent here."

The nun struggled to rise to her feet.

"Do not stand," Eleanor said. "God has sent you suffering enough, and your tale is hard to relate."

Ruth flushed but gratefully collapsed back into the chair. "You are most kind, my lady, and your compassion is an example to us all."

Impatient with what he considered dawdling, Davoir cleared his throat.

Sister Ruth glared at him.

Eleanor gazed with benign amusement at the nun. No matter how grieved her nemesis was, the woman had not lost her ability to display stern displeasure. For once the prioress was pleased. Father Etienne had deserved the look. "Take your time," she said sweetly. "The story is worth a careful telling."

Ruth sat up, back rigid, and hands modestly folded in her lap. "As I told you when you came to question me, Father, I was convinced that any accusation of unchaste conduct between our revered prioress and the respected Brother Thomas lacked all merit. Yet I remained troubled because of the utter falseness of the allegation and wondered why anyone would dare utter such outrageous lies." She briefly looked at the prioress and the monk with deep sorrow, then turned her attention to Davoir. "After you left my chambers, I thought more on this vile tale and, to my horror, realized the probable basis for the claim."

"Probable?" Davoir smiled with no attempt to conceal his disdain, then shook his head as if rebuking a wearisome child. "I need more than speculation as to intent and origin."

The nun reddened and grasped her hands more firmly. "I did not come to Prioress Eleanor with frivolous imaginings, Father. Our duties to God do not allow us time to indulge in such idle things."

The priest blinked. Once again, this woman pleased him with her plain speech and lack of foolishness. She would have made a fine prioress and must rule her charges with an iron hand, he thought, then bowed his head. The gesture lacked all hint of apology but did convey his acceptance of her argument.

"My brother is the source of this rumor sent to our abbess in Anjou," Ruth said, then winced. It was unclear whether the pain was the result of her admission or the gout in her toes. "I confess I do not have proof, but I have good cause to say so."

Eleanor fingered the carving on the arm of her chair as she addressed the priest. "Did Abbess Isabeau reveal to you the source of the accusation?"

"My sister did not tell me who had made the claim. I found no purpose in asking. The charge was so grave that the substance took precedence over the accuser, in my estimation."

"I am sure she knows and believed she had grounds to take the tale seriously," Ruth snapped. "Our abbess would not have asked you to leave court to come here if the source of the accusation had been truly unknown, probably mean-spirited, and she could resolve it by a simpler method." She took a deep breath. "I shall be brief, Father. My brother is of high rank, a baron in the service of our king. He is in Wales with Sir Hugh, the brother of our prioress. These two men have quarreled, which my brother told me in a letter received not long ago, and King Edward chose to support Sir Hugh." She looked at her prioress with a pained expression.

The prioress gestured to signify her opinion that quarrels were the nature of mortals and that kings must take sides.

"Why did they argue?" Davoir frowned.

"The subject of the dispute is irrelevant, Father Etienne," Eleanor said. "Suffice it to say that it involved a matter which touched family interests and therefore honor. The brother of Sister Ruth is not a man who would retaliate so fiercely for anything less." Her tone was surprisingly kind.

He sipped his wine, and then motioned for the nun to continue.

"I must tell you that my brother and I both resented the arrival of Prioress Eleanor to head Tyndal many years ago. I had been elected by the community to follow Prioress Felicia after her death. When King Henry chose to set aside my election, I suffered profound humiliation, as did my brother." Ruth's face turned the color of a mildewed cherry. "Satan entered our souls and cut a festering wound there that became as foul as gangrene. Since my brother is a man of the world, he might be quickly forgiven the sins of resentment and longing for retribution. As a bride of Christ, I cannot."

Sister Christina put a hand on the woman's shoulder and looked in the direction of Brother Thomas. Her eyes glistened with pleading.

The monk raised his hand, showed his palm so the infirmarian might see his gesture, and placed his hand against his heart.

At this sign that mercy was possible for the woman beside her, Sister Christina nodded, and closed her eyes with relief.

"After learning the king's response to this disagreement with Sir Hugh, my brother wrote to me, confessing his anger but also stating that he was now confident he had found a way to answer the insult and also return me to, as he called it, my rightful place as head of Tyndal Priory." Ruth pressed her hand against her eyes as if forbidding them to weep. "Not long after I received this message, Prioress Eleanor told us that Abbess Isabeau was sending her brother to our priory to conduct a thorough review of our practices here."

"Why did you not tell your prioress then about what your brother wrote?" Davoir raised his mazer so Gracia could fill it.

Sister Ruth narrowed her eyes at him. "Your visit was unusual but not completely unexpected, Father, and there was nothing in the abbess' message to suggest the grave magnitude of this investigation. Other priories are visited by the bishop under whose rule they live, but our Order answers to Rome and we to Abbess Isabeau. In the past, she has only required annual accounts. Prior Andrew has provided those. I had no reason to suspect there was a connection between my brother and your arrival here. None, that is, until you told me of the vile lie that brought you here." She sniffed in contempt. "Mold in the chapel, a badly repaired wall, or even incompetent accounting might bring advice or at most a rebuke, but a prioress condemned for immorality is removed from her office. It was then I saw my brother's hand."

Davoir gazed over the lip of his mazer at the prioress. "You said nothing about your own brother's quarrel with the baron when we spoke."

"My brother rarely sends me news," Eleanor replied. "I knew none of this."

The priest looked back at the nun. "Nor did you mention yours. You should have sent me a message as soon as you concluded that your brother had chosen to slander your prioress so you might regain the rank of leader here."

Sister Ruth grabbed the arms of her chair and rose to her feet, then cried out in pain and fell back into the chair.

Eleanor pointed toward the corner of the room.

Gracia ran to fetch a stool so the older woman's afflicted foot might rest more comfortably.

"My first duty is to my prioress, Father," the nun gasped, then caught her breath. "It was she who was injured by this folly, and I owed her the confession. I now sit before you and have told my tale. Is that not sufficient?"

He shrugged his shoulders, a gesture belittling the merit of her choice.

"Hear me well, Father!" The nun's voice rose, and her knuckles were white as she grasped the arms of the chair to control her fury. "I love and honor my brother. As his eldest sister, I helped raise him after the death of our mother. To imagine that he would cast filth on these two religious, known by all for their virtue and service to God, was unthinkable." Again she covered her eyes. "I spent hours on my knees to God, begging for guidance, even hoping that my suspicions were the result of my tormenting mortal pains. But the facts match and, although he has not said he was the source of this rumor, I am sure either he or Abbess Isabeau would confirm, if asked, that he wrote to her."

Davoir turned thoughtful. This woman was not one prone to fantasy, and the admission of this conclusion had cost her dear. That she had told Prioress Eleanor first might be a questionable decision, but he could understand it. In fact, their delay before informing him was a trifling thing.

As the nun looked at Prioress Eleanor, the woman's anger was replaced with sorrow. "Although I did not have pre-knowledge of this appalling deed by my brother, or any involvement in perpetrating his scheme, my sinful resentment and failure to completely rid my heart of bitterness over my humiliation years ago makes me complicit in the troubles brought upon these innocent people. I have resigned my position as sub-prioress and have begged to be reassigned to the lowliest duties normally done by a lay sister."

Prioress Eleanor let silence fall so that the full meaning of Sister Ruth's words would be understood. Finally, she said, "Are you satisfied, Father?"

He did not reply, choosing to study the color of his wine.

"Let me also clarify one other matter," the nun said, gritting her teeth. "I have learned that you accused Sister Anne of killing your clerk, either because she is incompetent or because she was trying to protect Prioress Eleanor."

Davoir looked up from his contemplation and nodded, but he seemed surprised that this issue was being mentioned at all.

"Then you must listen closely." The nun indicated her scarlet toe joint that was so inflamed it visibly throbbed. "Although I have often criticized our sub-infirmarian for using herbs and infusions when prayer is preferable, I cannot quarrel with the success of her cures. Our hospital is famous across the land for the efficacy of..." She hesitated, then gestured at Sister Christina, "...of the work done by these two women who toil unceasingly to save lives. Until you ordered her locked into a cell, Sister Anne used the same remedy for my gout that you say she used to kill your clerk. I have found much relief in that cure, until now when I cannot get any more of it due to her absence."

"Most regrettable," Davoir muttered.

"And if Sister Anne wanted to kill anyone to relieve Prioress Eleanor of a troublesome creature, Father, it would have been me. She knows how long I have resented our prioress, how often I have argued against her decisions, and how much I disagree with the sub-infirmarian on the care of the dying." Sister Ruth straightened in the chair and pointed to herself. "Yet I sit here, many years after the arrival of our beloved and honored prioress, quite alive. And, if you would admit your error and let her go, I might even become well again instead of suffering as I do!"

Chapter Twenty-nine

Father Davoir sat in silence.

Although Brother Thomas and Crowner Ralf remained, the two nuns had left the chambers.

Prioress Eleanor waited.

Gracia stood by the door, her eyes wide with curiosity. As she looked from priest to her mistress and back again, her shifting gaze was the only motion in the deceptively still room.

At last the priest spoke. "I am a judicious man, Prioress Eleanor. I did not come to Tyndal with an ardent desire to find you guilty of the charge against you. I wished to gather all the facts and dispassionately establish the truth based on reasoned judgement."

Reasoned judgement? Eleanor bit her lip. When he suggested she might have ordered the death of the clerk, he most certainly was not basing his decision on facts. When he ordered Sister Anne thrust into that cell, he did so out of anger and grief, not logic. The effort not to admonish him was almost more than she could bear.

But then she heard a low growl from Crowner Ralf and knew it was her responsibility to remain calm and keep this meeting civil. It did not matter whether she liked this priest or not, he was the brother of her abbess and a man of great influence in the French court.

If she said what she wished, she could endanger far more than the release of Sister Anne in time to help at Gytha's birthing and the conclusion that she and Brother Thomas were irrefutably innocent of the charge against them. Were she rash, the consequences of her actions might well nip at the pride of kings. The past was littered with corpses slaughtered in battles waged for lesser insults than what an English baron's daughter and prioress might inflict on a French religious whose head would soon wear a bishop's miter.

With effort, Eleanor's smile successfully conveyed the expected appreciation in response to Davoir's words.

"But when my clerk was killed and the only cause seemed to be the medicine sent by your sub-infirmarian, I had reason to suspect that she was either incompetent or had tried to protect you out of some benighted hope that I would be frightened away or perhaps less inclined to find you guilty of the charges against you." He raised his hands to suggest how obvious his conclusion must have been.

Eleanor nodded. Her neck ached from the effort to do so politely.

"Now I fear that someone wishes me ill and the attack against Renaud suggests that the death of Jean might not be solely due to your sub-infirmarian's incompetence."

Eleanor could understand why someone might want to wring this priest's neck. "Indeed," she said.

"I might still be inclined to suspect you had a hand in this, considering the seriousness of the allegations against you…"

Ralf stepped forward.

"Peace, Crowner," the prioress whispered.

"…but the words of your sub-prioress made me pause in thought. She had no love for you after your king sent you to replace her, a woman so respected by the religious of this house that she was duly elected to succeed the former prioress. Her great resentment is a sin, but, for once, truth was strengthened by her human wickedness." He smiled. "Her testimony on your behalf was powerful."

Eleanor smiled back. "I shall long remember that insight, Father."

For a moment, he said nothing and sat watching her with a preoccupied look. Then his brow smoothed, and he waved one hand in a gesture of surrender. "I have erred in suspecting you of complicity in murder," he said, "and your sub-prioress has convinced me that you are innocent of the charges laid against you."

"Although Sister Ruth is an honorable woman and strives to speak with honesty under all circumstances, I would not want you to take the word of only one member of our community, Father. I hope you will question others here as well."

"I have."

Of course, you have, Eleanor thought, but in this one instance I am glad you did pursue your investigation beyond all good sense. "And have you found support or condemnation? I do not ask for the names of those who gave witness to either."

"Nothing but praise," he replied. "Some have called you *blessed.*"

"Which I am not," she quickly replied with a modest bow of her head, "being a frail mortal and a lowly daughter of Eve." Seeing he was about to say more, she decided she must control the conversation until he had admitted all she wished in front of Crowner Ralf, the one presumed impartial witness. "I am sure you found none who had any criticism of Brother Thomas." She was tempted to smile up at the monk but deemed it unwise lest her gesture be misinterpreted.

"Again, I heard only acclaim. Some have even said he most resembles the founder of this Order in the strength of his virtue." Davoir looked briefly at the monk, his expression suggesting that he had found this discovery regrettable.

Brother Thomas followed the example of his prioress and lowered his gaze in silent humility.

"May I speak, my lady?"

Crowner Ralf rarely sounded so meek. Had the circumstances been different, Eleanor might have teased him. Instead, she gravely gave consent to his request. Looking at his eyes, she saw them glittering with fury, although his demeanor otherwise suggested calm. Taking a deep breath, she decided she must trust him not to decapitate the priest in front of her.

"The leader of the soldiers, who provided you with protection on the journey here, believes you are in danger. I concur. You now agree."

The priest clenched his jaw as if preparing for a test of wills.

"Since you have found Prioress Eleanor and Brother Thomas innocent of the foul lies leveled against them, I pray that you will allow them to join the captain and me in keeping you safe within the priory walls. In doing so, I believe we also have the opportunity to capture the miscreant who killed your beloved clerk, something for which you must deeply long."

Davoir said nothing, tapped his chin, and turned his gaze to a fat fly resting on the table nearby.

"Modesty prevents Prioress Eleanor and Brother Thomas from saying this," Ralf continued, "but they are both well-known in our land for their ability to bring evil men to justice." With a reverent expression and an unusual acknowledgement to God, the crowner looked heavenward. "Only those in His favor could do as well as these two in rendering His justice when we more flawed mortals fail."

Ralf lowered his gaze and shut his eyes so no one could read his thoughts, but Eleanor noted that he had blood on his lip from biting it. Although the crowner had long been a friend, and was the husband of her cherished Gytha, she suddenly loved him even more, knowing the effort it took for him not to rage against this man who had insulted his friends and put his wife in mortal danger with his arrogant blindness.

Davoir seemed oblivious to all the details and problems involved in finding the cause of the recent violence. The priest's face betrayed his profound struggle to determine what he thought was best. He shifted the honor of his gaze from the fly to the rushes under his feet.

Think of your bishopric, Eleanor prayed, and do what is in your own interest to survive long enough to enjoy it. Gritting her teeth, she forced herself to conclude that Davoir was not a truly evil man. The priest believed he had the gift of superior reason and thus his decisions must be beyond question. Yet if anyone was born unable to see beyond his nose, it was Father Etienne Davoir.

"You do think I am in danger of my life?" The priest continued to stare at the floor.

"We do," Ralf replied.

"If I may speak, my lady?"

Eleanor was surprised that her monk had broken his silence, but she quickly nodded.

"In order to more swiftly decide who might wish you ill, Father, we must know if you have acquired any enemies, men so angry that they would wreak violence against you." Brother Thomas' tone was respectful.

"Any man, especially one who has found favor with mortals of great standing and God, acquires enemies." Davoir glanced up, his expression revealing that he was perplexed by the question.

"As soon as you return to court, you will be elevated to a bishopric?" Thomas waited for the man to nod. "And you will carry your most talented clerks with you to higher rank as well, a well-known practice. When you arrived here, Jean and Renaud rode by your side, a position suggesting you held them in great favor." He paused.

"All of this is well known. Please be brief." Davoir glared at the monk as if Thomas were one of his clerks.

The monk ignored him. "Jean has been murdered. Renaud has been attacked. This violence suggests the culprit might bear a festering resentment against you. Perhaps he suffered some punishment you meted out or expected some favor you failed to grant. Are there any men who were once clerks but whom you sent away, or families who hoped you might accept a son into your service but for whom you found no position…?" His voice trailed off.

As Eleanor watched Davoir strive to put these elements together, she was grateful that her monk had asked the question. The priest would take that probing query better from him than from a woman, even if she was a prioress, or a man bound to secular law like Ralf.

Davoir frowned. "I have always made my decisions well-founded in logic."

"Even if their conclusion was in error, who might have disagreed with you despite the aptness of your judgement?"

Not for the first time, Eleanor was proud of her monk's calm.

"I am not in the habit of discharging clerks. My initial verdict on their suitability is rarely wrong, although I did choose one youth based on his father's service to my family. That was a mistake, but the family has not yet been informed of his pending dismissal." He thought a moment longer, and then raised one finger. "A few years ago, I had occasion to release one of my clerks. He was a promising lad from a respectable, albeit not titled, family. Sadly, he was found in a brothel and, when brought before me, confessed he spent much time there. I dismissed him."

Thomas glanced at his prioress.

That means something to him, she thought and grew hopeful that he had discovered a clue.

Davoir sighed. "His family begged me to reconsider. I could not, of course, but promised to find him a living suitable for a penitent. It was in a poor parish, and he died months after of a fever, but none of us is exempt from death. Later, I heard that his brother blamed me for the youth's fate and swore to take revenge, but nothing has ever come of these threats, perhaps because I rarely travel far from our king's court." He paled. "Until now."

"It is possible that the brother may have followed you here. I spoke to a man who swore he was on pilgrimage from France to Canterbury, claims to have injured his ankle, and is in our hospital. I have no proof…"

Davoir turned to the crowner and roared, "You must arrest him!"

"We have nothing but a vague suspicion." Ralf's tone betrayed his anger at the very idea of complying with Davoir's demand when the priest had also jailed Sister Anne with no evidence.

Eleanor winced at his ill-advised response.

Davoir jumped to his feet. "How dare you deny this request? I am in danger, a conclusion with which you all concur. You mention the logical suspect but now refuse to put him in irons." He rudely jabbed his finger at the prioress. "Is this revenge because I did my duty as my sister required?"

"No, Father, but I think you would agree that capturing the man, with enough proof of ill intent to keep him in custody while we get a full confession, would serve all far better than arresting him on suspicion alone." Eleanor tilted her head and glared at the priest, her patience at the snapping point.

"Without proof, he will be released." Thomas smiled without humor. "And would probably try again to harm you at a later date."

Defeated and frightened, Davoir sat back down with a thump. "I concur," he muttered.

Eleanor realized she had been holding her breath.

"Let us plan a trap for him," Thomas said.

"And release Sister Anne," Ralf added. "Her innocence is proven."

Slamming his hand down on the arm of the chair, Davoir shouted, "Not until there is as much proof of her innocence as you demand to establish the guilt of this alleged pilgrim! I am not yet convinced that she did not kill my clerk out of incompetence or malice."

Ralf turned scarlet with outrage.

"Ralf, be calm," Eleanor murmured. She knew the priest's outburst was the cry of pain from a proud man who had been humiliated. A man, who believed himself almost godlike in judgement, had been publicly proven wrong several times since arriving at Tyndal. She chose to let Davoir have a small victory in exchange for his cooperation. "Let us plan the capture of the real killer and then our sub-infirmarian will be free. It is only a short time longer, and she is not suffering great deprivation."

"If my wife…"

"If Gytha's pains begin, I swear that she will have the comfort and skill needed for her travail." And the prioress looked into the crowner's eyes with a promise she prayed he could read well.

"Very well," he snarled. "Now let us plan how to catch the real murderer."

Chapter Thirty

The wind struck like a berserk warrior slashing through a band of enemy soldiers.

"It will be a cold winter," Ralf growled, pulling his cloak tightly around his body.

"Sit closer to me, Crowner," Conan replied. "The shrubbery is thick here."

Hesitating a moment too long, Ralf moved only a fraction of an inch.

"You still do not trust me?"

The crowner was annoyed by Conan's deep chuckle. "Have you given me good reason not to be suspicious?" Ralf waited for a response, but his companion said nothing. "A man friendly to Jean is murdered on the road to the priory. When the clerk dies soon after, anyone responsible for the king's justice would find the circumstances troubling. You did offer an explanation I decided not to counter, but..." This time he let the sentence die in the chill air.

For a moment, the men said nothing, huddling to protect themselves as the wind grew in force and howled at them with primordial fury.

Just as quickly, it waned.

"True. Said clerk is murdered." Conan's teeth chattered.

"You suggest that an armed guard be set outside the priest's door, a proposal you surely realized would be offensive to a man devoted to the peaceful worship of God."

"And he was outraged. You claim I would have guessed as much, but I believed that the man had more sense than most of his vocation. I was mistaken."

Ralf laughed. "Well said and I concur, but that does not mean I suspect you less of devious motives." He rubbed at his nose which was dripping from the icy air. "After Davoir rejects your plan, Renaud offers a solution more acceptable to our priest, a godly resolution in which the clerks patrolled and offered prayers instead of carrying knives or cudgels."

Conan snorted, then uttered a curse as the wind swirled around them once again. "Tonight, I would prefer that they be here, not us." He looked over at the crowner. "If I thought it would help, I would even pray. But Heaven is supposed to be cooler than Hell, and I might choose Hell just to be warm again."

"I confess a growing fondness for your wit, but I have known killers who entertained the crowds with fine jests before they were hanged."

"Continue, Crowner. I shall save my breath to warm my hands."

"You tell the clerk that he would please his master by taking the duty at the bleakest hour, one that was probably the most dangerous time."

"I felt sorry for the lad. Davoir does not like him, and I wanted Renaud to do something that would please the man."

"He does as you suggest and is struck down. At that time, you also just happened to be nearby." Ralf wiggled stiff fingers at the captain to forestall a mordant reply.

"And I find him lying in the path outside the door to his master's chambers and swiftly carry him to the hospital so his life might be saved. What troubles you about that, Crowner?"

"Explain why I should not conclude that you struck the clerk yourself, with force that was not quite lethal, and took him to the hospital to avoid any suspicion sticking to your untanned hide? Since Davoir refused an armed guard, you would be able to slip through the watch of half-asleep clerks who were not as eager as Renaud to prove himself to his master. Remove him, and you have access to your target."

"Why even suggest Renaud patrol alone if I could have crept through a band of mewling clerks with greater ease? That conclusion was unworthy of you, Crowner! Instead, I propose to you that I might have come to the priory to watch for problems, knowing that the clerks might be fools, but still a company of fools. Renaud, by himself, would be a target, or at least a light enough guard that the culprit might be drawn out and caught by me. Is that not a more reasonable explanation for my actions?"

"I do not know you. Why should I trust any benevolent intent?"

Conon sighed. "You are making this very difficult, Crowner."

"My purpose is not to make matters comfortable for these who commit murder."

"You did not quarrel with me over the guard's death at the inn."

Ralf shrugged. "Since I do not have the time to confirm your tale about the man's past crimes and you have complete authority over those under your command, I conceded."

"If need be, I can give you a name, a man who will give you the proof you wish and one whom you will not doubt. Unless you arrest me, I see no need to do that. But, if you would assume for a moment that I am not lying about that incident, do you think I would do what was needed to protect Jean from harm then and kill him once he was here? Use logic, Crowner!"

Ralf bent closer. "If you have something to tell me that would relieve me of my suspicions, say it now."

"I was told you were a good man, if a trifle blunt. A soldier's soldier."

"Stop prancing, cokenay! You are not a womanish courtier posing in a silly dance. We are talking about a hanging offense."

Conan stiffened. "I might have killed another who said that to me."

The wind whistled through the shrubbery in which they hid, mocking all their attempts to avoid it.

Shivering, the men glared at each other in silence.

"Very well, Crowner. You have won this toss. To continue the dice game is neither efficient nor necessary. I know you are a man of honor who keeps his word so the only price I ask for the truth is your silence."

"Unless the silence puts me at odds with the law, you have my word."

Conan pointed to the sword resting in front of him and swore on the hilt.

"Quickly. My ears grow numb."

"You have heard that the accusations against Prioress Eleanor and her monk were made by a baron who quarreled with Sir Hugh and longed for retaliation. What no one here knows is that a man, who must remain nameless, learned early of this baron's plan to attack the reputation of Sir Hugh's sister and also achieve his old desire to have his own sister returned to the position she had lost."

"Your meaning," Ralf muttered.

Conan grinned and deliberately hesitated.

The crowner spat at the man, but the wind shifted direction and he rubbed his face dry in disgust.

"Our nameless man heard a rumor that this baron's petty act of revenge might be used as a cover for a more dangerous purpose than a minor struggle for power between two noble families. He urged the king to provide protection for the party coming from France. I was ordered to lead the guard that would protect Abbess Isabeau's brother and his herd of clerks during their entire journey in England."

"Petty? Minor?" Ralf's face was a shade of red brighter than could be blamed on the wind.

"Yes, Crowner, a trivial thing. There was no basis for the accusation, and the falsehood would swiftly become evident. A time-consuming, disturbing annoyance for Prioress Eleanor? Yes. More than that? No."

The crowner grunted. "It has become more than that, but I agree with you in principle." He nodded at Conan to continue.

"This same nameless man was afraid that the investigation ordered by Fontevraud Abbey might be used to create a deep rift between our king and Philip the Bold. If violence occurred on English soil against a man in high favor with the French king's brother, bitterness and desire for retaliation might result. Neither king wants that, but the skin protecting pride within royal breasts is thin. I have said this before, but this is not my conclusion alone, Crowner. It comes from a man far more knowledgeable than I in matters of State."

"Were you given any more specifics about this threat? The cause or names of those involved?"

"Neither the king nor his source said more, but the unnamed man is valued for his sources and loyalty to King Edward. Whether he knew the perpetrators or not, he would have responded to any threat of violence that might impact our king."

"Continue."

"My first concern was the inclusion of the now-dead guard whom I asked to be omitted from the company. As I told you, I was overruled. In my opinion, he became a threat to young Jean, but the guard died and relieved me of that apprehension. Once here, I came to the priory every night to make sure nothing untoward happened while all were sleeping. Sadly, the death of Jean by poison was unexpected. I failed in my duty."

"The priest accused Sister Anne of incompetence or murder."

"I did not believe that, Crowner. I was well-informed on those living within this priory. Since I did not know the clerks serving Davoir, however, I was pleased that they would all, except two, be housed with the monks. Watching for someone escaping the dormitory is easy. I could concentrate on looking for any other suspicious behavior."

"Are you certain none of the clerks are involved in the murder or the attack?"

"The poisoning troubles me, Crowner. I have no idea how that happened. As for the attack on Renaud, I doubt it was another clerk."

"Renaud claims to have seen the Jean's ghost in the shadows, yet he was struck from behind. Two clerks might be involved."

"I fear our lad sees the wandering damned when the branches of a shrub wave in the wind. It is a malady common amongst the religious—or so I have been told."

"Why are you so convinced it is not another in Davoir's company?"

"I saw someone hurrying over the bridge from the guest quarters and feared something had happened. I did not wait to see who it was but ran to the grounds, fearing injury to Davoir and cursing myself for being late. I was usually here earlier but was delayed because I suspected I had been followed and wanted to make sure no one was bent on killing me."

"You were followed by our innkeeper's foster son. She did not trust you either. When he saw you walk toward the guest chambers, he also saw the person coming across the bridge, and he ran back to the inn where I waited for his report."

"Which explains why you came so quickly, Crowner. Does it ease your heart that I now no longer add you to my list of men who might be involved in this perilous matter?"

Ralf stared at him in disbelief, but then realized the captain had cause to wonder why he had been on the priory land at the same time. If Conan was truly sent by the king, he had as much reason to suspect him as Ralf had to distrust the guard captain.

"I did not see who attacked Renaud," Conan said, "but I have seen a man lurking about on crutches. Once I noticed he was hiding in the bushes near the path to the guest quarters. The shadow that your young spy saw did not run toward the monk's dormitory but toward the main gate or perhaps the hospital."

"And what have you discovered about him?"

"Little enough. This hospital has several men on crutches. The lay brother told me there were many he could point out, and I had a poor description of him." Conan frowned. "And if he were injured, I thought it unlikely that he would be an assassin. Perhaps he simply wanted a glimpse of a foreigner of such high rank." He thought for a moment. "A man on crutches does not run as quickly as the escaping figure did."

"One of your own soldiers?" Ralf asked the question because he knew he must, but he also recalled what Brother Thomas had said in the audience chamber about the man from France with the injured ankle. Should he mention that to Conan?

"Many of them I know, having fought by their sides. A few I did not, but I sat apart at the inn and watched those I had no grounds to trust. No one left the inn that I did not follow, but their paths all led to some woman's bed."

Before giving a reply, Ralf suddenly reached over, grabbed Conan's arm, and pointed.

A shadow approached.

Ralf cautiously peeked through the shrub branches, then relaxed. "Greetings!" he shouted as the person drew near.

Renaud screamed.

"It is nothing, lad!" Ralf stood up as he called out. "We have no wish to harm you."

The clerk fell to his knees and raised his hands heavenward.

"What is your purpose in coming here?" Conan picked up his sword, climbed out of the shrubbery, and walked over to the clerk. The blade of his weapon glittered in the moonlight.

Renaud's mouth opened and shut but no sound came forth.

Conan grabbed him by his robe and dragged him to his feet. "Did the Devil castrate you?" He shook him gently. "If not, speak as a man ought."

"I have brought an urgent message from Anjou." The clerk squawked like a chicken.

Conan glared at him, then glanced over his shoulder at the crowner.

Ralf raised his hands, signifying that he saw no cause to question this.

"It is for my master," Renaud added. His voice still trembled.

Conan let go of the clerk's robe and gave him a slight shove. "Then go to him," he said.

Freed, Renaud fled toward the entrance to the quarters.

As they watched the clerk disappear into his master's chambers, Ralf walked over to join Conan. "Let us pray that Abbess Isabeau has learned that the accusation against Prioress Eleanor and Brother Thomas was fraudulent and has ordered her brother to return immediately to Anjou," he said and then muttered, "which means that our prioress may release Sister Anne in time for my child's birth."

"I shall pray for your wife," Conan replied.

Ralf looked surprised at this sudden display of piety.

The guard captain grinned, his teeth gleaming in the pale light. "With you as a husband, she needs God's mercy."

Ralf jabbed the man's shoulder with his fist.

Each now satisfied of the other's innocence, the two fell silent and waited for the expected killer.

The roaring wind from the north continued to slash with icy claws.

The subject of the pilgrim from France had been forgotten.

Chapter Thirty-one

The room reeked of sweat and candle smoke.

Thomas finished his prayers and glanced over at the murmuring priest beside him.

Perhaps Davoir had many worthy qualities he ought to admire, the monk thought, but they were not evident to him. If God was willing to forgive the penitent who had once eagerly leapt into the arms of the Evil One, as well as those who had merely stumbled, why did Davoir believe he could do less, especially for the negligible sinners? Although Thomas understood the reluctance to pardon the truly wicked, he scorned this man for his lack of compassion for any who did not match his own self-declared brilliance. Tonight the monk had prayed that God would force the priest to see, with brutal clarity, just how blind and ignorant he was.

The prie-dieu creaked as Father Etienne shifted his weight on the pillow under his knees.

Having suffered brutality in prison and seen mortals murder their fellows, Thomas was disinclined to accept the honeyed platitudes which excused cruelty. Most men would advise him to blunt his doubts and accept the judgements of influential men for it would serve his interests to do so.

He smiled at the thought. Any expectations of advancement had been shattered the morning he was taken from Giles' arms. For years he had mourned the loss of his beloved with the pain of a mortal illness. That he had forsaken all hope of high ecclesiastical status became meaningless in the face of such anguish. Now that he was healed of his grief, he remained content to be a man of no standing at Tyndal Priory and serve his prioress as she required.

Today he had been especially grateful to be in his position. He had seen the effort it took Prioress Eleanor to exercise the required diplomacy with this priest because he was a man of great influence. Thomas was pleased it would never become his duty to do this and that his disdain for self-absorbed ecclesiastics could remain between him and God.

Quietly backing further away, the monk rose to his feet.

Davoir was unaware that his fellow religious had moved and continued to mutter his prayers.

For his own devotions tonight, Thomas had knelt on the plain wooden prie-dieu placed in front of the simple altar where a cross was hung on the wall. All this was provided in the guest quarters for those who needed a place for private prayer while staying at Tyndal Priory. But the priest had ignored these and knelt on a finely embroidered pillow, at his own intricately carved and highly polished prie-dieu, in front of a bejeweled cross. Each item he had brought with him on the journey to England.

In the guttering candlelight, one blood-red gem embedded in that cross glittered unsteadily.

Thomas stared at it. At least he would not have to deal with this man's arrogance much longer, but he did pray that God would have mercy on the man's new flock which must. Yet miracles did occur, he reminded himself. Perhaps Davoir would repent someday, when he discovered that his soul had turned to dust, and finally become the man he now believed he was.

The monk shook his head. I have grown querulous, he thought. Considering his own bitter quarrels with God, over things he had done and felt which the Church condemned as more evil than anything Davoir might have committed, Thomas knew he had no right to throw stones at anyone.

Staring at the shadowy ceiling, Thomas silently confessed that he simply longed to be elsewhere this night, doing whatever brought peace to a soul or relief from mortal pains. Guarding a man whom he did not respect wore on him even if he knew he must do so. When this night was over, he would pray for forgiveness. Now, he could not.

Thomas eased into the shadows where the candlelight failed to penetrate. If he was going to think gloomy thoughts, he had best sit in the dark.

The priest continued to mumble.

Holding his nose to prevent a sneeze caused by the acrid candle smoke, the monk felt a twinge of guilt. Perhaps this man, to whom he had taken such a dislike, was confessing his deficiencies to God and suffering from the knowledge of his imperfections. After all, Thomas had not been asked to be Davoir's confessor and the state of the man's soul was not his responsibility, nor was the choice of penitential acts. Having conquered the sneeze, he forced himself to concentrate on what he was here to do.

Maybe Devoir had been right, he thought. Ralf should have taken the alleged pilgrim into custody rather than set a trap. Even with Conan and the crowner outside, there was still a chance that the man could slip through. Traps were risky things, which, of course, was the reason Prioress Eleanor had insisted that he stay by the priest's side.

Someone was likely to come here tonight, a man with murderous intent. Davoir had listened to this plan only because the prioress reminded him of his stated belief that no sword could match the power of prayer. When she added her final argument that the orisons of two priests would surely be the strongest defense of all, the priest had consented, albeit with ill-concealed reluctance to share the company of Brother Thomas.

At least Thomas felt comfortable with the probability that he might have to deal with the man from across the British Ocean. Even assuming that the alleged pilgrim did not suffer an injured ankle, the man from Picardy was slight of build. Thomas looked like a man born to swing a sword even if he had never been trained for battle. And, he thought, I have the advantage in this planned surprise and am more likely to keep my wits about me.

A knock at the door disturbed his thoughts.

As agreed, Thomas stayed where he was.

Davoir remained on his knees for a moment longer before turning his head and shouting permission to enter. His voice betrayed his annoyance at the interruption, and he bowed his head again as he returned to his recitations.

Renaud eased his way through the entrance with the reluctance of a child called for a scolding. Closing the door softly behind him, he hesitated.

Not the man expected, Thomas thought, then slipped back into even deeper shadows and squatted with his back against the wall. Of course he did not expect a killer to knock at the door and politely beg permission to come in so he might wreak havoc. The monk folded his arms and regretted that he must witness Davoir exercise his habitual humiliation of this clerk without interfering. Was it only a favored one or two whom he greeted with any kindness?

"Father?" The clerk's voice trembled.

Davoir looked up at his jeweled cross, shimmering in the dim light, and continued his prayers. When he came to a point where he chose to pause, he stopped but remained kneeling with his back to the clerk. "Why have you disturbed me? Have you no respect for my need to speak with God?"

"It was necessary," Renaud said as he inched closer, his hands clutched in a gesture of supplication.

"Has the king called me home? Has Abbess Isabeau sent further instructions?"

"No, Father."

The priest snorted. "Jean would never have troubled me for less. Leave me." And he returned to his recitations.

Renaud screamed, his howl like that of a frenzied beast. Drawing a knife from inside his robe, he rushed at the priest.

Thomas leapt to his feet and lunged at the clerk.

Chapter Thirty-two

Renaud lay bound on the floor, but he did not lie peacefully. Writhing, he grunted and yanked at his bindings, but they held fast.

Conan and Ralf stood in front of the culprit. For all the emotion their expressions betrayed, the clerk might have been a large fish flopping about on a wharf.

Thomas handed the knife to the crowner. "He missed his mark," he said, inclining his head toward the priest. The monk failed to mention the cut on his own arm which he pressed against his robe to stop the bleeding.

Davoir, eyes glazed with shock, knelt by the youth's side. "Why?" he whispered.

Squirming to one side, the clerk raised his head and spat at the priest.

As the spittle rolled down his cheek, Davoir grew rigid as a statue, but he continued to look bewildered as if he had just awakened into an incomprehensible world.

Putting a gentle hand on the priest's shoulder, Thomas said, "You should leave us, Father. These men must question your clerk."

Davoir leapt to his feet, all confusion melted by fury. "This clerk is under God's law, not your king's. I shall remain and hear all he has to say. Only I may be the judge in this matter, not these men." He waved at the guard and crowner, the gesture proclaiming his confidence that his mere will could make the men vanish.

Thomas looked down at the clerk. Whimpering like a hurt child, or else snarling like a maddened dog, the youth showed only glimpses of sense, but there was no hint in the clerk's eyes that the Evil One was peering out of his soul and mocking God. The monk pitied Renaud, despite the attack on Davoir's life. As a boy, Thomas had yearned for approval, although he had not been driven mad by it.

Surely someone other than Davoir would judge whether the clerk was mad or possessed. Thomas prayed for such to be the case. Although Davoir was right about jurisdiction, the monk doubted the man's ability to see beyond the attempted assassination and Renaud's maniacal rants to whatever torment had led to this longing to kill.

Thomas knew that men pointed to God's hand when murder was deemed righteous, or to Satan's touch when it was judged a wicked act. He wondered how often the cause was best sought in less significant places.

In the distance, a cock crowed. As the gray light of cold morning slipped into the room, the pale candlelight faltered.

With regret, Thomas turned to the crowner and guard captain. "Father Etienne must remain," he said.

Ralf looked at the priest. "He was one of your favored attendants. His words shall cause intense grief," he said, but his tone suggested he spoke only of facts and without compassion. "Should you leave the room, you may do so in confidence. I would never deny your right to take him away for Church judgement."

Although Thomas felt a momentary sympathy for the priest and what he must hear from Renaud, his pity swiftly disappeared. The arrogance he so detested in the priest glittered through the man's narrowed eyelids.

"I shall not leave," Davoir hissed. "I demand to know how and when he sold his soul to the Devil." Then he bent over and tore off the simple cross the cowering clerk wore around his neck. "You do not deserve the comfort of this, for you have denied the Lord and shall suffer the harshest punishment our Church can render."

Ralf's expression suggested he longed to hurl the priest out of the chambers, but instead he carefully stepped between the clerk and Davoir. "Nonetheless, Father, I must still question Renaud without any interruption from you," the crowner said. "He may have accomplices who do not fall within the Church's authority."

Davoir opened his mouth to protest.

This was not the time for a clash of wills, Thomas decided and quickly said, "Let me question the clerk, Crowner." He respectfully nodded at the sputtering priest. "Surely Father Etienne would agree that he ought not to do so now, for it was his life that Renaud wished to end." He forced himself to exude compassion when he addressed Davoir. "I know you have begun to pray for the strength to turn the other cheek after this attack, but God is merciful and would not expect you to obtain such grace without further prayer."

Davoir turned the color of watered wine, but his lips clamped together.

"As one trained in ecclesiastical law, and a man sworn to serve God, I believe I may ask the preliminary questions that both the Church and a crowner would deem necessary."

The priest's face became fully bathed in red. Opposition flashed from Davoir's eyes and threatened to drown his touted reason in a sea of defiance.

"I presume our abbess told you, before you left Anjou, that both Prioress Eleanor and Prior Andrew have reported on the quality of my legal advice in matters pertaining to the priory." Thomas did not wait for a response. "And our gracious prioress has also written of those times when she sought my opinion on matters of justice in the world outside our walls."

The monk was prepared for almost any reaction from the priest. The manifested surprise was not one of them. Despite the grave allegations brought against him, Thomas now realized Davoir had not been told anything about his education, work as a spy for the Church, or even the rank of his father. With bitter amusement, the monk chose to be grateful. Had Abbess Isabeau seen fit to elaborate beyond the present accusation, she might also have added *bastard* and *sodomite* as background to the claim he had broken his vows of chastity with his prioress.

But the priest chose not to confess his ignorance or argue against Thomas' proposal. He nodded an unenthusiastic acquiescence to the monk's plan.

Now Conan seemed ready to take issue with the suggestion, but the crowner put a hand on the man's arm. The guard captain stepped back without speaking.

"We consent, Brother," Ralf said.

Not allowing time for any further disagreement, the monk fell to his knees beside Renaud and bent to look into his eyes.

The clerk grew preternaturally still and stared back.

"What injustice so offended you?" Thomas murmured.

Davoir gasped with outrage. "I did not commit any injustice!" he shouted. "He turned to the Prince of Darkness because of…"

"As we all agreed, Father, let me do what I must without interruption." Thomas spoke with authority. No one had actually agreed to let him interrogate without interference, but he prayed the priest had forgotten that detail. At least, the monk thought, I want to keep the disruptions to a minimum.

"None of us should speak until Brother Thomas is done." Ralf lifted his right hand as if repeating his oath.

"As we all agreed," Conan added, also raising his hand.

Davoir was clearly annoyed but kept his thoughts unvoiced.

Thomas repeated his question with gentleness.

The clerk began to sob. "I did not mean to kill him." The words were barely audible.

"Your master?" Thomas bent closer.

"Jean!"

Davoir struck a fist into his open palm. "I knew you were a minion of the Devil!"

Conan walked to the priest's side. "Father Etienne, if the fear you suffered under the attack has so unmanned you that silence is impossible, I beg that you sit in that chair and have a mazer of wine." He pointed to a place at the far end of the chamber. "You will take charge of this clerk when the questioning is over.

At that time, you may say whatever you wish. Our needs will be satisfied, and we will have left."

The priest seemed about to protest this insult, then chose the wiser course, walked to the chair, and sat down.

"Continue," Thomas said softly to Renaud.

"I worked until my hands and knees bled to please our master, but the only good he ever acknowledged was what Jean did. Even when Jean sinned, Father Etienne praised the manner of his repentance. Yet if I so much as erred on a complex Latin verb tense, our master mocked me in front of all." He raised his head and yelled. "You were unjust!"

Thomas patted the youth's shoulder with a father's touch and hoped the lad's moment of lucidity would last long enough.

"I longed for Jean to be sent home in disgrace like the prior clerk. If he were, our master would look to me next and see my virtues. So I got Jean drunk in the inn the night before we arrived, but he again hid his disgrace too well." Pulling back from Thomas, Renaud shouted at the priest. "Or else you were so stupefied by him that you mistook the signs of drunkenness for holy rapture!"

Davoir stood, turned his back to the clerk, and walked to his prie-dieu where he stared at the bejeweled cross. "This sacred gift was from the king's brother in gratitude for my service to him," he muttered. "No matter what demonic abuse is flung at me by this churlish youth, I shall still receive a bishop's miter, an elevation that is my right as God's devout servant and the son of a noble family."

Thomas gently wiped spittle from Renaud's lips. "When your master asked for a treatment to cure Jean, what did you do?" he asked, hoping to keep the lad within the boundaries of sanity for just long enough.

With hacking gasps, Renaud began to weep. "I went to the apothecary hut and hid outside until Sister Anne finished preparing a remedy for a nun. They were discussing a gout treatment. As soon as she was alone, I approached Sister Anne for Jean's medicine, and she gave me something that I knew to be innocuous and suitable for uneasy stomachs."

"Did you disguise your identity or did you tell the sub-infirmarian who you were?"

Ralf quickly knelt next to the monk, lest the clerk's reply be inaudible.

"I hid my face and prayed that she would be called away. God blessed me. She was, and then the lay sister who had remained behind. Knowing something about herbs, I quickly read the labels on the shelves but found nothing to my purpose."

Thomas put a restraining hand on the crowner. Proving the innocence of Sister Anne meant too much to Ralf, and the monk feared he would speak despite his agreement. "What was your intent?" he asked the youth. Thomas longed to free the nun, but he had his prioress to protect as well and wanted nothing to interfere with either cause.

"To make Jean sicker. That was all! Signs of dissoluteness had failed to move our master from his unjustifiable preference. I knew my fellow clerk must therefore choose to leave Father Etienne's service. If Jean believed he suffered poor health, he would surely depart of his own volition."

"And if Jean did abandon his service for Father Etienne?" Thomas watched the clerk's eyes glaze as his mind slid from simple desire for approval to the madness of overweening ambition.

"When my brother clerk was no longer at his side, our master would choose me, and, when he became a bishop, my own fortune would rise higher because Jean would not be the recipient of all his munificence." Renaud began a high-pitched laugh. It swept the room like a scythe.

Ralf winced and moved away.

Thomas put a calming hand on the clerk's shoulder and whispered, "You were left alone in the apothecary hut. You had searched the shelves and found nothing you could use. What happened next?" The monk waited.

"I heard a voice and knew I must leave or be remembered too well. Then my eye fell on an open jar on the table. When I looked inside, I saw something that might be slipped into wine or ale. If it was the alleged gout treatment, so be it. I knew there was no such thing as a cure and assumed it was like most remedies, harmless in small amounts but upsetting to the humors if taken in larger quantities. Deciding it would have to serve my purpose, I took it and slipped away before anyone returned and caught me. "

Ralf turned around. "The jar was brown and had an ill-fitting lid?"

Thomas put a finger to his lips and bent his head in the direction of the priest.

Fortunately, the man seemed lost in contemplation of the altar wall.

Renaud winked as if sharing a mutual joke.

Ralf walked to the chamber door, opened it, and briefly spoke to someone outside.

"Did it not say what it was on the jar?" Thomas asked the youth.

"When I got back to our quarters, I read the label but did not know what *autumn crocus* was," Renaud wailed. "I assumed it might be a concoction to ease pain like poppy juice. If I used just a bit, I thought it would cause enough malaise that Jean would fear he suffered a mortal ailment."

Conan looked disgusted. "So out of ignorance and lust for position, he killed a man," he muttered.

Renaud shifted to stare at the guard captain, his mouth twisted into the rictus of a dead man's grin. "You, a man of the world, claim to know the justice of an act better than a man devoted to God?"

With a supreme act of will, Thomas kept himself from rebuking the youth for rank discourtesy. That was, after all, only a comment Renaud might have learned from his master. But the youth was quickly losing touch with reason. He was not willfully evil, and the monk decided to let the remark pass without comment.

Unfortunately, Conan laughed

Renaud twisted in his bindings and howled as he flung curses on the guard captain. If the monk had had any doubts left about the clerk's sanity, seeing this would have erased them.

"Stop this blasphemy!" Davoir rushed back from his prie-dieu, one fist raised, not at Renaud, but at Conan.

Thomas rose.

The clerk was now screaming words that were not in any language known to men.

Skidding to a stop and pointing to Renaud, the priest shouted, "He is talking to the Evil One!"

"Father, I must have peace to finish the few questions I have left," the monk said, then turned to Conan. "Both the priest and the crowner wish to understand what has happened here. Both have sworn to remain silent until I have gotten the tale from Renaud. I ask the same courtesy of silence from you. When I am done, all of you may pose your particular questions."

"You will learn nothing," growled the priest. "He is lost in hellish gibberish."

Ralf gestured to Conan.

The guard captain's lips curled into a sneer, but he swore to obey the monk's request and walked to join the crowner at the entrance door.

Renaud had ceased howling and began again to weep like a little boy with a scraped knee.

Davoir waved his hand at Thomas. "You do reach above your authority in this matter, and I am showing remarkable tolerance only out of deference to your prioress."

Thomas bowed his head. "You show a saintly patience, Father. I am humbled by your example." Not wishing to waste more time humoring the man, the monk quickly knelt at the clerk's side.

Renaud's eyes were tightly closed, and he repeatedly muttered, "I did not know I was killing him. I swear I did not know."

"But when Jean died, you hoped to take his place." The monk's voice was as soft as a feather.

The clerk's body jerked like one suffering a seizure. "Father Etienne mocked me! After I had risked my life to protect him, he told me that I could never replace his beloved Jean, that he had planned and still planned to dismiss me!" He began to strike his head on the floor. "Tell me where my reward is. The master is no master. He was sent by the Devil to torment me! Was it not right that I send him back to Hell like I sent Jean?"

Thomas grabbed the clerk before he reopened the wound in his head.

Renaud tried to bite him.

Ralf shouted at the priest. "If he is your creature, take responsibility for him!"

Stepping back in horror, Davoir cried out, "But he is possessed! His demon will attack us!"

"Pray?" Conan called out from the doorway. "Isn't that your chosen weapon?"

Suddenly, Renaud collapsed into Thomas' arms. "I didn't want to kill Jean! But he has come back as a damned soul to torment me. I saw him in the courtyard before he struck me down. I was sure his soul was cleansed before he died. I tried to tell him that. I did not mean to condemn him, but something went wrong." The clerk began to squirm in agony. "He is in Hell, and it is my fault!"

Thomas looked up at the trembling priest. "We have a confession from Renaud that he did kill your clerk, although I doubt there was any clear intent or malice in it. I witnessed his attempt to murder you. There was no accomplice. Tonight proves Sister Anne is innocent of all wrong, and we may free her and use that cell for Renaud."

The clerk began to scream that Jean was in the room and wearing a fiendish tail.

"Send for clerks from the monks´ quarters," Davoir said, his voice hoarse with terror.

"I have just done so," Ralf replied.

"And agree to Sister Anne's release," Thomas added before the crowner had a chance to demand it.

Swallowing what must have been bitter bile, Davoir agreed.

Renaud went limp in his restraints and wept like a whipped child.

"Are there any more questions?" Thomas asked. "Quickly, if you do, and be brief. His wits are fleeing."

"I shall ask mine when the Evil One is beaten out of his body," Davoir said.

"One," Ralf said. "Who was Brother Imbert?"

The monk bent over the wretched clerk and asked.

"I made him up," Renaud mumbled, then grinned as his eyes again grew unfocused. "Wasn't I clever?"

Thomas frowned. "You have said it was Jean who struck you down. Was it only…?"

Renaud twisted his head around and screamed, "It was Jean! I saw his spirit in the shadows, waving his arms and howling that he had come from Hell." The clerk began to foam at the mouth. "Ask him yourself! The hellish minion is there, standing by his priest!"

Conan looked uneasily at Davoir, shook his head, and then shrugged at the crowner.

Ralf raised an eyebrow at the monk.

"If Renaud truly believed he saw the ghost of his fellow clerk coming for vengeance," Thomas said, "he might have fainted from shock and struck his head on the stones of the path. That might have caused the wound."

The two men nodded.

Thomas was not convinced by his own argument, but he decided that the cause of the injury no longer mattered as much as he once thought it might.

In the distance, the church bell sounded for the morning Office. The men dutifully bowed their heads, but the call to prayer brought little peace to any and most certainly none to the guilty one who now lay still in a pool of his own urine.

Chapter Thirty-three

After that early morning prayer, Father Etienne reluctantly swore to his agreement that the sub-infirmarian be released, and Ralf left to take the news to Prioress Eleanor. Even faced with the indisputable fact of her innocence, the priest struggled against the truth. "Surely," he had muttered, "the woman is guilty of something."

When Thomas asked if he would accompany his wretched clerk to the cell, Davoir refused without explanation. The monk suspected that his decision had more to do with his unwillingness to see Sister Anne freed than it did with any pain he might have felt over Renaud's attempt to kill him. Thomas, however, looked forward to joining Prioress Eleanor and Crowner Ralf in welcoming the sub-infirmarian as she left the cell.

After Conan and the clerks bore Renaud away, the lad singing curious ditties under his breath, the priest returned to his prie-dieu and cross. In the ashen morning light, the jewels lost all color.

As he turned to leave the guest quarters as well, Thomas chose not to ask Father Etienne if he needed another priest's comfort.

When the cell door opened, and Sister Anne emerged to the joyful greetings of her friends, the nun stopped in horror as three clerks dragged the bound Renaud inside. The youth stank of excrement and urine.

The heavy wooden door of the cell slammed shut. Two more of Davoir's clerks remained outside and positioned themselves in front of it. Their boyish cheeks were round and utterly devoid of a man's beard, but they folded their arms with adult solemnity. Considering the tragic fate of their fellow clerk, their dedication to the assigned responsibility was poignant.

Prioress Eleanor quickly explained to her friend what had happened, and the nun gasped in dismay. Her expression grew solemn when she learned that the clerks must remain with the youth out of fear he might commit self-murder. Then tears wended their way down the sub-infirmarian's cheeks. "Surely he did this out of madness, not evil," she said to her friends, all of whom were inclined to agree.

Looking back at the door, which did not mute all screaming, Sister Anne asked how Renaud had been able to confess anything, considering how far his sense had fled.

Prioress Eleanor explained that Brother Thomas had been as gentle with his questions as a father might when a beloved son was in great pain.

The nun nodded. "If the clerk had received that kindness before, he might not have lost his reason so completely," she said. "Does He not command us to be compassionate?"

At no time did Sister Anne ask if Father Etienne had shown grief over these events or if he had sent an apology for misjudging her. She simply said she would pray for this youth who was so tormented that he might choose self-murder and an eternity in Hell to escape his temporal agony.

As the foursome left the corridor and Renaud's howls faded, Thomas thought about what must happen next. Of course the Church would not execute Renaud, although the alternative could be a more chilling punishment.

The monk shuddered. Exorcism would be performed. If that did not bring the youth back to his senses, Renaud might well spend the rest of his life chained in a tower or locked monastery cell where demons, real or imaginary, would infest his remaining days and nights with vicious mockery and obscene taunts.

Thomas had heard tales of men ripping off ears, and blinding or castrating themselves to escape the torments. None of this helped when nightmares had bored so deep into their souls.

Crowner Ralf would say the lad might be better off hanged. If Renaud were truly mad, Thomas asked himself, might that be the kinder justice? A cure for the satanic possession of a soul was possible. As he had once been told, the imp that allegedly forced his friend, Giles, to lie in sin with Thomas had been exorcised. But there was no cure for madness, a fate so cruel that many found a way to kill themselves despite all precautions and thus fell into an eternity of misery because they had done so.

Thomas wanted to raise his fist to the heavens and demand an explanation for this doom he believed unjust, but he was weary and the wound in his arm stung. Today, he must concentrate on his next duty. Tomorrow, he swore, he would spend the day on his knees and argue with God.

All but Davoir were delighted that Sister Anne was free, and the monk longed to share the joy to the fullest, but he knew he must talk with his prioress for advice about one more matter. Even if it was no longer urgent, he believed the question still called for an answer.

And if he needed the crowner, Ralf must be close to hand. As he now overheard, the crowner was begging Sister Anne to examine Gytha as soon as possible and swearing he would arrange for his wife to be brought to the priory. From the smile on the nun's face, the monk had no doubt of her reply.

He hurried to his prioress' side.

She turned with an expression of encouragement as if she had anticipated his request. "Of course, we may meet, Brother," she said. Inclining her head toward the pair discussing the perils of birth, she added, "And now might be the best time to do so."

Chapter Thirty-four

The north wind swept through the priory grounds, lashing the sea mist into razor-sharp swirls. Thomas pulled his cloak closer to his body. He had heard tales of northern lands covered in eternal ice. Today, he believed them.

Why had he decided he must make this effort? His treated knife wound still ached. Other monks were huddled around a warming fire in the Calefactory while his tonsure grew numb with the cold despite the hood over his head. But as he pressed against the wind he knew he had little choice. Some matters should be left to God for resolution. As his prioress said, this was not one of them.

Peering through the fog, he still could not distinguish any outline of the hospital even with its dark stone. In fact, he could only see a few feet in front of him on the path. At least he knew Sister Anne would soon be back at the apothecary hut, treating the suffering with her gentle touch and keen insights. That brought warmth to his heart, and the cold retreated just a little.

As the path curved, Thomas stopped, uncertain of his direction, and then realized he had taken the wrong turn. Instead of going to the hospital, he was walking to the main gate. Through the mist, he could just recognize the dim shape of the priory walls. Sighing, he decided he could find another way from the gate back to the hospital with ease. He certainly had no wish to retrace his steps in this bitter wind.

As he approached the gate, the fog suddenly thinned, and he noticed a party of men milling about. In that group, Thomas saw the one he had come to find. Picking up his pace, he hurried toward the man.

Philippe saw the monk coming toward him. He looked around as if seeking a way to escape, then grew still, his shoulders hunched with resignation. "You are seeking me," he said as Thomas reached his side. The words were a statement of fact, not a question.

"And I believe you know the reason," Thomas replied, keeping his voice low so those nearby could not overhear.

"Shall we step further away, Brother? These men are pilgrims on the way to Canterbury. I would not have them distracted from their pious intent by the tale of my unique wickedness."

"You expected to flee, hidden in their midst?" Thomas kept close to the man, although he had no great fear that the man would run off.

"I had meant to join them." Philippe's smile was thin-lipped. "There is a difference."

Thomas said nothing.

The man stared longingly at the pilgrims he had planned to accompany. His eyes lost the little hope they had briefly owned.

"Why did you attack the priest's clerk that night?" Thomas kept his voice low although he knew the fog muffled speech.

"I came to kill the priest." Philippe's reply was equally muted. "I did tell the truth about blood being the purpose for my journey here when you last asked, Brother. I failed to mention that it was blood I wished to shed."

The monk folded his arms and waited.

"You are a man, Brother. In the days before you took vows, did you ever wish to kill another?"

Of course he had, both before and after he took his enforced vows, but Thomas knew that did not matter. Only his acknowledgement of understanding did, and so he nodded once.

"We all do, I fear, but I did not know that there is a great difference between longing to do the deed, even planning it, and actually striking the blow."

With growing interest, Thomas encouraged him to go on.

"I came here under the guise of being a pilgrim, walking to Canterbury in expiation of my many sins." Philippe rubbed at his eyes. "Surely it is blasphemy to go on pilgrimage with the intention of committing murder. I did not think of that when I began my journey, but heated and willful obsessions blind us."

"You would not be the first to commit that sin," the monk replied as the events in Walsingham last year flooded his memory.

"After I had obtained a bed in the hospital, I decided to search the apothecary hut for a poison I could use to kill the priest." He shrugged. "My hope was to slip something lethal into Father Etienne's food." His laugh was a brittle thing. "I must thank you for catching me there, Brother. I think you brought God with you, for my eyes were opened slightly and I saw how foolish I had been to plan such a deed. I realized I could never come close enough to the priory kitchen, or to the lay brother who brought the meals, unless I wished to injure an innocent. My heart held no passion for that crime."

"Yet you struck the priest's clerk."

"With a very light blow. The youth lived. I saw him leave the hospital with his master after a brief stay. I now believe that God stayed my hand and allowed that clerk to take the blow in order to save his master's life."

And later try to kill the priest himself, Thomas thought sadly, but this information was also irrelevant to the man from Picardy. "We shall return to that," the monk said. "Go back in time with your tale. Did you know that Jean, the clerk, had died?"

"I did and that perplexed me. My fear was that someone else had arrived with a deep grievance and accidentally poisoned the clerk instead of the priest. Yet I knew of no one with a cause as terrible as mine, and so I assumed the clerk had been felled by a swift fever with no earthly cure." He hesitated. "Then I heard a rumor that his death was not from a fever but a deadly herb."

He began to shake. "I swear I had nothing to do with the lad's death, Brother. On the cross I give my word."

"Nor do I accuse you. The killer has confessed."

Philippe looked hopeful that the monk would elaborate.

The monk shook his head. "You have not told me the reason for following Father Etienne here with this murderous intent. After you have explained that, I want to hear how you pursued your desire, after you rejected poison as the means, and yet failed to accomplish it."

Philippe again looked into the fog at the ghostly figures of the gathering pilgrims. "My brother was once a clerk to Father Etienne, his most favored clerk in fact. But my brother fell from grace when it was discovered that he had a weakness for female flesh. Although he fought against it, he needed help to gain the strength to resist, a gift he dared not beg from his master. Father Etienne may be flawed like all mortals, but women have never tempted him, and he has no tolerance for men who copulate. My brother would have been banished in disgrace just for the sin of craving the act. Instead, he was caught in a brothel, dragged before his master, and mocked for his frailty."

"And sent away from the grace of his master's smile."

"To a poor parish, filled with whores, to whom he administered the compassion he had never received. Some might say the appointment was a blessing, for he lost all lust and was able to counsel the women in chaste encounters. But he ate little and drank only water until he grew too weak and fell victim to a plague that killed him slowly and in great agony."

Thomas suffered enough from weakness of the flesh, although mostly in his dreams. He shook his head, not in condemnation of the dead man, but out of profound sympathy.

"I blamed Father Etienne for his lack of charity. I saw him as my brother's murderer."

"And for that you chose to follow him here."

"And kill him, Brother, without the chance for confession, with all his sins festering in his soul. I wanted him to go to Hell."

The Church could not condone that, Thomas thought, for all mortals had the right to cleanse their souls before death. And yet he heard an insistent voice from his heart suggest that this favored priest might never recognize his harshness as a sin and never confess the wickedness. With such an inadequate confession, the man would certainly suffer longer in Purgatory. The image did not trouble him unduly, nor was this the first time he had felt this way about those he thought cruel.

Shaking the image from his mind, he continued. "After you learned of Jean's death, you were seen spying on the guest quarters."

"Something was not right, and I became curious. One of the lay brothers said the sub-infirmarian had been arrested for killing the lad, and yet there was talk of setting a guard for the priest. If she had been locked away or the lad had only died of a fever, I asked myself, why have a guard? Then I worried that the priest had learned of my arrival. He knew I had sworn to kill him after the death of my brother. Had he seen and recognized me?"

"He had not," Thomas said.

"I concluded I must swiftly act if I was to achieve my desire and even escape before the deed was discovered. That night, I found the gate to the guest quarters unlocked so eagerly slipped in. When I saw that only Renaud patrolled, I knew I had my best chance. As quietly as possible, I followed the clerk and waited for the right moment. When he stopped to peer into the shrubbery, I struck him down."

"You might have accomplished your intent, had you entered the chambers after hitting Renaud. The priest would surely have been asleep and most assuredly alone." The monk did not mention that Conan had been close by and might have caught him in the act. It was this man's failure to proceed that interested Thomas. "What stopped you from entering the guest quarters and killing the priest?"

"God took mercy on my soul and his. As I looked on the fallen clerk, I knew I had only rendered him unconscious. If I did not kill him, he might awaken and raise the hue and cry. May God forgive my evil heart! I raised my hand for the fatal blow, but my hand inexplicably faltered and slipped to my side. I knew I would be unable to crack open his skull and sent him for judgement. Like Saint Paul on the road to Damascus, I fell to the ground as if the hand of God had struck me. It was then I heard a voice telling me that murder is an act beloved by Satan, one forbidden by the Commandments and abhorred by Him. I rose and fled the grounds."

And in that moment Thomas believed God had spoken to the man whose eyes were glazed with the wonder he had experienced. The monk waited to hear what more this would-be assassin might say.

Philippe covered his eyes as if he could no longer bear what they now saw. "My brother feeds worms in his grave, whether or not I kill the priest. Were I to plunge a dagger into Father Etienne's heart as reprisal, I would still never hold my brother in my arms again. I would only add the horror of my crime to the pain of loss. How could I live with the understanding that I had willingly committed a great wickedness and was no better than the man I hated? Revenge is not the balm for grief. At least my brother was shriven of his sins before he died. God has said that such men will not suffer the agonies of Hell."

"And the suffering he endured on earth may also cut short his time in Purgatory."

"I confess that I still can not forgive Father Etienne for what he did to my brother. May God give me the strength to do so! But He did stop me from committing an act that would never heal my heart and would only add to the chains which may yet drag me down to Hell."

"Father Etienne must face God's judgement for the sins he has committed against your brother and others."

"Henceforth, I shall try to find peace in that, but I fear he will never see his condemnation of my brother as the heartlessness it was."

Thomas remained silent about his own condemnation of the priest's soul. Instead, he smiled approval for the man's resolution. "And so you fled the quarters to avoid killing the priest."

"And went back to the hospital chapel where I lay prostrate before the altar, weeping and begging God to show me how to expiate my sins."

"Did He answer your prayer?"

"His reply came from the quiet flickering of a candle." Philippe gestured at the men close by. "That small group of penitents had just arrived on their way to Canterbury and had been given mats next to mine on which to sleep one night. I was to join them in their journey, but this time I must do so as a true pilgrim. After which, I might return home to my wife and children. Holy vows are not my calling, but my wife has long urged me to give more of the income from my trade to the poor. As I rose from my knees, I could hear my wife's joyous cry when I returned from Becket's shrine and announced that I would follow her pious advice and found a small hospital, based on what I had seen here, for the sick and dying poor."

Thomas solemnly nodded. "But now I keep you from your devout journey and holy purpose."

"I conclude that is God's will, Brother. The innocent clerk meant only to protect his master and did nothing to merit the wound I gave him. It is only just that you take me to the crowner for punishment."

Thomas quietly looked at this man but found the struggle to decide what was best easier than he had imagined.

Philippe had folded his hands and meekly waited for the monk to lead him off to chains and the king's justice.

"Go to Canterbury," Thomas said and pointed to the other penitents waiting for the fog to lift so they could commence their travel on the road to a saint's tomb. "There is no reason for you to remain here." With a brief blessing, he walked away.

Had Thomas looked back, he would have seen Philippe fall to his knees, his arms raised to heaven, and his heart filled with astounded gratitude.

Chapter Thirty-five

Although the sea mist had finally dissipated, the earth remained wet with its tears. Multicolored leaves, once proudly announcing the rich harvest in the priory orchard, lay on the ground, dull with mold and rotting into the soil. The chill, eager to herald the coming months of bitter cold, lingered in the air. It was that time when men's souls grow fearful, for the dark season is when Death most loves to garner souls.

Brother Thomas and Prioress Eleanor were not part of that tremulous multitude. As they approached the courtyard inside the main gate, their expressions spoke of keen anticipation.

"Have you received any news?' he asked.

The prioress nodded. "Nute was chosen to be the messenger for Gytha's travail. He has confirmed that Sister Anne arrived at the manor and immediately ordered Ralf out of the house. After she had examined Gytha, she sent Signy outside long enough to announce that our sub-infirmarian was pleased with the progress of the child's birth." Eleanor smiled. "The crowner is sweating drops the size of crossbow bolts. Nute said that Ralf had even fallen to his knees in prayer at least once."

Thomas looked surprised. "If Ralf is doing that on a day that is neither a Sunday nor a feast day, he is truly frightened."

"Our crowner may growl and sputter about the Church, but he tithes faithfully," she replied with a smile. "And he may not attend Mass every Sunday, but he most certainly can recite all of the Seven Deadly Sins."

"His wife may help him forget a few of those," Thomas replied with a lighter heart, then grew solemn. "Sister Anne is certain there is no problem with the birthing?"

"I did not want to postpone Nute's return to the manor with questions he could not answer, but I am confident that our beloved Gytha is doing well. Before Sister Anne sent the boy to us, she urged him to emphasize that Gytha was having as easy a time as any woman could with birth pains." The prioress looked quickly behind her as if hoping to see the lad arrive with word that the babe had been born and all was well. "Nute vowed to come to the priory every time there was news."

"After we wish Godspeed to our abbess' brother, I beg leave to go to the manor and help Ralf through this time. Men may not give birth, but it would be a heartless husband who did not weep when he heard his wife scream with pain. Ralf cherishes Gytha, and he recently asked me if God minded the curses he gave Eve for burdening good women with such agony just because their foremother couldn't resist a pretty apple." Thomas grinned. "I told him God might condemn him if he didn't."

Looking at him with fondness, Eleanor said, "You would have been a good husband had you chosen another calling." Then she flushed with embarrassment and quickly added, "Of course you must give comfort to our dear friend. I would suggest you leave now, but we both must see Father Etienne off." She grimaced at the very thought of the man. "I need your strength to prevent me from saying something I should not."

"My lady, it is your strength I shall need not to forget my vows and strike him."

At that, they both laughed.

"Fear not, my lady," he said. "I have never regretted my oaths, although they are not always easy to obey." Those were words he would not have meant years ago when he was forced to take the vows, but they had become true since—with one unsettling exception.

Although he no longer mourned the loss of the man he had once deeply loved, he now found he often thought of Durant,

a wine merchant he had met in Walsingham. Surely the cause
was Gytha's pregnancy, he decided, for Durant had spoken of
the longing he and his wife had for a child. When Thomas
and the wine merchant last parted, the monk had given him
a blessing and added his prayers that the union between husband and wife would be fruitful. A babe would bring much
joy to Durant, he thought, and wondered again if God had
heard his plea.

"Not once have I doubted your devotion," the prioress
replied, then paused. "Before we see Father Etienne, you should
tell me the details of your recent meeting with the man from
Picardy. Was he interested in our honored guest?"

It was Thomas' turn to blush as he prayed Prioress Eleanor
would never discover his longing for a man's love. To hide his
face, he bowed his head and told her the tale of Philippe as well
as the reason for letting the man go. "I beg forgiveness for doing
this without consulting you," he said.

She stopped and looked up at him, her gray eyes warm. "We
often think as one in serving God, Brother. Had you sought
advice, I would have agreed that justice was best honored by
letting the man expiate his sins as he wished. Perhaps God did
enlighten him on how murder blights the mortal soul. Despite
the Commandments, many try to distinguish between righteous
and sinful killing, an often confusing difference." She sighed.
"Our world has become so violent. Under King Henry, we had
longer periods of peace, but his son has changed that."

"Your clemency is gracious, my lady." But he knew that her
comments on the world reflected her fears for her brother's safety
in Wales. "I pray daily for Sir Hugh," he added softly.

"Prayers for which he and I are most grateful." Although she
never knew exactly why her eldest brother had initially disliked
Brother Thomas, the monk had saved Sir Hugh's life. Since then,
there had been no discord between the men. "After the service
you have rendered all of us in my father's family, you have become
my third brother in the world as well as my spiritual kin."

He bowed his head with humility, and the two fell silent, lost in their particular thoughts as they hurried on to the meeting with the soon-to-be Bishop Etienne Davoir.

Clerks tossed their meager bundles of possessions to others and clambered into the wagons that had brought them to Tyndal Priory. Their shouts and laughter at departure contrasted with their sedate hush on arrival.

No one rebuked them for the din, or suggested it was unseemly. Even Father Etienne turned his back on it as if accepting their eagerness to return to more peaceful lodgings where the worst violence might be an impassioned quarrel over a tiny theological detail.

Outside the gates, the party of mounted guards had gathered, ready to escort the Frenchmen back to the coast and their waiting ship. Even their horses seemed impatient to leave, snorting and shaking their heads.

As a reminder of Jean's tragic death, a riderless horse was tied to the back of one wagon which had been filled with all the records of this visitation, a carved prie-dieu and a bejeweled cross. No one approached the horse. Three passing clerks suddenly changed direction when they realized they would be passing too near.

Bereft of attending clerks, Davoir stood with Prior Andrew. The prior was assuring him that the lay brothers of Tyndal would take care in preparing Jean's corpse so it could be sent home without an embarrassing incident.

Thomas noticed Conan dismount and walk through the gate. He hoped the guard captain would rotate the soldiers assigned to watch over Renaud. The clerk's ranting, day and night, would be torture. As the monk leaned to one side, he could see Renaud bound and tied to his horse. Although the general noise of departure muted the sound, Thomas could see the youth opening and shutting his mouth as he alternated between raving and weeping. He had heard that the youth had refused all nourishment and wondered if he would survive the voyage home.

◇◇◇

Glancing up, Davoir saw the prioress approaching. He nodded to Prior Andrew and went to meet her, his head bowed. "I beg forgiveness for any sorrow I have caused you, my lady, with these wicked and false accusations."

"A most serious allegation had been made against me, Father. You came seeking the truth and found it," she replied. "There is no shame in doing as you were commanded or wishing to serve our abbess well." But Eleanor could not help thinking that few men could perform an act of humility, as Davoir had just done, and still retain an arrogant demeanor. It was not uncommon for younger sons of great families to enter the Church more out of ambition than faith, but the prioress had met some whose hearts God had softened. This man was not one of those.

"But I accused your sub-infirmarian and you of far worse than breaking vows of chastity. For that, I shall beg a harsh penance."

"We knew we were innocent and had faith in God's justice." The prioress tried not to bite her tongue too hard to keep from saying more. Tempting as it was to ignore or even refuse his request for forgiveness, Eleanor knew she could not. "What we might have suffered was over in a moment, and our hearts are joyful that we have been vindicated. Forgiveness is not needed, Father. You had a duty to perform. God cast His light on the facts as we knew He would." She wondered if he would mention Renaud now and express some sorrow or regret. Surely the priest knew he bore some responsibility for what had happened.

Davoir clutched his hands together. "Your sub-prioress has resigned her office because of her brother's actions, but she is a worthy woman and a good servant of God. I pray you will have mercy on her."

"I have accepted her plea to be released from the duty she has long performed with honor, Father. It is her wish, not mine. Once she has returned to health, I shall speak with her about her desired path of service, as well as what is best for our priory, but I assure you that I bear her no enmity. It was her brother who sinned against us, not Sister Ruth." It seems he has entirely forgotten about Renaud, she thought, but then the clerk was a steward's son. All souls might be equal in God's judgement, but rank still raised some above others in the eyes of mortals.

He smiled with relief. "It is with great joy that I return to my sister at Fontevraud Abbey, not only with complete repudiation of the false claims against you, but a fine report on your leadership in all aspects at this daughter house." He swallowed and looked away for a moment. "She has always held you in especial regard, among all her daughters, for the work you do in God's service. She will not be surprised at my laudatory report, but she will be most pleased."

Since he was so much taller than she, the priest stared down at her. His smile and gaze made her uneasy until she realized that they reminded her of her cat when he approached a fine piece of fish she had saved for him. She struggled not to laugh. Then, with exemplary humility, Eleanor knelt. "Give this unworthy woman your blessing, Father, for I am mortal and suffer many sins."

Standing as straight and grave as the bishop he would soon become, Davoir granted the request and waited for her to rise. Briefly, he glanced at Thomas but chose to ignore him.

The monk managed not to smile. He was pleased that the priest knew nothing of his father's rank or the man might have been more conciliatory despite Thomas' illegitimacy. At least one king's bastard had held higher rank in the Church than this man ever will, the monk thought. But he was grateful he would always be a simple monk within the priory he happily called his home.

He stepped away but kept his head bowed while his prioress and the prior bid their guest a formal farewell.

"Brother, may I interrupt your meditations?"

Startled, Thomas looked up to see Conan by his side.

"I have a message for you."

The monk brightened. "Gytha…"

"No, I have no message from the manor house, but I do have word of another birth."

Thomas blinked, then noticed the smile twinkling in the guard captain's eyes. Suddenly, he felt his face grow hot.

"Durant of Norwich wishes you to know that your blessing last year brought great joy. His wife has been safely delivered of a healthy son. Although the good wine merchant has vowed to return here with them both at some future date, he will first send a worthy gift to this priory in gratitude for God's kindness—and yours." The guard bowed.

"Will you see Master Durant soon?" Thomas knew his voice trembled.

"After I have delivered this company to their ships, I return to court to report on my adventures." Conan's expression was inscrutable. "Master Durant provides some of the king's wine and is often in attendance there. I believe I may meet him."

"Will you tell him…?" Thomas turned away, and then forced himself to finish his sentence. "Will you say that I continue to consider him my brother after our time together in Walsingham? I pray daily for his health, that of his wife, and now his babe." With a genuine smile, he looked back at the captain. "You say a son? What is the babe's name?"

Conan grinned. "He was named after his mother's favorite uncle, a man who died only a few months before the birth. Coincidentally, his name was *Thomas*."

The monk did not bother to hide this blush, suspecting this man might not care about the cause. "I am sure the boy will be a credit to his good kin and will become a far worthier man than another who also bears that name."

Conan agreed to relay the message, and, with a pat on the monk's shoulder, returned to his horse and men outside the priory gate.

◇◇◇

When the party had left, and the sound of the travelers' horses had faded, a great sigh rose from the three monastics who could now return to the tasks that had been set aside for no better reason than a man's petty longing for revenge.

Although Prioress Eleanor had given the priest her forgiveness, and most certainly forgave her former sub-prioress, she was not so sure she could forgive Sister Ruth's brother. She did ask herself if she should tell her own brother about what had happened, then rejected the idea. To do so would be as petty as what the baron had done. In time, she decided, God would render some justice on him, and she was glad to let Him do it.

After some discussion with her prior about what tasks must be done first, Eleanor and Thomas walked back along the path that led to the hospital and to her own quarters.

Before they had gone far, they heard a voice calling out.

Nute raced down the path toward them.

"What news?" the two monastics shouted in unison.

Nute skidded to a halt in front of them, stood up straight, and took a deep breath. "Sister Anne has announced that Mistress Gytha was safely delivered of a healthy son. He shall be named *Fulke.*" Then he frowned. "I could hear the babe outside the manor house, my lady. He has the crowner's lungs."

And with great relief, Prioress Eleanor and Brother Thomas laughed and shouted for joy.

Author's Notes

A few years ago, while enjoying an author tea at The Poisoned Pen in Scottsdale, Arizona, I had a delightful conversation about medieval history with fellow reader, Paula Davidon. When she asked if I had read Archbishop Eudes Rigaud's account of his travels around his archdiocese in thirteenth-century Normandy, I confessed I hadn't. In such moments the process of plot development often begins.

Not long after, Paula sent me a copy of the archbishop's dictated chronicle in which he discusses, with fascinating detail, his visits to the religious houses under his authority, the inadequacies he found, and the remedies he recommended. I knew then that I would have to put Prioress Eleanor through this ordeal. Life must never get too comfortable for her.

There was one problem. Almost all Orders did live under the oversight of a local prelate, like Archbishop Eudes Rigaud of Rouen, and received regular visits from him to make sure the physical buildings were maintained, fiscal affairs were in order, and everyone kept to their vows in both major and minor ways. The Order of Fontevraud was different.

Instead of the local prelate, Fontevraud was under the rule of Rome and placed there in 1244, with the approval of Pope Innocent IV, which suggests that the Order was well-regarded and skillfully run. Popes did not allow lax Orders to have this privilege because it gave the Order leaders more leeway in decision-making and control over their daughter houses. The abbots and abbesses of houses under Rome's rule could order the investigative reviews as they saw fit. Records indicate that they were a little less dedicated about scheduling them than Eudes' chronicle would suggest he was.

Although the abbesses in Anjou approved some visitations, very few have been recorded for the English daughter houses of Fontevraud and these were almost exclusively concerned with fiscal affairs. The pattern suggests that Prioress Eleanor would have had good cause indeed to wonder why her religious house was being singled out if Abbess Isabeau ordered an assessment of all aspects of Tyndal Priory from fish ponds to monastic shoes.

Isabeau Davoir (or d'Avoir) was the fourteenth abbess at Fontevraud Abbey and ruling head of the Order from 1276 to 1284. Her kin were the noble family of d'Avoir in Anjou, and her problem with querulous monks, who did not like female rule, is part of historical record. Eventually, she got papal approval to send the rebellious ones off to other priories. Her second notable achievement was the successful acquisition of a relic from the true cross for the abbey.

Nothing else is known about her, including anything about brothers. Presumably there was one to inherit the family title. If she also had a younger one, he might well have opted for a career in the Church. His birth would have put him on the fast track for ecclesiastical promotion much like the fictional Father Etienne Davoir, a man who bears absolutely no resemblance to Archbishop Eudes whom I found quite charming.

There is a general assumption about religion in the medieval era. This can be summed up by the image of Christians kneeling in a church, a group whose frequent adherence to ritual was set in stone and whose beliefs were standardized or else deemed heretical.

The image is fallacious. First, not everyone in Europe was Christian, although that was the dominant creed. Second, the average Christian had little in-depth understanding of the faith, and practices deemed common today in Catholicism were not always honored. Third, there were long periods in which a fair tolerance for differences of opinion existed as long as certain fundamentals weren't questioned. (Jesus was the messiah, for instance.)

In this book, I do portray some differences amongst the professional religious. Prioress Eleanor believes in a compassionate and tolerant God who is outraged most by cruelty and injustice. Brother Thomas feels free to argue constantly with his. Father Etienne sees God as a stern, unbending task master who must be strictly obeyed without question. Some theologians said a Christian must never doubt or question but just accept the faith as preached by the professionals. Others argued that Christian tenets could and must be proven with reasoned arguments and that questioning was an acceptable path to faith.

If the theologians exhibited variety in their approach to the Christian religion, the laity was just as diverse. *Canterbury Tales* offers a good survey course. In my series, Gytha and Signy are conventionally devout, but the critical and casual approach, suggested by Ralf and Conan, was not unusual.

In all religions, faith leaders worry about the laxity of the lay folk. Will they follow those in religious authority on morals, compliance with financial support, and attendance at group rituals? For medieval Christians, it was no different.

Baptism was a non-negotiable, basic requirement for entrance into the faith, and Christian families did this dutifully. Once that was done, however, there was surprising variance in almost everything else having to do with the faith. Some of this was understandable. The complex rules over when a dutiful Christian couple might have sex would drive a modern computer mad, let alone a medieval human. There was a lot of disobedience going on with that.

What might surprise many is that knowledge about the intricacies of faith was not obligatory for the laity. Robert Grosseteste, the mid-thirteenth century bishop of Lincoln, clarified that the average Christian was only required to know the Ten Commandments, the seven Deadly Sins, and have a rudimentary understanding of the seven sacraments. (Others did think memorizing a prayer or two was good.) Those with vocations to serve God were expected to have a far greater understanding in order to advise and preach. In reality, many of those, especially the local priests, were as ignorant of the rules and details of the faith as the laity.

In general, attendance at Mass on Sundays and feast days was expected, but non-attendance was so common it was regularly bewailed. Tithing was part of a Christian's obligation, but tithes were not always collected with any regularity, except in England where compliance seems to have been rather good. Annual confession was a duty around Easter as was taking the Eucharist. Many did adhere to that. Many others did not.

As for respect due the professional religious, the literature of the day was filled with mockery of the foibles of priests, monks, and nuns. Bishops came in for their share when they chose to chastise local priests for having unsanctioned wives—despite having mistresses themselves. (And I won't even get into the Borgias.) Like an archaeological dig of the town dump that brings us a picture of life amongst the common folk, secular literature provides us with a peek into what the average Christian practiced (or didn't) and thought.

So Ralf's contempt for the more lenient punishments given clerics is echoed in historical quotes by kings; his snide comments about the professional religious, his friends excepted, is repeated in much literature of the time; his infrequent church attendance is supported by recorded theological wailing. Conan's remarks and behavior also fall into that category. Unapproved scoffing and lax adherence to ritualistic practices was scolded but not ardently punished most of the time.

That noted, medievals, like many moderns, were frightened of the afterlife. This terror eventually brought most medieval Christians back to the fold in times of stress or on their death-beds. Ralf is a different man when faced with the possibility that his wife could die in childbirth. Even Conan might utter a prayer before he next faces the Welsh. Rulers, notorious for lifetimes of brutality and rampant greed, often donned a monk's robe and took religious vows on their deathbeds. King William Rufus, overcome with fear during a dire illness, piously chose a later sainted Archbishop of Canterbury, a decision he came to rue when his health crisis passed. Like Rufus, Ralf will probably return to his irreverent self after the child is born.

Autumn crocus is an ancient remedy. The first mention is in the Egyptian *Ebers Papyrus,* the oldest known medical text from approximately 1500 BCE, where parts of the plant were mentioned as useful in the treatment of inflammation. Later, the Greeks discovered it could be an effective remedy for acute cases of gout, although Alexander of Tralles in the sixth century CE wrote the most complete treatise on its specific value as a gout medication. The medicine was composed of the plant's dried seeds, flowers, and corms. It wasn't until 1820 that the alkaloid *colchicine* was isolated and discovered to be the valuable element. Today, modern medicine still prescribes the vital part of autumn crocus for acute gout attacks in the form of a tiny purple pill called Colchicine.

The problem with autumn crocus is its toxicity. Before 1820, it was very difficult to concoct a remedy with it that didn't cause serious side effects or even death. In fact, the plant was best known as a poison. The amount of the alkaloid colchicine in the various parts of the plant varies dramatically, and a safe dosage would not have been easily measurable many hundreds of years ago.

Since physicians were reluctant to put their lives on the line with their noble patients, a jar of autumn crocus was not the first thing they reached for to treat gout. History might have been a tad less bloody if a few kings had gotten the remedy. On the other hand, a few more royal doctors would have gotten their necks stretched on the scaffold if the gout cure killed the patient. Even today, a patient is at risk for unpleasant or even severe side effects, but, in medieval times, the correct dosage would have been difficult. Obviously, autumn crocus could be used successfully or the Greeks and others wouldn't have written so enthusiastically about it.

I have always presented Sister Anne as observant, analytical, and well-educated, thanks to her father who had access to medical treatises not always available to most western physicians. With her education, use of a conservative dose and careful observation, all possible with a resident sub-prioress, Sister Anne could have successfully used the remedy, but even she would not have used autumn crocus on a regular basis or with a transient patient.

Many of us may assume that only men suffer gout since afflicted women are rarely mentioned. It is true that men get the disease more often and earlier in life. My father did. So imagine my surprise when I awoke one morning to a very red and increasingly painful toe joint. Post-menopausal women with a family history can and often do suffer from gout. I was not pleased by the paternal gift.

Fortunately, I am a writer so found distraction from the flare-up in researching the background of that wonderful, little purple pill. Once I discovered what a fascinating history it had, I knew the treatment must show up in a book. I also wanted company in my misery and decided that Eleanor's sub-prioress was the perfect person to benefit from my experience. After what Sister Ruth's brother tried to do to Prioress Eleanor and Brother Thomas in *Satan's Lullaby*, I also hope that brother shares the family medical tendency to painful little uric acid crystals.

Sneezing was problematic in the medieval period. One belief, of the many prevalent theories, was that a sneeze expelled the soul from the body. Another was the fear that demonic creatures filled the void in the body left by the sneeze. In order to call the soul back, or to keep Satan at bay, the words "God bless you" were uttered. The expression is still used.

As a final note, the term *English Channel* was not used in the thirteenth century. The most common name for that body of water separating the British Isles from the continent was *British Ocean* (*Oceanus Britannicus*) or *British Sea* (*Mare Anglicanum*). The first known reference to the *English Channel* (*Canalites Anglie*) was on an Italian map of 1450 within a translation of Claudius Ptolemy's second century *Geographia*.

Bibliography

In the course of researching any new book, I always find useful and entertaining sources that I love to share with readers. Here the joy of fiction and the excitement of academic discovery can join in a common, harmonious purpose. The following titles are a few of the latest which I hope you will enjoy as much as I have.

Bishops, Clerks, and Diocesan Governance in Thirteenth-Century England, by Michael Burger, Cambridge University Press, 2012.

Episcopal Visitation of Monasteries in the Thirteenth Century, (second, revised edition), by C. R. Cheney, Manchester University Press, 1983.

The Holy Bureaucrat: Eudes Rigaud and Religious Reform in Thirteenth-Century Normandy, by Adam J. Davis, Cornell University Press, 2006.

The Register of Eudes of Rouen, translated by Sydney M. Brown and edited by Jeremiah F. O'Sullivan, Columbia University Press, 1964.

Religious Life for Women c.1100-c.1350 (Fontevraud in England), By Berenice Kerr, Oxford University Press, 1999.

Oxford Dictionary of Popes, by J.N.D. Kelly, Oxford University Press, 1986.

Medieval Travellers: the Rich and Restless, by Margaret Wade Labarge, Orion Books, 1982.

To receive a free catalog of Poisoned Pen Press titles, please provide your name and address through one of the following ways:

Phone: 1-800-421-3976
Facsimile: 1-480-949-1707
Email: info@poisonedpenpress.com
Website: www.poisonedpenpress.com

Poisoned Pen Press
6962 E. First Ave. Ste 103
Scottsdale, AZ 85251